The Delivera

The Deliverance

RICHARD S. WHEELER

A TOM DOHERTY ASSOCIATES BOOK / NEW YORK

THE DELIVERANCE

A Forge Book
Published by Tom Doherty Associates, LLC
175 Fifth Avenue
New York, NY 10010

www.tor.com

Forge® is a registered trademark of Tom Doherty Associates, LLC.

Library of Congress Cataloging-in-Publication Data

Wheeler, Richard S.
    The deliverance / Richard S. Wheeler.—1st ed.
      p. cm.
    "A Tom Doherty Associates book."
    ISBN 0-312-87844-3 (alk. paper)
    1. Skye, Barnaby (Fictitious character)—Fiction. 2. Mexican American Border Region—Fiction. 3. Kidnapping victims—Fiction. 4. Cheyenne Indians—Fiction. 5. New Mexico—Fiction. 6. Trappers—Fiction. I. Title.

PS3573.H4345 D45   2003
813'.54—dc21

                                  2002032544

First Edition: March 2003

Printed in the United States of America

0 9 8 7 6 5 4 3 2 1

For Jean Sandberg, who suggested it

The Deliverance

one

With the quickening of the grass, the Cheyenne woman came once again to Bent's Fort. Barnaby Skye saw her from a great distance, a small, blue-blanketed woman crouched in her usual spot just outside the massive gate where she could watch every mortal who entered or left. He knew her sad story; everyone in the post did.

He had been out hunting, along with his Crow wife he had named Victoria, and now they were returning at sundown with a groaning wagonload of buffalo meat, butchered and wrapped in the hide against the year's first green flies.

He rode his shaggy, winter-haired buckskin down the slight grade and out upon the velvet-grassed bottoms of the Arkansas River, which severed the plains and two nations as well. He hoped to escape the sharp March wind that reddened and chafed his flesh, but he knew it would harry him clear to the post and even into his rooms.

William Bent's great adobe post lorded over a riverside pasture on the Mountain Branch of the Santa Fe Trail, just within United States territory, a lonely outpost hundreds of miles from settlements; a haven and refuge for weary travelers; a source of white men's magic for the Indians.

Victoria drove the mule team that was hauling the remains of two skinny cow buffalo. Poor doings. This hard day's toil would supply the post with meat for barely a day, but the buffalo were scarce and had wintered down to bones and hide.

The Cheyenne woman saw them coming but didn't move; it was only when strangers arrived, a Missouri wagon train, or St. Louis teamsters, or Santa Fe muleteers, or a band of Kiowas or Utes or Arapahos or Jicarillas riding in for some trading, that she stirred. Thus it had been ever since Skye arrived in the fall of 1838; thus it was now in the spring of 1841.

Her name was Standing Alone. He wondered whether the winter in Black Dog's camp had been good to her; whether her copper flesh had withered prematurely, or her jet hair had grayed, or whether her stocky Cheyenne body had begun to shrink with her sorrow. She wasn't old; perhaps upper twenties, early thirties, but her ordeal had added twenty years, and she peered at the world from eyes that had seen centuries of torment.

She would soon be given some of this very meat. William Bent himself saw to it. Once each day, Archibald the cook took a wooden bowl full of scraps through the creaking cottonwood gate, and handed her whatever was that day's fare. She would eat swiftly, nod her thanks, and settle again at her post, to continue her vigil. Some said she was there because she never got over the tragedy and was obsessed. Others said that she was there because she had received those instructions in a sacred vision. Injun hoodoo, they called it. There was also the possibility that she was mad. Her husband, Cloud Watcher, respected her desires, and brought her each spring, and left her there to watch for the missing ones.

No one ever touched her; not even the cruel Comanches when they came to trade. They despised the Cheyenne and murdered them on sight, but not Standing Alone; no blood flowed below the towering tan adobe ramparts of Bent's Fort. Indeed, even these mortal enemies of her people called her

Grandmother, this vigiling woman, and passed gently by.

Skye paused to let Victoria draw up beside him. She sat
on the hard wagon seat, hunched against the wind, her wiry
frame fierce against the weather and weariness, ready to subdue the mutinous mules with great oaths and swift lashes of
her whip. Upon her rite of passage into womanhood she had
been named Many Quill Woman, of the Otter Clan, of the
Kicked-in-the-Belly band of Mountain Crows, and now she
was a long way from home, and a white man's woman.

The earth had softened under the winter's wetness, and
made hard work for the mules. But Victoria spoke mule language even better than English, understood mule wiles and
extortions, and knew how to compel these beasts of burden
to her small, iron will. She had mastered all the oaths of white
men, employed them enthusiastically, and the mules listened
respectfully to her music.

"She's there," he said. "Never so early as this."

"Something's different," Victoria said.

Skye felt it, too.

The biting wind harried them toward the post. No one
was out in the fields; not on such a cruel day. Bent's Fort rose
amazingly out of nothing; a tawny apparition, made of cottonwood logs and golden mud, its round bastions promising
protection, and its towering walls promising respite from nature. It was a laird's castle, the seat of empire, the work of
hard-willed men who had found fortune in the wilderness
of the southern plains. The Bents of Missouri had built it out
of nothing but iron hearts and a vision of empire.

Skye rode ahead, eager now to escape the wind and warm
his chilled body before a cottonwood blaze in one of the massive fireplaces within. He reached the gate, expecting to pass
through the portcullis into the great yard within. But this
time, Standing Alone rose suddenly, her blue blanket
wrapped about her, and blocked his way, her black eyes surveying him boldly.

"Grandmother," he said politely. "How are you?"

She could not understand a word, nor could he fathom the Cheyenne tongue, so he could not translate the torrent of words pouring from her. He turned helplessly to Victoria, who had stopped the mules just behind, but he could see no comprehension in Victoria's face.

"Dammit, I don't know what the hell she's spouting," she said.

He lifted his battered beaver hat, and settled it again. It stayed aboard his head no matter how treacherous the wind, but just how was a secret that only Skye knew. The hat was his hallmark. Anyone within a mile could recognize Barnaby Skye by his black beaver hat. Anyone closer up might recognize him by his small bleached-blue eyes, deep-set in a ruddy face occasionally shaved; a formidable hogback of a nose, much battered and pulped by fisticuffs and hard use; great slabs of bristly jowl that hung to either side, giving him the look of a bulldog; and the stocky, short body and seaman's roll to his gait that was familiar to men anywhere in the mountains or the plains.

Standing Alone had recognized him from afar, and this time she wanted something.

"Can you make out what she wants?" he asked Victoria.

"Something awful damn bad," Victoria replied. She didn't like Cheyennes, ancient and bitter enemies of her Crow people.

Skye released his looped rein, wondering whether his unruly buckskin would behave, and hand-signaled to the woman.

"What say?" his hands asked.

She responded at once, her hands flashing. "Talk to you."

"I will later."

She nodded.

He would have to find William Bent or Kit Carson to translate. It was certainly odd.

He lifted his black hat to her once again, and settled it on the shaggy brown hair that reached his shoulders and helped keep his neck and ears warm in the winter. The hair was showing its first streaks of gray, which had shocked him. How could he be getting gray when he was still young? But he knew. His had been the hardest and most brutal of lives.

"Cheyenne killer bastards," Victoria said.

Around the fort, Victoria was celebrated as the most advanced cusser in all the Indian nations. She had honed her skills by listening to profane mountain men, and not even the fort's legendary chief trader, Goddam Murray, could match her.

But Skye never cursed at all. He touched the flanks of his horse with his winter moccasins, and steered toward the kitchen. The cooks would be glad to add this meat to the larder even if it was fit for nothing more than stew.

He steered his buckskin hard left, toward an alley that led to the corrals. Victoria steered her wagon across the yard, stopping at the far corner before the kitchen and cook's quarters. Skye swiftly unsaddled, turned the horse loose, and hurried to help her. No one else was going to pitch in. The cooks were busy, or pretended to be, and besides, dragging hunks of meat wrapped in bloody hide was beneath them.

Wordlessly, Skye opened the wagon gate, rolled a massive quarter of meat to the ground, and dragged it into the hot kitchen, where cooks were preparing a supper for the fifty mouths they were expected to feed twice a day. Skye yanked and tugged, pulling the meat past cursing cooks, until he reached a cool locker area to the rear. He and Victoria repeated the process, winning only curses from the harried cooks. That happened often. He often arrived while a meal was in the making, so they waved bloody butcher knives at him and snarled.

By the time he and Victoria had finished, they were both even grimier than before. Skye touched her arm, and she smiled gratefully. She would scrape the gore off of her arms and hands and face, and somehow make herself clean.

Skye clambered onto the wagon seat and turned the

mules, only to discover the post's bourgeois, Alexander Barclay, observing him.

"Two cows, poor doings," Skye said.

"Buffalo aplenty here."

Skye repressed his anger. It had been hard enough to come up even with that. Barclay, like himself, was an Englishman, but there the resemblance ended. Barclay knew all about Skye, the deserter from the Royal Navy who had jumped ship at Fort Vancouver and become a mountain man. His obdurate disapproval of Skye stood between them, and had made life at Bent's Fort grim at times, and never joyous.

Skye, not wishing to talk further, hawed the mules, and steered the wagon around to the rear of the post and into the spacious corrals there. He was bone tired but he compelled himself to remove the harness, hang it up on its pegs, rub down and grain the mules, and check their feet for hoof cracks and stone bruises.

By the time he had finished, the gong had sounded. But he headed for his apartment, a cubicle partitioned off from the hunters' quarters, to clean himself. Victoria was there, freshened and ready to eat. She was one of few women on the post, and the only pureblooded Indian, and that made for uneasy circumstances. Some of the engagés resented her; others eyed her intently, their designs plain in their gazes. Skye suspected she had fought several off with the glint of her skinning knife, and had chosen not to tell him about it.

He sighed. Bent's Fort had given them security, comfort, a modest wage, and a refuge from weather. But Victoria was too much alone among so many white men, and Skye knew she was enduring life rather than enjoying it. He wasn't faring much better. But the beaver trade was plumb belly-up and a man had few places to turn.

They exited their quarters, passed through the empty dormitory and into the yard, where they encountered Lucas Goddam Murray, the chief trader.

"Say, mate," said Skye, falling in with the trader, "you mind translating for a minute?"

"Planned to eat."

"Standing Alone wants to talk with me."

"Cold meat." He glared. "Well, the day's been ruined enough, so I guess I can translate for the Cheyenne and eat cold stew."

"I'm obliged," Skye said. He steered Lucas and Victoria toward the great cottonwood gate, to see what the savage woman wanted.

two

The chief trader veered resolutely toward the gates, stepped under the portcullis, and stopped without. The Cheyenne woman stirred at the sight of him. Skye and Victoria followed.

"Grandmother," Murray said, using the Cheyenne word of greatest respect. "Grandmother, we will talk in the trading room."

He held out his big white hand to her, and she stood gracefully, peering into his face, then into Skye's, and finally into Victoria's. She nodded, drew her blue blanket about her as if it were a queen's ermine, and walked toward the trading store, the place where Murray and his squinty black-clad traders pulled the proffered robes and other peltries onto the worn counter, examined each one, offered a miserable price, and bartered the pelts for the white men's wonders on the rough shelves.

This was Murray's lair; he even knew where the dust was thickest. The Skyes followed.

Standing Alone seemed much younger when she stood; erect and slim, and not so worn. The transformation was startling, and did not escape Skye and his woman.

"I am here to tell them what you say to me," Murray said

in her tongue, wanting to get it over with. He looked at her impatiently, wanting food in his belly.

She nodded, touched his wrist, and turned toward the Skyes. "All of my people know this man," she said. "All of my people know this woman too," she said.

Goddam Murray translated hastily, hoping that Standing Alone wouldn't sink into the redskin oratory that could consume hours.

"I say this: For four winters I have waited for my boy and my girl to return here to the place I last saw them and they last saw me. I have waited upon the westwind and the eastwind. I have waited upon the southwind and the northwind. But the winds have not brought my son and my daughter back to me. Now the four winds have passed, and I have not seen my children. They are far away."

He turned to the Skyes. "She's waited four years for her children, and they haven't come."

Standing Alone had a sweet, melancholy voice, and he listened closely as she continued. "I say this: Now I will go look for my children. In a vision I saw this man and woman leading me. They will know where to go and who to talk to."

Murray turned to the Skyes. "She wants to hire you to find her children. She'll go with you."

Skye looked nonplused. Victoria muttered something that Goddam Murray thought was a curse. The Crow and Cheyenne weren't bosom friends.

"I have brought them a present," Standing Alone said. "This comes from my people. It is a sacred bundle, with great powers. This I give to Mister Skye to wear."

She pulled open her blanket and lifted a small medicine bundle, no larger than the palm of her hand, from her bosom, and passed the cord over her neck, stirring her silken jet hair.

"Medicine bundle's for you, Skye. That's her gift for taking her."

"Me? Me?"

Such a sacred gift could not be refused and Skye accepted it reluctantly, cupping his brown hand to receive the leather-bound packet. He could not ask what was in it, nor its powers, nor how to honor it.

Victoria lifted the bundle, examined it with a keen eye, and slipped the thong over Skye's neck. It hung over his bear-claw necklace.

"Thank her, mate."

Murray did: "Mister Skye is honored to receive the sacred gift of the Cheyenne."

"I say this: Tell the man I am ready to go whenever he is ready to go. We will find my children."

"She's ready when you're ready, Skye. You'll find her wayward ones."

Skye lifted his black beaver and settled it on his stringy hair. "I can't say as I'm ready to go, mate."

"You've got the bundle on your chest, Skye."

"I'll find some excuse. Is that it? That's what Standing Alone wanted to say?"

The Cheyenne woman seemed to understand, and nodded. That was it. Go with her. Find her children. Take the sacred bundle and wear it.

Murray thought to pour oil on those turbulent waters. "Grandmother, our hunter may not wish to go to find your children and he will want to talk to his woman about this."

The Cheyenne nodded.

"I can't do this. Tell her," said Skye.

"Wait. We'll talk," Victoria said.

"Go? With what? A bundle of pebbles and bird bones wrapped in leather?"

"You are blind, dammit, Skye. She's paid you honor."

"It's not an honor I want."

The Cheyenne woman waited for a translation, so Murray provided it. "They are thinking about it."

"They are disagreeing."

"Yes, Grandmother."

"I say this: It is honor enough, the sacred bundle. It was given to me by Strong Runner, a keeper of the arrows."

Big medicine, Murray thought.

Skye looked desperate. "I will talk with her in the morning. Will you translate?"

Murray nodded. "If I'm not in the store, Wagner knows the tongue."

"Grandmother, we will take you back to your place, and soon the cooks will bring you your bowl."

"Thank you, Grandfather Murray," she said. She turned to the Skyes, peered into each of their faces, touched each one on the hand, touched the bundle on Skye's chest, and pulled her blue blanket about her.

Murray escorted her out the door and through the gates, and then returned to the silent yard.

"You satisfied, Skye?"

Skye lifted his beaver and settled it. "It's Mister Skye, mate."

Murray laughed. The man in charge, Barclay, had ridiculed Skye's pretensions from the moment the renegade had applied at the post for a position. The seaman off the docks of East London had taken on airs, and the post's chief factor had seen through them and made light of Skye's peculiar manner. The mockery had spread through the post, and for two years no one had honored Skye's request that he be addressed as "Mister." But Skye never stopped requesting that he be addressed as he wished.

"In the new world, I will be Mister, not Subject," he had said, amiably, when anyone asked.

"Tell me again how she chose me," Skye said.

Goddam Murray shrugged. "Indian hoodoo."

"I will think about it."

"Don't."

Murray pushed the great doors closed, sealing out the

savage world and its savage inhabitants, including Standing Alone. He dropped a heavy bar, which fell in its iron slot with a slap.

"Skye, that was four years ago. That Ute band doesn't even have the same chief. The trail's colder than the bottom layer of hell. You could spend the rest of your goddam life going from rancho to hacienda and never find them."

"I'll think about it."

"Did you hear me?"

Murray was annoyed that the Limey even was taking the request seriously. The supper was probably over, and he'd be picking at cold meat.

Skye didn't answer. He was peering at the heavens, as if some secret of the universe was about to be unveiled. Murray left them there in the shadowed yard and hastened to the kitchens, peeved at the world. Maybe they should evict Standing Alone. Get rid of her. Tell her to go sit in the bulrushes, but stay a mile from the post. That would do it. The old bat. Costing the post a meal every day, and for what? Because they all felt sorry for her?

He spat.

Her story was simple, and old, and known to everyone on the southern plains, Indian and white, Mexican and Yank. Over four years earlier, in the spring of 1837, Standing Alone's Cheyenne band, led by Black Dog, had come to trade with William Bent, their white brother and protector of their people. They had set up their lodges north of the post in a grassy flat and spent their time lazily dickering away the fine, winter-haired buffalo pelts and dressed robes for all the plunder on Bent's shelves.

Then one day, a band of Utes rode in to trade; the two tribes weren't friends but Bent imposed peace everywhere in the vicinity of his great adobe fortress, so the Utes camped well to the west, leaving a no-man's-land strip between the tribes. Even so, they got along. Stocky Ute warriors gambled against taller Cheyenne warriors, playing the stick game. The women shyly visited, their nimble fingers making words. The boys swiftly organized war games against each other. The girls traded dolls.

Each of those breezy spring days, Standing Alone plucked up some good fox or wolf or buffalo skins and wandered happily into the trading room to see what marvels she might have: blue beads, awls, sharp steel knives, jingle bells, keen hatchets, bolts of gingham or flannel, needles and thread, sugar by the pound . . .

On this day, the last that the Ute band intended to stay at the post, she had brought her nine-year-old son, Grasshopper, and her twelve-year-old daughter, Little Moon, to the gates.

Wait, she had said. They would each receive a surprise from their mother. And into the trading store she went to begin the process of turning peltries into little gifts for her children. And even as she whiled away the time, the Utes finished their trading and left.

Standing Alone could not find her children when she left the post but that didn't disturb her. They had probably gotten weary of waiting and had gone back to the camp. Hours later, they still were missing. Night fell, and they had not returned. It was only then that she realized, with a chilling wail heard through her village and in every corner of the hushed post, that the Utes, famous stealers of children and slave traders, had stolen her son and stolen her daughter and were long gone.

three

rritably, Skye sawed at a haunch of buffalo and added some boiled maize to his trencher. His mood matched that of the cooks, who were cleaning up when he and Victoria wandered in. Victoria sawed a huge piece of buffalo and scorned the vegetable.

Skye sat down at a vacant trestle table and Victoria joined him. The last of the engagés were mopping up their food. The post's officers, including Murray, ate separately.

"That is big damn medicine," Victoria said, eyeing the bundle.

Skye didn't answer. It was nothing but a leather pouch with feathers and pebbles and God knows what else in it. He was feeling trapped. He knew what he had to do. At dawn, he would find Standing Alone and return the thing. If she thought a leather pouch with some totems inside of it committed him to anything, she was mistaken.

He had no intention of going out to hunt for those children, long gone and probably dead. Northern Mexico was full of Indian slaves, many of them sold to hacendados by the Utes, who made the traffic of human flesh a good business. They abducted children of working age from neighboring tribes and peddled them in Taos for cash. The docile children made good field hands, doomed to hoe and weed and scythe and harvest until they died at a young age from sheer exhaustion. Some ended up in the mines, hauling heavy baskets of ore, fed just enough to keep them going, until they, too, died at a young age, their bones twisted and backs curved.

Mexican officials averted their eyes; the church also looked elsewhere, upon heavenly vistas. There was wealth in the slave traffic; cheap stoop labor for the haciendas, mines, and plantations. And the wily Utes, in their mountain lair, were the principal suppliers of human flesh.

Skye pondered all that as he masticated tough and stringy buffalo, which the cooks had scarcely bothered to subdue with fire. Meals for engaged men, hunters, laborers, and others like himself, tended to be perfunctory at best. Men up the ladder ate better here and at any other large western post. Skye remembered the officers and clerks' meals he had seen, or eaten, at Fort Vancouver, run by the Hudson Bay Company, and Fort Union, the great outpost of American Fur. This was no different.

No, he wouldn't go. Not that this post offered him anything but subsistence. He hadn't advanced and didn't expect to, not with Barclay the chief factor. Skye's formidable reputation as a mountaineer mattered little here. His recent experience as a brigade leader counted for naught. His youthful history, however, counted for all too much. But the post offered company, security, food, and comfort. Many were the winter days when he cherished being behind its thick walls, beside a crackling fire. Here he slept in a bunk, defied weather, enjoyed the safety, and got a regular pittance for his troubles. When the beaver trade faded he didn't know what he would do. Bent had given him his answer.

No, he wouldn't leave. Not for some wild-goose chase. Not to track two children lost four years ago, first by heading into the dangerous warrens of the Utes to find out where the children went, and then probably wandering around, illegally, in Mexico, hunting two slaves. And if he did find one or both, getting them out would be still another problem. Hacendados commanded small merciless armies.

He couldn't even buy the children's freedom; he had scarcely ten dollars to his name. The rest had gone to sustain himself, clothe Victoria, and gradually replenish his outfit. But most had gone for aguardiente, Taos Lightning.

When the Utes had fled Bent's Fort with the Cheyenne children, William Bent had swiftly organized a pursuit; he and his best men tracked the band for days, only to be defeated by veils of rain and the wily maneuvers of the warrior Utes. He didn't stop there; William Bent would do anything to help his wife's people. He had written Governor Armijo of New Mexico, asking that the children be returned. He had posted rewards. The Cheyenne themselves had sallied into Ute fastnesses, all to no avail.

And then Standing Along began her vigil, and had stood her watches at the gate long before Skye had first set eyes on the post. He had never known a summer season without the sight of her huddled beside the gate.

What had changed her mind now? He knew the answer to that, at least. She had dreamed it; her spirit guide had ordained it. Her husband had understood, and brought her there in the spring, and returned for her when the geese flew south.

Victoria was glaring at him. "You gotta go," she said.

"For what? I need money."

"Because of the bundle."

"I'll return it."

"You are dumb."

There were moments when Skye sunk deep into himself, especially when Victoria was needling him, as she was now. He picked stringy buffalo out of his teeth and let her gusts of importuning sail past him.

He halfway wanted to go; the idea of finding the children and restoring them to their mother appealed to him. The idea of righting a wrong, wreaking trouble on the damnable Utes, stealing them from some heartless and cruel hacendado, delighted him. But most of all, that face of Standing Alone, the suffering in it, the hope in it, the trust and dream, all worked on his heart.

But all the practical considerations warred against such a quixotic adventure. Money, food, security, clothing, weapons, horses. Why throw all that away?

Murray was right: don't even think about it.

"I'm going upstairs," Skye said, sullenly.

Upstairs at Bent's Fort was the billiard room and saloon. It had started as Bent's offices, and had evolved into a place for the men at the post to congregate. Amazingly, it had a billiard table dragged out the trail from St. Louis, more than half a thousand miles away. William Bent's saloon probably soaked up most of the monthly salaries of the post's men; for a little Taos Lightning, a brandy made of agave leaves, he got his wages back.

"You'll get drunk, dammit. You got to be ready to go," she said.

He laughed. Soon she would follow him, and together they would drink up half a month's wage and forget about Standing Alone.

This evening, in a velvety twilight, as cool air eddied into the second-story saloon, Skye found few men. It was the middle of the week and the middle of the month. But one of those present was William Bent himself, lounging at a table with Goddam.

"Skye," Bent said, "let me see that bundle."

"You've been talking to Murray."

"You'd be crazy to go, Skye."

"Mister Skye, mate."

Bent laughed. The man was actually younger than Skye, but the sheer force of his personality, and his lordship over this amazing castle in the wilds, made him seem ten years older.

Bent drew an oil lamp close and studied the bundle pending from Skye's neck. He turned to Murray. "That's it. I know that one."

"What is it?" Skye asked.

"Owl Woman's talked about it," Bent said. "That's the bundle worn by Strong Runner, keeper of one of the sacred arrows. He was wearing it when he led the famous attack on the Pawnees, who'd stolen the arrow. For my wife's people, that's quite a piece of merchandise."

Bent talked like that. A sacred item became merchandise.

"I'm giving it back when the gate opens."

Bent smiled. "I would too. That thing obligates you to lead the whole Cheyenne nation. When Strong Runner died, that bundle went to his senior wife, and then it was hung in a special lodge, and after that . . . I'm not sure. Say, Skye, fetch a dram and sit here. I don't want you to go on that wild-goose chase, and I'll list the reasons why."

Skye nodded, headed for the bar, where a clerk delivered a dram drawn from a cask and made a notation. Skye knew he was in for more than his next payday would yield; a position the Bents wanted to keep him in.

Bent sipped, felt the fiery stuff lava down his throat, and settled down beside Bent and Murray. The aguardiente felt just fine, and he sipped again.

"Skye, first of all, Standing Alone's crazy. You know that. Secondly, you haven't a chance of finding that boy and girl. They're probably a few provinces down, in Sinaloa or Sonora or Chihuahua. The Utes probably traded them off in Taos, but there are half a dozen slavers there who carry the flesh south, deep into Mexico."

"Why'd she pick me?"

Bent shrugged. "Hoodoo."

"Why not one of her own?"

"A Cheyenne can't do it. He'd be butchered trying to talk to Utes or dealing with Mexicans. It has to be a white man.

She elected you. Carson tells me you had something of a reputation up north. That's why."

"Why now?"

"More hoodoo. They do everything in fours. Sacred number. She waited four years. Her brats didn't show up. Skye, amigo, that trail's so cold and those children are so dead you'll waste a year of your life. And besides, you're a good hunter and we need you here."

"What happens when I return the bundle?"

Bent sighed, obviously searching for words. "That's one of the most revered bundles the Cheyenne have. Might be an insult to return it. But make no mistake, she picked you. She got that bundle from her elders or chiefs, and gave it to you. It's flattering, Skye. That's honor. That's a passport, too. You show that to any Cheyenne and you'll get help."

"What's in it?"

"Who knows? Strong Runner's totems. It's not what's in it, it's what happened. He got the stolen sacred arrow back from the Pawnees, wearing that thing around his dusky neck."

Skye sipped, feeling the heat build in his belly. The damned bundle somehow seized him and he knew what he was going to do, and William Bent wouldn't like it, and everyone at the post, save for Victoria, would consider him a lunatic. She would just grin.

But William Bent had the last word: "Skye, don't do it. I mean it."

four

Skye tossed in his robes that night. He was remembering things he desperately wanted to forget; those years of virtual slavery in the Royal Navy, powerless to live his own life or choose his destiny. He had been pressed into the navy at the age of thirteen, lifted right off the cobbled streets of East London by a press gang. He never saw his family again. He never felt the sweetness of liberty until he jumped ship at Fort Vancouver.

But most of all, he remembered the cruelty. He remembered being tied to the deck gratings and lashed with a cat-o'-nine-tails until his back ran with his own blood. He remembered being brutally beaten by boatswains. He remembered being robbed of porridge by older seamen; being reduced to a starving bundle of muscles subdued to the will of 'tween-decks tyrants and captains.

He wallowed in his bunk, remembering the brutal punishment every time he protested, the despair, the hopelessness of ever living his own life, the prison of the forecastle, the desolation that he meant no more to others than useful muscle and bone.

He remembered how they took away even his pittance as punishment for imagined infractions, so he was not only a slave, but without a pence to his name.

Many was the night, lying in his hammock in the fore-castle, that he would gladly have jumped overboard and given himself to the sea but for some glimmering sense that he was not alone; somewhere, God hovered, offering hope. And yet it hadn't all been bad. He remembered the dolphins sporting in the green sea, the strange tropical shores, the sea-men's hornpipes and rough humor, their pride in their skills. He remembered the breathtaking views of the endless gray seas from the crow's nest as it swayed to the tides. But all that was part of a life not chosen or desired.

Out of that seven-year ordeal was born in him a loathing of slavery that ran so deep and fierce that he despised every form of it, from the indenture of pressed seamen in the navies of the world, to the wage peonage and perpetual debt that bound a man to his creditor, to convict labor, to the obscene slavery of black men that stained and tarnished the American South. In every case, people were being used; human beings were forcibly denied their right to live their own lives. In every case, the oppressed lived in hopelessness and sorrow.

And so he thrashed in his bunk until Victoria slipped over to him in the darkness and placed a small, cool hand on his forehead.

"It is a bad night," she said.

Skye came fully awake at once, and all the dark phantasms slithered away. He clasped that small hand and held it.

"Bad dreams," he said.

"Dreams? You were asleep?"

"Memories, then. When I was a sailor."

She had heard of all these horrors. "Aiee, it is bad to think of that."

"Can't help it."

He felt her hands on him, comforting him, sending messages of love and grace to him.

"No master commands you," she said.

"I'm not so sure."

"Only in your thoughts."

"You want to go after those children? Go on the wild-goose chase?"

"What is this, a wild-goose chase?"

"A foolish quest. A futile effort."

"If it makes you think such bad memories, maybe we shouldn't."

"If I go, it's because of those memories. If those children are still alive, they're probably slaves in Mexico. That's what the Utes do. Sell them into slavery. They would be down there somewhere, being ruined, hopeless, denied happiness, used and used and used and used until they die."

"Let's go, Skye." Her voice was urgent.

He pulled her to him until her head nestled into the hollow of his shoulder. He liked that; liked sharing life with her.

"You opposed to slavery so much? Your people got slaves."

"It's for her. Standing Alone."

She pitied the woman even if she was Cheyenne. He did too, but not so much. She was free to do what she wanted. It was the two captive children whose fate stirred him.

"We have different reasons," he said.

"Not so different."

"It's a stupid thing to do. No money in it."

"Skye, you are so damned dumb."

He laughed. She always did that to him when he was being buffalo-witted. "I'll talk to Bent in the morning. We've got problems from the get-go."

"Like what?"

"We can't even talk to Standing Alone. Except in signs. How's she going to tell us anything? We need someone with us who knows Cheyenne."

"I don't want anyone with us. Just me, you, and her."

"That's just one thing. I'm in debt to Bent. We've been sipping a lot of Taos Lightning. How can I get out of that?"

"We just go!"

"I am a man of honor."

"Well, who says he is, eh? He charges too damn much."

"There's a few more problems than that. If we find her children, how do we free them?"

She grunted. He knew she had no reply.

"I don't have any money," he added.

"We got to steal them children, then."

He didn't reply to that. He knew what the odds were.

And so they spent the night snugged together but in the morning Skye felt exhausted. He splashed himself with water and called that his toilet, and headed into the quiet yard just as Goddam Murray was opening the front gates.

As always, Standing Alone huddled against the mud walls, greeting the day.

Skye stepped outside into the golden hush. The Cheyenne woman saw him, and stood slowly. She was waiting for an answer, and her gaze enveloped him, missing nothing.

He had to think of the signs. The finger language was so poor it never sufficed. But finally, he signaled her: Grandmother, I will go. Soon. Not today. Much to do first.

Standing Alone nodded and touched him with her hand. He felt a strange power flowing from that gentle touch, from the tips of her fingers upon his wrist. There were things about life he never would grasp, and one of them was this strange touch that sent something deep into his heart, something that was more than gratitude or encouragement; something that bonded him to this Cheyenne woman.

He felt mesmerized by the force of it and then shied away from her, fearful of this strange force.

"Soon, Grandmother. I must talk to Bent. Quit this place and get my horses and all. Then we'll go."

It was English, but she nodded. Odd how meanings sometimes conveyed, even if words failed.

She stood solemnly in that gold dawn light, the level rays

of the sun strong on her face, her features once again young. He knew she was barely thirty and yet all those years at the gate she had been an old woman.

He left her there, and hunted down Bent but failed to find him. He looked for Barclay, intending to give notice. It was too early. The post didn't stir until midmorning.

He crossed the quiet yard again, and then up the stairs to the hunters' rooms. He would need to look at his outfit. He would need powder and balls and caps at the least. The outfitting worried him. He owed the company. Many a night he had squandered his future pay in that billiards parlor and saloon.

He found Victoria in their room, packing up gear.

"We going?"

"Soon as we can."

"You ain't got much powder."

"That's going to be tricky."

He left Victoria to the packing and headed for the pens to round up his three horses. Two of these he saddled. The third would carry a pack. Someone of them would be walking.

That done, he headed for the store and there at last he found Bent.

"Mr. Bent, I'm resigning."

"No you're not. You owe the company three months of back wages."

"I'll write you an IOU."

"No you won't. You're going to stay here and hunt. If it's Standing Alone, forget it. I told you, leave her alone."

"I've told her I'm going."

Bent was growing angry. "Well I'll tell her otherwise. You will not duck out on me."

Skye sighed. "What I owe is just about the price of a horse. I'll give you a bill of sale."

"The hell you will, Skye." Bent loomed over him, beetle-browed and tough.

"All right, what are your terms?" Skye asked.

"Terms? Terms? There are none. You'll go hunting today as usual and you'll give me your word you'll return this evening. Your wife stays here. Your outfit stays here."

"You didn't hear me, Bent. I've quit. You'll get a horse for what I owe. I'm going to do something that will make the Cheyenne happy. If you pen me up, they are not going to be happy."

He glared at Bent, ready to pound the man if it came to that. No one, no one on earth, would imprison him again if he could help it.

Bent retreated. "Your funeral," he said.

"I need powder and ball and some other stuff."

"Your problem, not mine." He turned to the chief trader. "Murray, he's got no credit. Don't give him any."

"My word is my credit."

Bent laughed. "Don't come back," he said.

five

Two young hunters, Tom Boggs and Lyle Lilburn, braced Skye while he was packing his duffel in the plaza.

"We hear you're leaving us, Mister Skye," Boggs said.

"Word gets around fast."

"You going to help that crazy Cheyenne woman?"

Skye nodded.

"That's a fine thing to do," Boggs said.

That wasn't what Skye had expected. He supposed they would all echo William Bent, and greet his decision with a horselaugh, or consider it a self-imposed death sentence.

Goddam Murray and the clerks had been talking, and it took only about two minutes for gossip to work through Bent's Fort.

"You're doing it for nothing, too," Lyle said.

"No, I'm being paid," Skye replied.

"Yeah, with that." Lilburn pointed at the Cheyenne medicine bundle. "That don't buy DuPont."

Skye shrugged. "It's just something I want to do. That's pay enough."

Boggs shook his head. "You're likely going to get yourself killed, if not by a pack of mean Utes, then by some ornery greasers. You're walking into the devil's own lair."

Skye nodded. There was no point in denying it.

"You're doing it to help Standing Alone?"

Skye straightened, lifted his top hat and settled it. "I suppose I am."

"You *suppose* you are!"

"Maybe help those children, then."

Lilburn grinned. "Now that sounds more like the Skye I know. Help those young 'uns escape from ten years of stoop labor and an early death. That wouldn't have something to do with your sailor past, would it?"

Skye grinned.

Boggs eyed the heap of goods. "You outfitted proper?"

Skye evaded that. These boys were relatives by marriage to the Bents.

"No, you ain't," Boggs said, relentlessly. "I heard they wouldn't even spare you powder."

"I've enough," Skye replied, tightly.

"It's bad enough you going off on this grouse hunt, like you're after the Holy Grail, but it's worse you going off half fixed."

"I can live like an Indian," Skye said.

"Indians don't live like Indians anymore; they get stuff from us. How long since you seen a stone arrowhead?"

Lilburn lifted Skye's powderhorn and shook it. "Thought so," he said. "A man going off into Ute country without spare powder is a man gonna push up flowers. Skye, you just stay right here."

"I'm busy, mate."

But Lilburn ran up the stairs and into the dormitory where the trappers and hunters bunked. Skye could hear him up there, and moments later half a dozen of his comrades and rowdies burst out the door, clattered down the stairs, and surrounded Skye. There was something afoot, and it made Skye uncomfortable.

Then Will Gibbs thrust a powderhorn at him. "This here's for you, Mister Skye. I got me another. It's full of DuPont."

He hung the horn over Skye's neck, and patted Skye's arm.

"What a thing, helping that savage," he said.

Johnny Case was next. "I got a spare bullet mold, fifty caliber like yours, and here's a few pigs." He dropped the one-pound lead bars into Skye's duffel, and added the mold. "This'll let you throw something that stings."

"I think maybe we'd better get us a proper pen and paper so I can record what I owe," Skye said.

"You don't owe nothing," Boggs said. "Not one in a thousand would do it. Risk his life like this for nothing."

"It's not for nothing," Skye said, uncomfortably.

"I seen that woman there at the gate all this time, and I feel bad for her, but you're the one who's doing something about it."

"She chose me, mate."

"So I heard, but you said yes."

Skye felt itchy. He wasn't used to anything like this. He saw Victoria watching quietly, approval in her face. The crowd grew, until most of the engaged men in Bent's Fort crowded the plaza around Skye. And one by one, they brought him sustenance.

"Mister Skye," said Walt Gillis, "this here's cowhide shoe leather; real sole leather, tougher than any buffler hide you'll ever find. You'll need it."

Skye accepted it gratefully. He and Victoria and Standing Alone would be walking because they lacked horses.

One by one they brought him valuable things: from the clerks in the store, some trading items, including the prized blue beads the tribes loved so much. From the cooks, some jerky, tallow, cornmeal, sugar, flour, salt, and tea. From the engagés, spare flints and steels, a spare blanket, soap, half a candlestick, a canvas poncho, thong.

Skye watched the pile grow, wondering whether he could fit it all on his two remaining horses, wondering what he had done to earn this sudden outpouring of honor and esteem.

Now a silent crowd stood around him in the plaza. Skye saw Victoria standing proudly by; and there at the gate was Standing Alone herself, oddly isolated, as if this blanket squaw had no connection to the portentous events unfolding a few yards away.

Above, on the broad deck of the galleries, stood those in command: William Bent himself, his posture dour and his face furrowed. Beside him the chief factor, Alexander Barclay, exuding disapproval as only the English can disapprove. And the excitable Goddam Murray, rising up and down on his toes like a tottering barrel. The entire post had come to see the Skyes off.

The heap of offerings exceeded what his horses could carry. And offerings they were, as if a church's collection plate had passed through this motley crowd of bearded men, and they had spilled their very substance into it. They were honoring him. He had never been so honored. These were a bold race of men, whose imaginations were fired by this quest for the Holy Grail, two imprisoned children; or more likely, the news of their deaths. Not for money was Skye setting out into dangerous lands, nor for fame, but only to help a woman whose presence had haunted the post for years.

Skye scarcely knew what to say, so he pulled off his top hat and bowed his head.

When he lifted his gaze again, he discovered Bent racing down the stairs, and that spelled trouble. He'd get out just as fast as he could.

Bent pushed through the silent crowd until he reached Skye.

"I'll lend you the horse," he said. "You'll need it."

Skye nodded. "I do need it."

"And another. You need another."

"Mr. Bent, I can't assure you that I'll ever—"

Bent wasn't listening. "Get that horse, and the dun pack mule, rigged up."

The stable man, Voller Campbell, leaped to the command.

"It's yours. Skye, I can steer you a little, if you're so determined to commit suicide. The Ute band you want isn't the Mouache who live around here. Those were maybe Weeminuche or Capotes. We think Capotes, from the San Luis Valley. We don't know. We looked hard, offered bribes and rewards. They're trouble, the Utes. Treacherous buzzards. I don't have to tell you what you're facing. You know the Utes. Dangerous and unpredictable. All smiles and murder. Likely to sell these women into slavery if they can."

Bent offered his hand, and Skye found the grip strong and affectionate. "I will remember this," Skye said.

"We'll remember you."

The stable man brought the bay horse Skye had turned over to Bent to pay debts, and a mule, each rigged with a packsaddle.

Then, while Skye hastily wrapped and balanced his loads among the animals, Stands Alone slowly walked to the heart of the plaza, her gaze soft upon them all. She had seen the hunters and trappers, and finally the whole post, contribute something to this venture, and now she passed through them, touching each, mumbling something in her own tongue that Skye knew was a thanksgiving. She paused long before Bent; he understood the woman's Cheyenne, and nodded.

Then the moment came.

Skye nodded to Victoria, who grabbed the halter rope of one horse.

"Thank you all," he said. "With all these things, we'll succeed."

"It'll take more than things, Mister Skye," William Bent said. "My wife's people will remember."

Skye nodded. Nothing more needed saying. He beckoned to Standing Alone, who took up a halter rope, and he collected the other two, and they made their way out the gate and into the morning.

It seemed oddly silent. No breeze hummed through grass. No crows gossiped. No sounds emerged from the great yellow fort. He led his bride, and Stands Alone, along the river trail west, scarcely knowing where to go.

They reached a point where cottonwoods and a slope threatened to conceal Bent's Fort, and paused to look back. Skye had an odd, hollow feeling as he stared at that solemn walled city, a strange island of safety and comfort in a wild land. Something about the place tugged him back even if he had not had the happiest sojourn there.

He turned to Standing Alone, whose gaze was sharp upon the silent white man's castle. But then she smiled, first at Victoria and then at Skye. Her few possessions had been heaped upon the old mule so she could walk beside them unburdened. But it was her face that caught his eye.

She had come alive. The woman who had huddled at the gate, awaiting her loved ones, had seemed ancient, but this majestic woman standing proudly beside Skye and Victoria had shed thirty years overnight, and her strong-boned face was alive with hope.

six

Straight toward the Utes. Skye didn't quite know what his hurry was. And yet he chafed at every delay, as if the children had been abducted four days ago instead of four years ago. But he knew why he hurried. Less for the Cheyenne woman's sake than for theirs.

Walking pained him. His ungainly gait, comfortable on the rolling teak deck of a man-o'-war, served him ill on land. The women walked easily, each leading horses, but he felt the hard clay hammer his feet and calves with every step.

The Taos Trail took him where he wanted to go, straight up the Arkansas River. Mexico lay on one side; the United States of America on the other. He belonged to neither and probably would always be a man without a country, a friend of suffering people whoever they might be. For he had suffered, and knew how much any small kindness meant.

The river coursed through rolling plains, short-grass country, dry all summer but verdant now with spring rains. At least the weather was bearable. Later on, this blistered and blistering land would be impassible from midafternoon until dusk, and one would be wise to shade up until the worst of the day had passed.

Even so, the walking sweated him. He paused frequently and always with the same salutation:

"You ladies will wish to rest," he said, his courtliness concealing other motives.

But Victoria only laughed as she watched him collapse into grass, undo his laced-up bullhide moccasins, and massage his white feet. She was more careful than he, scanning the distant vistas and studying the hilltops before she settled herself.

Skye splashed river water on his face, and sometimes threw it down his shirt to cool off. But the heavy mountain rifle was always at his side, and even during his ablutions he was aware of everything: the gossip of the crows, the sudden silences, the flight of hawks, and subtle alterations of nature.

He knew he was virtually helpless, alone with two women. The Comanches would make quick sport of all three and so would the Jicarilla Apaches. The Utes themselves could go either direction depending on their mood. But his octagon-barreled rifle spoke with authority, especially when pointed casually at a headman.

He chose his campsites carefully, sometimes half a mile off the trail, and in a hollow where they could scratch up a cook fire and not be seen. He didn't want to meet anyone, not even friendly traders.

During those first days, he quietly studied Standing Alone. She was a mystery to him. Questions teemed in his mind but he could not converse with her, and the finger signs were crude and unhelpful. What had impelled her to huddle through four travel seasons at the gate of Bent's Fort waiting for children who would never return? Why couldn't she simply surrender, grieve, and go on living? What did her tribe, her husband, her clan and parents think of this strange conduct?

She had built a small wickiup downriver from the fort, and had repaired to that place many evenings to cleanse herself and do her toilet. The hut was known to all the tribes trading at the fort, and was sacrosanct. No one disturbed one item within it. But always, when daylight stirred and travelers arrived or departed, she could be found at her self-appointed post, wrapped in her blue blanket, watching them with a keen and searching eye.

Sometimes she had cried out and leapt to her feet, run toward some youth or girl who looked like her own, only to wither back into inert sorrow. Most of the men at the post had seen her do that; they could only shake their heads. Some wondered whether she was mad, but Skye had never seen any suggestion of it. He had seen a determined mother, waiting for her children.

But Victoria was making progress with the woman, and somehow they were conversing in simple terms. Standing Alone had absorbed many English words over those years, and while she could not put them together she had acquired some understanding. With fingers, a few words in common, much pointing, and sheer guesswork they were starting to talk.

"Skye, dammit, you know she's got a younger daughter?" Victoria asked, one late hour in the dark.

"Daughter? Where?"

"In her band. Aunts take care of her, like mothers."

"What do her relatives think of her?"

Victoria shrugged. "It's her way. She has chosen a way, and they got no more say in it."

"But her husband—"

"Dog Soldier." She spat it out. The hated Dog Soldiers of the Cheyenne were deadly, lived for war, and bullied others.

"Why are there no more children?"

"She wears the rope."

That was a cord worn between the legs and around the thighs by Cheyenne women to announce and protect their virginity if they were unmarried girls, or to signal their wish to avoid mating, if married. Men usually honored it when girls were wearing it; husbands sometimes did not. Skye knew of no other tribe with a tradition like that.

"For four years?"

Victoria nodded. "Me, you never get me to wear some rope," she snapped.

Skye responded with an arm around her shoulders and she nestled into his chest. "What does her man think about that?"

"He don't question her medicine. She got it from somewhere, and she live by it. He got other wives now. Pretty lucky, eh? There's something else she don't tell me. She's big stuff in that band. She got big powers. She can make a bird fall out of the sky. Maybe someday she will say what her medicine is."

"If we find her children are dead, then what?"

Victoria sighed. "How the hell should I know. I'm some dumb Absaroka, not some beautiful Cheyenne saint that blinks her eyes and talks you into getting her children for her."

Skye sensed something in that; maybe envy. Was Victoria envious of the grieving mother, Standing Alone, who had somehow gotten a white man to hunt for her lost children?

"Don't," he said, roughly.

She turned silent, and the moment passed.

Standing Alone always unrolled her robes a little distant from them, as much to preserve her own privacy as to give them theirs. She was as solitary as her name.

She had been an able and willing travel companion, wordlessly helping Victoria with everything from building a fire to butchering an antelope. She knew her way around horses even though Victoria sniffed at that for a while. Crows considered themselves the best horsemen of the North, and no mere Cheyenne woman could possibly possess the fund of horse-knowing that Victoria possessed. But Skye knew differently. This Cheyenne woman knew horses from the hooves up, and understood their natures, too. And she handled the balky mule in a ruthless way that revealed deep familiarity with the most obstreperous of four-foots.

The enigma of Standing Alone remained on his mind as

43

he took the women farther and farther west. What had led her to pick an obscure white man to find her children? What did she expect if she found one or both? The children would scarcely recognize her now. What manner of medicine had she bestowed on him? Sometimes her gaze was miles away from anywhere; as if she had a world into which no other mortal was permitted. *Madness*?

They traveled twelve or fifteen miles each day along the river, mostly in utter solitude. A few sharp showers were all that marred the exodus, but mostly they trudged through long silences keeping their thoughts to themselves. The world was vast. In the southern and western distances, snowy mountains lifted from horizons, but a day's travel scarcely brought them any closer.

Skye himself was holding up the progress. The women and pack horses could have walked twenty miles easily, but Skye's legs and feet rebelled, and he needed to pause for rest every little while, rub his feet and doctor his blisters, while the women grinned.

They pierced, at last, into a sunny flat where Fountain Creek tumbled into the Arkansas. It had always been a favorite trading place among the tribes; a place that looked eastward over the plains, but backed against isolated ranges of the Rockies. And it was here that they discovered in the distance a crude cottonwood log trading post, brand-new, with a few bearded white men lounging in the shade of its broad veranda. Who were they? Small-time traders and renegades, doing a lively business with the surrounding tribes, including the Utes?

Skye stood at some distance, assessing the quiet, sunlit place, which had no name that he knew of, though he knew that traders and Indians had rendezvoused there. Such places could bring swift and brutal grief to a man, and even worse to a woman. Victoria and Standing Alone pulled up beside him to study this new phenomenon, a white men's building where there had not been one only weeks before by all accounts of travelers.

"I'll go in; you wait," he said to Victoria.

"Alone? Hell no," she said, drawing her bow and quiver from the back of a horse.

"Easy pickings for them," he said, eyeing the pack horses, the mule, and the women.

Victoria glared, and he knew he had offended her. Victoria would never be easy pickings for anyone.

They walked slowly in, across a barren flat denuded of grass by livestock, and knew that they were being watched. But Skye saw no steel poking from shuttered windows. And the three white men on the rude veranda made no move.

They proceeded through afternoon sunlight toward the porch, but saw no sign of activity from the lounging men shaded up there.

"Hello the fort," Skye cried.

"Well, are you all coming in or pickin' a fight?" someone yelled back.

"Coming in," Skye yelled.

He nodded to the women and walked forward, and saw no sign of trouble. One of the men on the veranda did bestir himself, and stood up.

"You looking to trade?" he asked.

"Might be. Looking for some information, too."

"We got both, and they all got a price," the gent said.

Skye looked him over: rail thin, black bearded, squinty, and probably a man with a past, judging by the wariness he showed. These men were armed with horse pistols and had a military bearing, though they wore no uniform. They also were barbered and clean, with trimmed beards, a great rarity in the wilds.

He had reached the veranda, studying them all, and decided there would be no trouble. Not at least for a while.

"I'm Mister Skye," he said. "My wife, Victoria, and our

friend Standing Alone. Maybe you could tell us how to find the Utes."

The man laughed. "You all don't need to do that; the Utes will find you."

"And separate you from them delicious horses and wimmin," added another of the loungers.

"And likely sell the whole lot of you down deep in old Mexico, Sah," added still another, a rotund gent with a goatee, muttonchops, a wide straw planter's hat, and a sweat-stained white shirt.

"Skye, is it?" said the thin one. "I know the moniker. Working for Bent?"

A sudden wariness stretched through the shaded veranda. Skye understood it. These were the opposition; small-time traders wanting to horn in on William Bent's empire.

"Quit 'em," said Skye. "Good people, but I'm on my own."

That's when the big-lipped hairy monkey swung down from the rafters, jumped on the fat one's shoulder, and started chattering.

Seven

Victoria shrieked.

"Aiee!" she cried, and whipped behind her
horses.

Never had she seen such a thing. It sat there, grinning at
her, picking its nose, a Little Person crouched on the sweating
fat man, its tail curling lazily around his neck.

A person from the other world. A person long gone, come
back to this world to haunt her. Truly, she was seeing the
dead. It was a perfect Little Person, with wide-set, bright eyes,
little hands that picked at its reddish-gray fur, long skinny
limbs, and that strange hairy tail that had wrapped itself
around log rafters to enable it to float in the sky.

She covered her eyes with her hands, and furtively
squinted at it through her fingers.

Standing Alone had retreated behind her horses too,
punched backward by an invisible hand, and now looked as
if she were preparing for her own death. Or maybe, yes! She
was seeing her own dead son come back from the other side.
Never had Victoria seen such a haunted look upon a woman's
face.

Skye grinned. "Where'd you get him?"

The fat man chucked his hand under the bewhiskered
chin of the little monkey and scratched. "Panama," he said.

She did not know this place, Panama, but it must be a vast distance away, and in some other world.

"First one I've seen on this continent," Skye said.

"He's my helper," the fat man said. "Can't get along without him. He fetches wood, entertains the savages, and can even make war."

Aiee! A real Little Person. The Absaroka had always known about the Little People, the secret ones who could help them or cause them big trouble, purely on whim. She had never seen one of the Little People but now she was staring at the very first.

"Saw a lot of 'em when I was in the navy," Skye said. "Along the coast of Africa and Asia. They hardly let me off the ships, but still I saw a few. Rhesus, gibbons, apes, lots of 'em. Never expected to see one here. This one's South American, then."

"Spider," said the fat man. "Central America. Some have more hair."

Victoria listened carefully, her hand on her skinning knife. If this Little Person came too close, she would dispatch it.

Skye lifted his battered topper. "I didn't catch your name, sir," he said, offering a hand. But it was the Little Person who took it and shook it cheerfully. Aiee! Her man was a friend of this Little Person. Maybe she should flee to her people before worse happened.

"I'm called the Colonel," the man said.

"Colonel?"

"Call me that; it'll do. The Colonel, Sah, rules all things including Shine. That's the name of this business associate of mine, Shine."

"The monkey's called Shine?"

"No other. I first named him Cayenne, after the robust pepper, but no one called him that. He became Shine, but he's no less spicy. He's uncommonly smart. Wiggle your finger and call him."

Skye lifted his thick hand and wiggled a finger. The monkey gathered itself and leaped gracefully, settling on Skye's shoulder. It reached for Skye's black top hat and stole it, turning it around in its little hands, then biting the rim and spitting.

"Guess it tastes bad," the Colonel said.

Victoria squinted at this apparition. Never in all her years with Skye did she suspect him of truckling to such evil. Maybe she should nock an arrow and kill that thing.

"Colonel, this is my wife, Victoria, and yonder is our friend Standing Alone of the Cheyenne People," Skye said.

The fat man stared right at Victoria, much to her horror, and didn't even avert his bright blue eyes. He doffed his fine straw Panama, and settled it.

"It's my great pleasure, and indeed an honor," he said.

She nodded curtly.

"Mister Skye," she said, "we go now."

Skye studied her. The Little Person on his shoulder grinned and patted Skye and tugged Skye's earlobe.

"Victoria, this is a monkey from South America. There are many types. This type lives in the trees. His long tail is like a spare hand or arm. They are friendly little fellows and often mimic mortals."

The thing leered at her.

She had nothing to say to that. Plainly he had a Little Person on his shoulder, and this was an evil unspeakable. But she saw Standing Alone eyeing the monkey with curiosity. Aiee, what would a stupid Cheyenne woman know about Little People? She felt a flood of scorn for such an ignorant tribe.

Skye saw he had made no dent in Victoria's fears, so he turned to the Colonel.

"Shine is your servant, I gather?"

"He is, Sah. I need one because of my girth. I weigh twenty stone, as you can see, and I would not trade an ounce of it. Twice I have been pierced by arrows, but my avoirdupois is my shield, and neither arrow reached my vitals. It's the perfect means of survival in Indian country."

Victoria was fascinated. She had never seen anyone so fat. How could he even bend over, or lift himself off the ground, or dress himself?

The Little Person dropped off of Skye and bounded to the top of Victoria's packhorse, chattering cheerfully as it began undoing the pack.

"Aiee! Stop him!" she cried, reaching for her skinning knife.

"Shine, conduct yourself in a gentlemanly manner," the Colonel said sternly.

The Little Person rested on his haunches atop the horse, sucking his odd-shaped right thumb. Victoria loosed her knife just in case. But Standing Alone was grinning.

"I will answer your questions before you ask them, Mister Skye. You, by the way, are known to us all as a brave-hearted man of the wilds. I am, Sah, a trader by profession, owner of Childress and McIntyre, Outfitters—we're from the Republic of Texas—and my current project is to supply the Utes with whatever they desire from my stores, while I in turn rake in valuable robes, hides, peltries, and leathers, which in turn I sell here and there or ship downriver."

"The Utes?" Skye asked. "Here?"

"These gents take care of our store. I travel by myself, preferring the open road."

"Alone, in Ute country?"

"Sah, I am never alone with Shine at my side. I have a cart rigged with a seat and storage for my merchandise. We are welcomed everywhere, and my friends the Utes will come from great distances to befriend Shine."

The Little Person held out a hand to Victoria, who shrank from it.

"You . . . Lakota!" she cried, hoping to offend the beast. She would never touch such an abomination. It would destroy her medicine. Let him hold his paw out forever; nothing would alter the stony resolution of her heart.

Shine grinned, sighed, and jumped straight at Victoria.

"Aieee!" she howled, contorting herself in such a way that the Little Person could gain no purchase on her, and landed in the grass.

Standing Alone smirked.

Victoria was angry. She tried to kick the Little Person but it scampered toward Skye and with one bound landed on Skye's shoulder, where it turned and chattered meanly at Victoria, and ended up spitting and clacking its teeth.

"I go back to Yellowstone River now," Victoria said. "Absaroka country."

Skye started laughing. Her man, *laughing* at her. Nothing like this had ever befouled their marriage.

"Madam will come to enjoy Shine; nary a soul does he fail to win to his bosom," the Colonel said.

That was pretty fancy talk. Sometimes Skye talked like that, instead of like the trappers and mountain men.

"As it happens, Mister Skye, Shine is my manservant. If I say build a fire, he gathers the wood for me, lays up the sticks, ignites some kindling with a flint and striker, fetches a kettle, and prepares my repast."

This time Skye was silent, but plainly he was wondering whether there was a scintilla of truth in it. The Little Person was playing with Skye's medicine pouch, the very one given him by Standing Alone. Victoria recoiled at the very sight of it.

"He is also my counselor, Mister Skye. If something goes amiss, I listen to the monkey."

"And what if he's wrong, Colonel?"

"The monkey accepts blame without cavil."

Skye laughed. "One more question, Colonel. How do the tribes respond to Shine?"

Victoria listened closely. If the scheming, forked-tongue Utes liked that thing, then it would be clear that they are even more evil than she imagined.

"They enjoy him," the Colonel said. "Shine is my passport.

When fat Colonel Childress and Shine the spider monkey show up, they welcome us with a feast, and Shine entertains them deep into the night. They call him The Thief, because he pilfers anything he can put his hands on. He jumps from shoulder to shoulder, pats them all for anything he can extract, and then races off to a tree, chittering and chattering and laughing."

Victoria squinted at Shine, having learned of some new reasons to despise the monkey.

Standing Alone studied the monkey silently, and the men, no doubt comprehending very little, and Victoria thought the woman was fortunate to be so ignorant of such an evil, ill-mannered animal.

Then Shine glided off his perch atop the packhorse, and landed at Victoria's feet, hugging her high moccasins.

"See, madam, he likes you," the Colonel said.

"Aiee! I am attacked!"

The monkey scurried off while the men laughed. Let them laugh! They would suffer if they knew this thing was a Little Person, bent on making trouble. Victoria smoothed her skirts and calmed her ruffled composure.

"Mister Skye, let us go," she said.

But her man shook his head gently. "I was thinking maybe the Colonel and his monkey might be the perfect passport to the Utes and the Mexicans," he said softly. He turned to the fat man. "Your name is Childress, sir?"

"Jean Lafitte Childress, of Galveston Bay, Republic of Texas. I come from a long line of privateers and soldiers of fortune."

"I hear London in your voice."

"London? London? No, but I did spend a year at a seminary in Canterbury before choosing a vocation as a privateer."

"What brings you here, then?"

"I am seeking my fortune, Sah."

"This is not your usual line of work," Skye said. Victoria heard the skepticism in his voice.

The Colonel sighed. "I am the black sheep of my family, Mr. Skye. I might have enjoyed a perfectly respectable career flying the Jolly Roger, but the sea terrifies me, death curdles my blood, my nature is gentle and romantic, and I have had to make a living on my own terms, much to the despair of my family."

Skye laughed. Victoria wondered what was so damned funny.

"Perhaps you're the man we want to talk to, Colonel Childress. Ah, where does the title come from?"

"To confess my private intentions, Sah: it is my purpose to detach a vast portion of this wild land from Mexico and set up an empire from here to the Pacific, the empire of Childress, devoted to the nurture of the humble, the weak, the needful, the oppressed, and of course to advance my own fortune. My men share my ideals, and call me 'Colonel' as a courtesy."

Skye laughed softly, and again Victoria wondered what the hell she was missing.

"A filibuster," Skye said.

The Colonel looked pained. "You make it sound so crass, sir. In fact, I am at the service of large and noble ideals."

"In that case, perhaps you could help us. We're looking for a gentleman who knows the Utes and can talk their tongue, as well as the Mexicans and can talk Spanish. Your reward would be exactly nothing in terms of wealth, but deep satisfaction in other respects."

The Colonel turned serious. "Mister Skye, Sah, your purposes are unknown to me and my partners. You may think me excessively cautious, but I assure you, there is calculation in all that I do, and further, Shine is an important reason I am harvesting furs from the Utes as no one has ever done before. I must know every detail of your intentions, and then I will judge."

Skye didn't reply for a while. He gazed at these ruffians, at the fat man and his monkey, and at Standing Alone.

"Our purposes are nothing but charity," he said. "There's not a peso in it. Let us put up our horses, pay you for some feed for man and beast, and then I'll tell you a story. And I'd like to hear yours, Colonel Childress."

eight

Skye and the women cared for their horses and the mule, splashed water bucketed from a shallow well over themselves, and settled on the veranda in time for a quiet twilight visit. The man who called himself Colonel Childress always enjoyed that time of day at this arid place not far from where the Arkansas River erupted from the mountains. The place cooled swiftly except in midsummer, and the air was so dry that his armpits chafed.

The Colonel knew of Skye; so did the Colonel's colleagues. No man of the western borders was ignorant of this legend of the mountains. The Colonel also knew about the Cheyenne woman, and that excited his curiosity more than anything else. Why was the storied Standing Alone with Skye and Victoria Skye?

Well, there would be an answer soon enough—if Skye was willing to tell the whole story.

"Tell us about your post, Colonel," Skye said, after completing his ablutions.

"Why, Sah, we're six in all, out of the Texas Republic but we trade in Taos and sometimes Fort William, up on Laramie's River. We've two Mex boys also, from the ranchos down below, and they herd and do our chores."

"That's a goodly number."

"Dangerous land, Mister Skye; not for greenhorns and fools. But the post has loopholes and a small tower, and we can defend."

Skye turned toward the others. "Gentlemen, I am Mister Skye, and whom do I address?"

The Colonel caught the glances, and nodded. One by one, his militia proffered a name. Crowsnest Jones, Horace, Spade, and Deuce. Men with ugly scars, squinty eyes, and a loose-limbed quickness that made them deadly. Men with long knives, dragoon pistols, and rifles standing nearby.

"Men of the borders?" Skye asked blandly.

"Every one a Texan and a water man. We're a seafaring nation, Sah. Texas is. Most of them have walked a teak deck and climbed rigging. Not men to tangle with."

"I would not think of it," Skye said. "I always want to know who I am with. Especially when I may have business to transact."

"Business," the Colonel said, sardonically. "Business or charity?"

Skye stared at the Colonel with a gaze so intense that the Colonel was taken aback.

Crowsnest Jones, his skinny cook, hustled around inside the hot building, putting some corn tortillas on a trencher for the guests. He added some cold chorizo and beans, and brought the platter out. The guests could build their own meals from that. Crowsnest Jones was a sailor once, a soldier now. The surname probably had not been Jones until recently. His shirt covered a Louisiana convict brand. All of the Colonel's men had been handpicked for the reconnaissance.

Shine stole a tortilla and some beans, and retreated with one graceful leap to the log vigas, where it ate and slurped and licked its little fingers.

Victoria Skye hissed at him. But Standing Alone laughed, and looked to be ready to toss more tortillas at the bandit.

Skye finished eating, belched luxuriously, and settled back against the log wall.

"Victoria and I are assisting our friend here, Standing Alone of the Cheyennes," he said. "If you haven't heard of her, I'll tell her story."

He waited, but not a man responded.

"We are looking for her children," he said.

Sheer amazement flooded through Childress.

The astonishment was palpable. No one said a word. The Colonel thought that such a quest was the most quixotic venture he had ever heard of, and he had heard of plenty of foolish things. But he was smitten by the whole idea, because he was a born Don Quixote. And for other, more profound reasons. His interest quickened, and he began to see possibilities in this.

"Good luck," he said.

"We're going to find that boy and girl and return them to their mother, and to their people. Wherever they are, we'll find them. Some thread will lead the way. If they're alive, down in the Mexican silver mines or hoeing the fields or herding the cattle, we'll find them. I'm hoping you might help us deal with the Utes who stole them and probably sold them—to someone, somewhere."

"My dear Mister Skye, Sah. A most admirable enterprise, but we can't help. We're not in the brat business." He laughed. "Maybe we should be. Steal flesh and peddle it. Beats trading for buffalo robes."

"How long have you been open for business here?"

"A week. But we've been in this country for some while, scouting and trading from our wagons. We decided on this place, got out the axes, and began laying up logs a fortnight ago."

"I thought so. New logs. No one at Bent's Fort knows of this post. Any band show up here yet?"

"No. They'll find us. We're open for business. Mister Skye, Sah, what you'll do is head straight into Mexico. There's slave markets in every town. Taos first, then the city of the Sacred Faith, and then the duke of Albuquerque's town, and on down the royal road clear to the City of Mexico or beyond. You have an entire walled and private nation to search, and you no doubt can devote a lifetime to the task. Some hacendado down there has the brats, if they're still alive. Not the Utes."

"Why not the Utes, mate?"

"Because stolen children are commodities to them; they even sell their own. A working-age brat is worth a horse, and Utes lack horses because they're a mountain tribe. Sometimes they keep a little nit a few months, looking for a place to peddle him. But not four years. There are two choices: the children are dead or the children are alive in Mexico trapped in slavery."

Skye nodded.

Shine leaped from viga to viga, using his prehensile tail to swing through the air, until he landed on Skye's bench, and then he sprang gracefully to Skye's shoulder and stole his battered black hat.

"Hey!" roared Skye, as the top hat sailed toward Victoria, who caught it.

But Shine wasn't done. He plucked the medicine bundle from Skye's chest, lifted the thong over Skye's head, and ran off with it.

Standing Alone leaped to her feat, stricken, and cried out.

The thieving monkey whirled the sacred bundle around and around merrily, and then sprang toward the Colonel and lowered the thong over the Colonel's head. Childress stared at the small leather packet that contained some redskin's totems, stared at the delicately dyed leather full of symbols that meant something to those people.

Standing Alone trilled like a wounded bird, and staggered toward the Colonel, stared at the bundle as it rested on a new bosom, and wailed.

"Grandmother," he said in his rudimentary Cheyenne, "what is this?"

She squeezed her eyes shut and shook her head, as if this sight were too much for mortal eyes.

"Grandmother?"

"I will say this: Whoever wears the sacred bundle must help me find my children. I gave the sacred bundle to Mister Skye, and now it is no longer upon his breast." She began a strange chant, dolorous and sad, like a death song the Colonel once had heard sung by an ancient Aztec. But something melodic and haunting about her song told him she was singing about life at its very roots, not death.

He fingered the bundle and found it light, and yet oh, so heavy.

"What did she say, mate?" Skye asked.

"It seems you were the one to find the boy and the girl, Sah," the Colonel said. "My monkey has upset her universe. The sacred bundle obligates whoever wears it."

But the Cheyenne woman tugged at his sleeve.

"Grandfather," she whispered, "now you have worn the bundle, and now you must help me find my children, for that is the meaning of this. It is your fate."

"She says, Mister Skye, that now I'm committed to her cause, because I have worn the bundle."

Skye held out a hand, wanting the bundle back, but Childress was in no hurry to return it.

Maybe there was merit in it. Childress had always lent himself to any good cause, and maybe he could lend himself to this one, and serve several good causes at once. Maybe this would be a way to serve President Mirabeau Buonaparte Lamar. Maybe . . . it would offer concealment for his other designs, the original ones, worked out long ago in another land.

He weighed the risks. The things he had told Skye about himself were true enough, but there was so much more to it. He was indeed engaged in a filibuster but not on his own behalf. He was serving Lamar's great vision of a Republic of Texas stretching from sea to sea. He had come here with a few picked members of the Texas militia to reconnoiter northern New Mexico in advance of the army that was even then being marshaled in Texas. The whole of this province was being held by scarcely a hundred armed Mexicans, and was there for the plucking. Ah! What an enterprise! But of this Skye knew nothing. Childress believed in smoke as the best way to conceal true purpose.

Thus did Colonel Childress sit on that veranda pondering this sudden turn of events. And the more he pondered them, the more opportunity he saw.

"Mister Skye, Sah, I do believe I greatly favor your cause. What a noble heart you have, gallantly assisting this lovely princess of the Cheyennes. My own jaded heart is soft and tendah toward any urchin trapped by the greed of cruel masters. If you should desire my company whilst you roam northern Mexico in pursuit of mercy and grace and communion with saints, Sah, I think I might join you. I am not a bad companion of the road. Perhaps I can even contribute a bit to your enterprise, for I have an able tongue, and a sturdy cart, and the assistance of the little pirate and thief Shine, who has talents you cannot fathom, all of which will become manifest as we ransack Mexico, each in our own fashion."

Skye was staring again. "Colonel, the bundle, please," he said, holding out his hand. The mountaineer meant business.

nine

*J*he bundle," said Skye, holding out his hand.

But Childress was not surrendering it. The monkey jumped to the trader's shoulder and scolded Skye.

"The bundle," Skye repeated.

Childress did not lift the thong over his head.

"Make your Little Person give the sacred medicine bag back," Victoria snapped. "It is Skye's."

Childress addressed her, inflating himself in his chair. "Ah! If it were a mere thing of material value, gold, rubies, aphrodisia, rupees, Grecian statuary, anything of that miserable sort, I would remove the dead weight from my neck at once, for I have no patience with mere wealth. But this is purely a mystical gift and it was intended that I should receive it so that I might be empowered by the Spirits. Thus it represents my destiny, my incubus, which my discerning monkey at once recognizes."

He scratched the simian's jaw.

"The bundle," said Skye.

Childress addressed Victoria. "Shine didn't steal it; he merely bestowed it, and now I am committed to your noble cause, without reservation or cavil. Someday, when this is over, I will return it to your esteemed husband . . ." He peered at her. "But let us ask the woman whose will and intention matters most to us."

He turned to Standing Alone, who stood transfixed, understanding little of this, and spoke to her in her tongue, his fingers lifting the sacred bundle even as he spoke to her.

Standing Alone replied in the simplest manner: she approached the fat Colonel, lifted the bundle from his possession, and gently gave it to Skye. He felt its mysterious power as it lay in his hand, and then he lifted his hat and settled the medicine bundle upon his chest, where it belonged. That made things right. The Cheyenne woman nodded.

But Standing Alone was not through. She was talking in her tongue to Childress, and pointing at the monkey.

"She says, Sah, that I must come with you. The monkey is very wise. I am at your service, Sah."

Skye saw how it would be. He had gotten in with a daft adventurer, a self-confessed privateer and soldier of fortune, alleged Texan, and only God knew what else. Those gents on the veranda were not traders. Skye had spent years among Indian traders, and none of them resembled this phalanx of cutthroats. Colonel, indeed! Buccaneer, fraud, mountebank, confidence man, these were the correct titles. Skye had made mistakes in his life, but this would not be one of them.

"Colonel, tell our friend Standing Alone that we respect her wisdom, and we are honored that she asked us to look for her children. But we're going on our way now, without your help."

"Skye—"

Standing Alone somehow fathomed what Skye was saying. She probably grasped plenty of English after all those seasons at the gate of Bent's Fort, though she didn't speak it.

She did not hesitate, but rushed to Skye, a tall, proud woman who each day seemed younger than the previous day, and gently pressed her hands over his.

"All come," she said, and then spoke in her own tongue to Childress.

The Colonel translated. "She wants me to help you to find the Utes and look for her children in the nation across the river; she means the Mexicans, Sah. The monkey has told her that I must come with you on this great quest for justice and liberty and reunion. I accepted with pleasure."

Craziness. The woman had never seen a monkey before, so the monkey was a new god.

Skye had rarely felt such misgivings. He felt trapped. Here he was, committed to Standing Alone, being pulled and tugged by a Cheyenne tribal medicine bundle and a thieving monkey named Shine and a fat trader who sounded more like a pirate, and probably was one.

He turned to Victoria.

"Big medicine," she said. "Little Person gives the fat man the medicine bundle. Skye, we go get them damned Cheyenne Dog Soldier children, and he comes with us," said Victoria, gesturing toward Childress. "You and me and Standing Alone and the fat man and the Little Person."

Monkey or not, Victoria wanted Childress along. Skye gawked at her. Suddenly he laughed, the miraculous, booming Skye laugh that shook the mountains and shivered the grasses, and settled his mind and lifted his heart.

"All right, we will."

All those hard-eyed scoundrels on the porch stared. He wondered whether the warrants for their arrest numbered in the twenties, fifties, or hundreds. They weren't border men; they were men a thousand miles beyond the borders, and for good reason.

Skye eyed the fat man. "How are you going to travel?" he asked. "Not by horse, that's certain."

"I have a cart and a dray."

"We need more horses."

"I'll arrange it. What will you offer?"

"I need the loan of them."

"I will do it."

"At dawn, then, Colonel?"

"I sleep late," he said.

"We'll be ready whenever you are."

"Our accommodations leave something to be desired, but you are welcome." He waved toward the gloomy chamber.

Skye had already peered into the rectangular dirt-floored room stacked with trade goods but redolent of sweat and viler odors. This outfit had yet to erect bunks or build an outhouse, and were simply making their beds among the spiders and snakes.

"Think we'll camp down by the river, Colonel."

"As you wish, Sah."

He led his silent women down to a flat near the water where they could bathe. The sky didn't threaten, and they could unroll their robes on soft dry silt that would shape to their bodies.

Standing Alone retreated to her own space thirty or forty yards distant, as usual, leaving Skye and Victoria alone under the bright canopy of stars. A chill breeze swept out of the western mountains, and by dawn Skye would be pulling his robes tight around him.

He could hear the water lapping. Far off, a coyote barked. He listened closely. Not all coyote sounds were coyotes.

Victoria huddled close this time, which was not like her.

"Skye, that thing you call monkey. I know what it is," she whispered.

"It's just a critter from far south."

"No! It is a Little Person!"

Skye sat up. "What is that?"

"Only my people know them. A few Absaroka have seen them. But that is one. Aiee! I never thought I would see one."

Skye waited intently. If Victoria didn't want to say more, nothing could persuade her to.

"Sometimes they are friends and help us. Sometimes one of our warriors or hunters is in trouble, and a Little Person helps him. He brings a lost horse, or brings wood to splint a broken leg, or finds water. They live in caves and hidden places. This man the Colonel, he does not know this, but I know."

"Then we have a helper," Skye said.

"Ha! Skye, you don't know nothing. The Little People are tricksters too, like the coyote, making everyone miserable. Maybe this Little Person makes us miserable. They steal, too, and that is how I know. This Little Person, he would steal everything we got and hide it if he could." She paused. "Don't you trust no Little Person."

"The Colonel obviously does."

Victoria laughed sardonically. "Look at him. Fat man run by a Little Person like a gelded horse hitched to a wagon and he don't even know it."

Skye didn't reply. Sometimes silence was best. He squeezed her hand. It wasn't the monkey he was worried about; it was the erratic and strange Colonel from Galveston Bay who could put them all into a parcel of trouble. But when he thought of those missing Cheyenne children, and the ever-blooming Standing Alone, who was so filled with hope now, he didn't have any regrets.

ten

To Skye's discerning eye, the Colonel's equipage was as bizarre as the man. His men loaded a scarlet enameled cart with trade items and then backed a huge draft horse between the hardwood shafts and hitched it.

"A Clydesdale," Childress said. "Brown or black, blaze nose, stockings, and a spray of hair around the fetlocks."

"I wouldn't know one from another," Skye replied.

"Came out with traders, but draft animals don't do on the Santa Fe Trail; trader sold his six-hitch in Santa Fe, and I bought a pair."

"And the cart?"

"Best carriage for overland travel. Goes where wagons can't."

This one was fitted with a bench, though most carts had no seating at all; their drivers walked beside the horse or mule.

Most startling of all was a familiar insignia enameled on the side of the cart. It was a Jolly Roger, white skull and crossbones on a black field. It gave Skye the chills. All his years in the navy, he had heard forecastle stories about the outlaws of the sea.

"I'm an old, watersoaked pirate," the Colonel explained. "Hard to get rid of old habits."

"So it seems."

"Some take the Jolly Roger for a pirate's death's head, but they're wrong," he said. "It is a signal that quarter will be given if there is no resistance. That's my motto. I give the redskins quarter if they don't resist."

"Who would resist, and why, Colonel?"

The fat man smiled and let the question hang. When all was ready, he slapped the lines over the back of the draft horse. From the shade of the veranda, his ruffians watched lazily. He had given them no instructions; not even a time when he expected to return. Skye could not even discern which of them was in charge.

Skye had a thousand doubts, but after all, this fat entrepreneur was going only to hunt down some Utes, and do some translating.

They departed in a cloud of dust, the colonel and his cart leading, followed by the Skyes and Standing Alone, all mounted now on sturdy nags, and trailing the packhorses. The little monkey sat calmly on the Clydesdale's withers, but occasionally bounded back to perch on the Colonel's shoulder.

They crossed the frothing Arkansas River at a hard-rock ford and headed into Mexico along a dusty trail, through arid slopes and building heat. Skye often rode beside the Colonel, wanting to talk to the man as well as observe him. The trader was so bizarre and unpredictable that Skye felt an urgent need to fathom the man and foresee trouble.

"Where are we going?" Skye asked.

"San Luis valley. That's home to one band of Utes, the Capotes. Pestiferous lot. They should be boiled in oil. Probably the child thieves you're after."

"Bright red wagon with a Jolly Roger. You want to be seen."

"I never hide. It says the Fat Trader is coming. The trader can be seen twenty miles away."

"What do the Utes see in the Jolly Roger?"

"They see their own death if they harm me. That is what it tells them."

"You told them that?"

"Their own shamans did, after studying the device."

"That's what you intended?"

The colonel grinned from under his straw Panama. "We are safe, and you can thank my hard calculation, my understanding of savages, the bright red cart, the monkey, and the ensign, which I had painted onto my cart in Santa Fe by a devout and grandfatherly monk who relished the task. I told him I was a Lafitte by marriage and I could cut his heart out if he refused, and he told me he would have the priest perform an exorcism after he had finished the artwork."

The trader was already sweating. Skye imagined that by the time the midday heat built, Childress's flowing clothes would be soaked. He sat upon the red bench, his flesh bobbing with every lurch, growing stains under his armpits.

"Did you cut his heart out?"

"Only in my dreams, Skye."

Skye eyed the monkey, who leered insolently. Shine was calculating evil. Skye's gray horse laid its ears back and pitched slightly. The horse had been unruly from the start, and didn't like walking beside the cart, didn't like that monkey, and probably had it in for the Clydesdale as well. Skye had learned to deal gently with horseflesh, so he did nothing. The horse would settle down eventually. The reddish-gray monkey clacked teeth and tugged its ear.

"What happens when we meet other bands? Apaches, Paiutes? Comanches?"

"I am known, Sah, in this region quite as well as you are known among the border fraternity."

"Indians roam, Childress."

"And so do reputations, Mister Skye."

They toiled southwest through the cool spring morning, passing into rougher and higher country. The gray sagebrush gave way to juniper, and ahead Skye could see slopes dotted with piñon pine. The well-used trail took them through long gulches, some of which showed signs of running snowmelt not long before.

The Sangre de Cristo pass lay ahead, and if the grade was no worse than this, the Clydesdale might yet pull that mountain of flesh and loaded cart over the top and down the other side. Skye watched the hardwood shafts closely, saw them flex at every pothole and bump, and wondered what Childress would do if one snapped.

As the sun neared Zenith, Childress pointed to an island of bright green ahead.

"A pool. We'll refresh. I always stop there."

Skye discovered a pool, all right, far below the trail, in a narrow gulch. Cattails surrounded it; birds flitted close to it, and numerous narrow animal trails descended to it.

"We'll rest the nags," Childress said.

Skye nodded and dismounted, ready to help Childress unhook the harness from the shafts, but the fat man shooed him off. Laboriously, he clambered to earth and sighed. He lumbered forward, released the harness, and handed the lines to Shine.

"Water," Childress commanded

Shine sprang forward and led the draft horse out of the shafts and down the steep path to the pond.

Skye stared. The fifteen-hundred-pound draft horse placidly followed the monkey to water, shambling down the steep slope while the little monkey tugged him onward, chittering at the horse.

"Sonofabitch," Victoria snarled. "Little Person."

To her this was further proof that the thing Skye called monkey was one of the tribe of small people known only to the Absaroka. But Skye just shook his head.

Shine led the Clydesdale not only to water, but also to succulent grasses that lay just below the pond, and there the giant horse munched contentedly while the monkey hung on to the lines.

Standing Alone laughed, enchanted with the sight.

"I am beginning to see the utility of that little rascal," Skye said to Childress.

"You've seen only the beginning. He's a phenomenon. And I've been training him for six years."

In due course, without any instruction from Childress, the monkey led the gentle draft horse upslope, and backed him between the shafts, and Childress hooked up.

Skye thought surely a man so enormous would want to chow down, but Childress seemed content as he stepped into the creaking cart and settled himself on the red seat. Shine handed him the lines.

The women had completed their ablutions and the cavalcade started down the trail once again. This time Shine nestled in Childress's lap and went to sleep.

The day passed uneventfully except for a chafing wind. They encountered no one, but that was the usual in these wilds. Twilight caught them well upslope, in scattered piñon woods, with plenty of parks to graze the horses. A rivulet splashed its way toward the dusty plains far below.

"We shall halt here in this demiparadise," Childress announced. "Here we shall be provisioned, the horses succored, and all of us hydrated."

Judging from the sopping black stains on Childress's clothing, Skye supposed he needed hydrating worst of all.

Once again the monkey turned itself into manservant for the gargantuan trader. Little Shine led the huge draft horse to the runnel, let it drink, and brought it back for Childress to halter. The giant horse drifted off, snapping at good grasses with each step, belching and farting in horse heaven.

"You gonna picket him?" Skye asked.

The response was a withering stare.

Skye's women prepared a camp and set off to gather deadwood, but Shine had already beat them to it, and was heaping it at the feet of his master.

Skye wasn't sure who was master; monkey or man, but

it made no difference. They each had a high order of intelligence, but so did many madmen.

Skye knew he would sleep well that night. He was saddle sore and weary, but the sweet smell of piñon pine floated through the evening breezes; the air was fresh and gentle; the clouds promised no rain but a good sunset, and all in all, they were off to a hopeful start. The only unhappy person in the party was Victoria, who was locked in mortal terror of Shine.

eleven

our days later they reached the summit of Sangre de Cristo pass, a grassy plateau, and there ran smack into Utes. A dozen warriors, brightly dressed with all their war honors on display, raced their fleet mounts straight toward the red cart, whooping ever closer.

Skye slipped his rifle from its beaded sheath, checked to see whether a cap was on the nipple, and waited for whatever came.

"It's the Capotes," Childress proclaimed as the advance guard hurried forth and surrounded Skye and his women. He lifted his broad-brimmed straw hat and waved them on, with a gallant and cavalier swoop.

All but two or three of these bronze, lean, bare-chested warriors were young and ready for anything. But Skye saw no nocked bows, and their war clubs hung from saddles. He slipped the rifle back into its nest. Shine fairly bounced and somersaulted on the back of the draft horse, chittering and yammering at the Utes, who pointed and laughed. They were all familiar with the monkey. Shine, not the trader, was the cynosure.

Skye saw Victoria ease back on her horse. Her skirts were hiked high, baring slim brown legs. Standing Alone rode in the same fashion, but she was not relaxed and her gaze was somber and piercing as she looked over these rawboned warriors. Something malign rose from within the Cheyenne woman.

Childress immediately plunged into intense talk with a graying warrior, probably a subchief, and for once Skye regretted having a translator present because there was no finger talk he could read. The crafty Utes spoke a Shoshonean tongue, similar to that of the Comanches and Shoshones, and Skye wished he might understand.

The likelihood of trouble seemed remote, but with these Utes one could not know. He saw no easy escape. The open plateau offered no concealment, no help. He would have to wait and see how things went.

At last Childress turned to his fellow travelers.

"They're heading out to the plains on a big spring buffalo hunt. They're hungry. Whole band's following, every last one. Back a way is Chief Tamuche and the rest of them."

Skye nodded. "What have you told them?"

"I'm trading; you're with me. That's all."

"Do they know what we're about?"

"No."

"Would they recognize Standing Alone?"

Childress shrugged. "This woman, Skye, looks two decades younger than the one huddled at the gate of Bent's Fort. I saw her there last summer."

"Please tell Standing Alone all this."

Childress switched to the Cheyenne tongue, which he spoke hesitantly, and Standing Alone absorbed his news without a flicker of emotion. Several of the warriors listened intently, barely controlling their restless horses, and Skye suspected that some of them understood Cheyenne, and maybe English.

Skye didn't like it. He lifted his hands to draw attention to them, and addressed the older one who bore the scars of war upon his torso, Skye's fingers and palms and wrists and elbows spelled out messages.

Friend, peace, who are you?

The warrior pointed at himself. "Degadito," he said aloud. *Chief, friend, buffalo hunter. You trade? Hungry. Who are you?*

Skye replied. *Maybe, few things. Looking for lost people.*

Ah, looking for people. The subchieftain nodded.

Skye made the sign for the heavens, and pointed at himself.

"Ah! Skye!" the headman said. The name was obviously known. Skye marveled that his name was so well known from tribe to tribe and band to band. The warrior studied him, examined Victoria, and then gazed at the beautiful Cheyenne woman, registering curiosity in his face.

The rest of the village rounded a copse of pine, and rode majestically forward. Now other warriors and headmen raced ahead, the red cart galvanizing them all. Soon Childress's wagon was surrounded, ten deep, and Shine put on a show, swinging gayly from horse to cart to the ground, where he shook hands with squealing children. Soon the women were crowding close, wanting to see Shine. He obliged them by tugging at skirts and grinning broadly.

Skye saw the value of the monkey who entertained these Utes but was looking for other things: children who looked Cheyenne, or any other color or race or breed, and there were plenty of them to consider. The Utes seemed even more varied in racial composition than most tribes, and Skye thought he saw Hispanic and other European blood in the younger ones. The men were lean; the women stocky.

Standing Alone, too, was studying the Utes from the back of her horse. Here was an entire village on the road, the lodges loaded onto travois, households bundled onto the backs of burros and mules and horses, and even a few oxen. There was no place to hide a child.

The Ute women were smiling, poking fingers at the monkey, and obviously having a grand time, while Childress continued a conversation with the Utes. But Standing Alone was sliding off her horse. She handed the rein to Victoria, who was muttering things, and then Standing Alone walked slowly through the throng, her piercing gaze resting on each young man and woman, missing not one young person. Her back was arched and she walked proudly, as if to say that she was a Cheyenne woman and not afraid. Once she cried out, only to turn away after staring at a girl.

All this suited Skye fine; Standing Alone could examine the entire band without making her purpose known. In a settled village, with lodges erected and life within them hidden, it would be much harder.

Victoria edged her shaggy horse closer to Skye. "We damn well got big luck this time," she said. "They don't know her. We don't have to say."

Skye nodded, lifted his top hat, and settled it.

Tamuche had dismounted and sent a boy to summon them; he wanted to be introduced. Childress did the honors, hastening across the flat with Shine riding his shoulder. Skye and his women followed. Tamuche stood on his tiptoes, erect, wiry, intense, dark as mahogany. Some black chin whiskers curled around his jaw, his eyes glowed like agates, and his demeanor was a studied indifference, a theatrical yawn. Tamuche plainly considered it beneath him to be impressed. The chief and headmen and shamans looked Skye over, nodded, and talked among themselves. Eventually, they turned to Childress.

"We'll have a fiesta," the Colonel said. "They want to trade with me and have a big Bear Dance in your honor. They got them a gander at that grizzly bear-claw necklace around your neck, Sah, and think that's big medicine. There's a spring around the bend, and that's where they'll break out the champagne and caviar."

"I'm agreeable," Skye said.

"They're inclined toward anything bearish, Mister Skye. They have an affinity for bears, and think of themselves as bear people. Their Bear Dance is mighty medicine. So you're being highly honored. They look upon you as a good omen; a bear-claw man like you, can only mean a good hunt."

"Sonofabitch," said Victoria.

"Your wife expresses herself poignantly, Mister Skye. I am at a loss when it comes to matching her elocution."

Victoria laughed. Skye could read her mind. If she was lucky, she might even get some hooch this dance night under the stars.

Childress continued: "I'll tell them about our new store and hand out a few trinkets; I'll remind them they'll be passing it en route to the buffalo grounds. And I'll probably sell some iron arrow points, and some powder, perhaps, but not a dozen of them have muskets. This outfit's low on food, too."

That all seemed just fine to Skye. He wanted to observe the Utes; watch them trade, study their physiognomy, and maybe learn how to approach them about the children—and stay out of trouble.

The Utes retreated to the small spring that dribbled icy water into a green pool with no outlet, while Childress drove his red rig there. Soon the squaws had some fires lit and the warriors were watering the ponies at the small spring. When Shine led the big draft horse to the spring, the warriors parted at once to observe this amazing thing, twenty pounds of monkey leading fifteen hundred pounds of horse.

No meat. The Utes didn't have any, which was why they were en route to buffalo country. The squaws stood about, waiting for some provisions from the traders, but Skye had none to spare and Childress wasn't carrying much. It was going to be a hungry night.

The Utes had a small herd, heavily guarded by the boys, and Skye looked them over carefully, unsure of what a Cheyenne boy would look like. But Standing Alone had already done that, walking imperiously among the laughing and joking Utes, her face a mask but her will and determination springing from every step.

The fat trader opened his store with a majestic flourish

and gymnastic entertainment from Shine, who plucked up awls and blue beads and arrowheads and flasks of powder and held them up, clacking and dancing before the studious Utes. Soon the cart contained some heavy buffalo robes and a few glistening beaver pelts, and the Indians were busy ogling their ribbons and beads.

Some cooking smells drifted on the breeze, along with piñon pine smoke, the sweetest aroma Skye had ever smelled, and in time he realized they were boiling a few dogs. He would gladly have rolled up in his blankets by then, but the night's festivities were just beginning. Chief Tamuche invited the Colonel's party to sit beside him, smoke the pipe as twilight thickened, and then see the great Dance of the Bears.

The dogs vanished down Ute gullets, and Skye saw Childress watching. But the Colonel asked for nothing, and contented himself with some tea, which he brewed in a small kettle all by himself. That in itself seemed to be a mystery: a fat man who didn't need food. Shine had no trouble at all stealing a meal. In time, Tamuche's wives presented Skye and his women with a half a dozen fat roasted lizards, glistening and yellow, with black collars, on a slab of bark. Some piñon nuts, Ute emergency food, completed the repast. Skye ate. He had learned to eat when he could and what he could, because the natural world provided nothing else. The whole meal consisted of a few smoky, stringy bites, and some starchy nuts.

Victoria laughed. She preferred the cuisine of the plains tribes.

The Bear Dance began in the velvet quiet of the evening, softly at first, each portion of it varying from the next. Skye listened to the metronomic drumming, the low gutterals, the honoring of all bears, the pantomimic capture and killing of a bear, the portioning of its spirit to the bear dancers, and then he nodded.

He awakened with a start as silence enveloped the encampment. A chill spring wind cut through the uplands, scattering orange sparks. Skye worried about his horses, which were being herded with all the rest. He worried about the Utes' famous propensity to lift whatever they could lift. The women were slipping into their blankets. Childress was snoring under his cart. Skye had never found raw ground comfortable to sleep on, and knew that few mountaineers did either, though they bragged about their toughness. This ground was hard as stone and he could not shape it. The night would be long and wakeful. But all things considered, maybe that was good, not bad.

But it was Standing Alone who filled his mind that night. Among these Utes, she was a different and forbidding woman.

twelve

kye awakened at the earliest gray light of dawn
thinking something was wrong. But nothing seemed
wrong. The Utes slept. Childress's red cart, perched
on its wheels and its shafts, still sheltered the trader. The draft
horse grazed nearby, its halter rope trailing. No one stirred.
No cook fires burned. None of these people had erected a
lodge, but lay on the cold ground, grouped as families or
clans.

He felt about for his rifle and powderhorn, and found
them beside his robes. Victoria's quiver and bow lay beside
her. Standing Alone's few things, captured in a parfleche, lay
at her blankets. The Skye provisions, heaped where they had
been lifted off the horses, had not been touched. Nothing stolen. It was not going to storm. No hostile warriors were fil-
tering through the slumbering encampment. There were
fewer dogs this morning than last night, and those that survived the cookpots were not roaming. Nothing was wrong.

He turned and found Victoria staring at him silently.

"What?" he muttered.

"I don't know, dammit," she replied.

They began a systematic search as they often had done
when they sensed danger. Stare at each twenty degrees of the

compass, wait for movement, wait for whatever it was they were waiting for.

Skye ran his hands over the stubble of his jaws, and down his chest, finding the bear-claw necklace, a treasure any Ute warrior would have coveted. He picked up his short-barreled mountain rifle, which felt sweet and heavy in his chapped hands. There was nothing to shoot at.

The light improved perceptibly, and the first hints of color began to tint the grayness. Skye could not shake the feeling that something was amiss. The one thing he could not see from where he lay was the horse herd. But no alarm had sounded and he had no reason to suppose that this Capote band had lost their four-foots to marauders.

Then, as the light quickened, Victoria pointed. On a distant knoll, ghostly in the murk, stood Standing Alone, her arms stretched upward, her back arched, her fingers reaching for something that lay in the beyond.

"Praying, big damn bad medicine, makes the world ache," Victoria whispered.

Skye nodded. He could not fathom this mystery. The woman's morning prayer was infecting this place, making him jumpy, as if she had called down pox and plague upon these Utes and demons were cursing the land under him.

"Maybe she wants these here damn Utes to get scabs, starve, sicken, and die," Victoria muttered.

Whatever it was, the Cheyenne woman had wrought an uncanny malaise upon this place, and it resonated in his bones.

He stood; Victoria did, too. It felt good to escape the cast-iron hardpan that had formed his bed. His body ached as it often did when sleeping in the wilds. Life lived in nature was no lark: bitter cold, fierce heat, mosquitos, horseflies, hornets, hunger, thirst, bad water, rain, hail, snow, frozen toes, chafing wind, and solid rock for a bed.

The Utes would probably not sleep late into the morning; they would leave for the plains in a rush to find buffalo for their bellies, their sleeping robes, their lodges, their war shields. Buffalo weren't easy to find and were hard to kill. Butchering them was brutal work. Tanning their hides was just as toilsome.

He glanced around sharply, still ill at ease, stretching the ache out of his muscles. Now he could see the horses scattered on a grassy slope just beyond. They looked unattended, but he knew Ute boys had been entrusted with the task of keeping them close and chasing off predators.

The camp stirred. An old man padded to the edge of camp and made water. A woman stood, wrapped a blanket about herself, and walked toward some brush. Off in the distance, Standing Alone finished her incantations and walked slowly toward the encampment. Skye sensed a strange force radiating from her.

There was indeed one unaccounted for, and that was Shine. Where was the little pirate? A dread crept through Skye. He could think of scores of reasons why these people might want to kidnap Childress's monkey, maybe even to worship a creature that so resembled human beings. Whoever possessed Shine would possess great medicine. Worried, Skye edged toward the trader's cart looking for the spider monkey, and found him curled up under it, next to his master. Or was the monkey the master? The monkey was safe with Childress, and Skye felt sheepish about his strange foreboding.

By the time the sun's orange light was lancing the treetops, the Utes were up and preparing to move. Skye saw no cookfires this morning. There was little to do at this impromptu camp but load the travois and packhorses and start. One by one, the men headed into the herd and caught horses for the women. They were good horsemen and able to drop a braided leather loop over a horse's neck without stirring the herd. They had probably learned equestrian skills from the Spanish.

Skye and Victoria caught their horses, bridled them, and led them back to the encampment.

He found Childress up and brewing tea at a tiny fire, the only one in the camp. Shine had vanished.

"How are you and the monkey this morning, Colonel?"

"We're fine; Shine's hungry. He's fetching himself a meal."

"And you?"

"I live on my padding, Sah. It is a great asset at times, on the road."

"You know the Utes. Would this be a good time to ask about the missing children?"

"There is never a good time for that, Mister Skye," Childress said, pouring steaming tea from a tin pot into a battered cup.

"Would you ask Tamuche?"

Childress turned silent and stared at the ground. Finally, he nodded. "It is a great and just and noble cause we pursue, my friend Mister Skye. I'll commence a powwow with the devil."

"How would you approach the chief?"

"You brought something to give him?"

"Blue beads, a few tools and knives."

"He might prefer food. This band is down to pine nuts."

"I have a little."

"There's no time like the present, Mister Skye."

The heavy man rose nimbly to his feet while Skye extracted some gifts from his meager supplies: beads, a knife, a pound of sugar in a cotton sack. Most Indians loved sugar and he suspected Tamuche would too.

They walked to the chief's bedground and stood at the edge, awaiting an invitation. The wiry man was watching his wives toil.

Eventually the chief nodded, and Childress began a colloquy with him in the Ute tongue, finally turning to Skye.

"He says not now; no talk. They are going to find buffalo. Their stomachs are empty. They are in a hurry."

"Tell him I have a gift if he would answer some questions

about missing children. A pound of sugar. A knife."

This was conveyed to Tamuche, who shook his head.

"They cannot delay," Childress said.

Skye set the gifts before Tamuche and added an awl to the knife and sugar sack and skein of beads. "A pound of sugar, an awl, a knife, and a string of blue beads for his women. Very quickly. A few questions. All for some knowledge he might possess."

Tamuche replied with a question: About what?

"About two Cheyenne children, a boy and a girl, who disappeared from Bent's Fort four winters ago. Their mother is with us. We want to find them."

Tamuche listened and fell into silence. Skye noticed that two headmen had gathered also and were monitoring this exchange. He saw no change of expression among the Utes, yet something had changed.

Childress spoke, and there was a vast silence, broken only by the soughing of the zephyrs through pine boughs.

Tamuche spoke sharply, and Skye thought all was lost, but Childress conveyed an unexpected message. "We will smoke," he said.

That was good news. The great ritual of negotiation would begin. So time didn't matter. Reaching the buffalo didn't either. A smoke could last half a day.

A brief word to one of his wives brought Tamuche a long-stemmed pipe with a red pipestone bowl, an alien pipe for this country, along with a beaded leather pouch of loose tobacco. He signaled that all should be seated.

A Ute boy appeared with a glowing coal from Childress's fire, borne on a green leaf. Tamuche accepted the coal, used it to fire the pipe, then offered the smoke to the four winds, and passed it in the small circle. By now, a dozen Ute headmen had gathered around and stood watching. The camp itself was largely ready to travel. Time had stopped; this was ritual, and no white man's clock governed it.

But at last, after the pipe had circled the seated Utes and

white men, Tamuche began with a question, translated by Childress.

"Is the Cheyenne woman with you the one we hear of, who huddles at the gate and awaits her children? We have heard of this woman. We admire her, and believe she is following her own bright pathway, and all the Utes talk well of her."

Childress answered without waiting for Skye, saying yes, this is the very woman. Indeed, Standing Alone was standing apart, outside the circle, a strange bleak aura separating her from other mortals.

"But she is young; the one we know of is very old."

"It is the same woman, Standing Alone, of the Cheyenne. She has washed her hair, put on a new dress, and wears spirit moccasins that take her where she must go. And so her years fall away. Her spirit helpers have told her the time has come to go find her children, and now she has enlisted us." All this Childress explained, this time fingering the sacred medicine bundle.

"Ah!" exclaimed Tamuche, studying the bundle. "Why does this Cheyenne woman think I might know such a thing? The Utes are accused of many bad things. Many lies! We have many enemies, and they tell lies about us. We are nothing but a poor band of mountain people who cannot find enough food and must get horses and food any way we can."

When this was translated, Skye thought it amounted to an admission that the Utes did indeed traffic in children.

In any case, Childress was earnestly conversing and all Skye could do was sit there and wait, and interpret the occasional gestures that accompanied their talk.

"He says the gifts are not enough."

"Tell him maybe his information isn't enough."

Tamuche's face registered nothing upon hearing that. He was a master of diplomacy in his own way, Skye thought.

"Enough of this, he says. He will go to the buffalo lands now and kill the hairy ones and fill their empty bellies. He says, Have we not been good hosts, fed you from our poor stores? Have we not given you enough? We go in peace. You have not given us enough, but we will accept it anyway."

Skye nodded, but Tamuche was talking again.

"He says, go to the Weeminuche and talk to White Coyote," Childress said.

A thread of something.

Skye nodded. "We thank the chief of the Utes, and wish him great success."

Within minutes, the Utes headed east, and Skye and his women, Childress and his monkey, and all their horses and equipment headed west, down the long grade into the San Luis valley.

thirteen

The farther Skye pierced into Mexico, the more he felt its brooding silences. For days after they had descended into the San Luis Valley, Skye and his entourage had progressed southward through a moody and austere land. Scarcely a breeze stirred the air. The skies were a transparent indigo that he had never before seen in all his wanderings, and he found this heaven utterly strange and marvelous, as if God had fashioned a different firmament for a different nation.

But most of all, Skye felt the fearsome silence. Mexico was a land of such deep silences that the slightest noise was startling, like a lamentation in heaven. They rode their docile mounts along a dry trail toward the village of San Luis, northernmost of Nuevo Mexico's settlements, or so Childress said.

So transparent was the air that Skye was sure he could see peaks a hundred miles distant, brooding and mysterious, harboring secrets. Crystal air, deep silences, and forbidding ranches in hidden havens.

Where would the children be? This country was so vast that a glance could sweep hundreds of square miles and yield nothing. Yet it was an illusion. They had passed hidden valleys verdant with foliage, which were invisible from the plain. Ranchos could be tucked into any of them. How would they search? Who would guide them? The sheer grandeur of the country they were slowly penetrating humbled Skye.

Somewhere off to the west the Rio Grande tumbled through a gorge, according to Childress, and in various places its bottoms were farmed and settled. Yet none of that was visible from the trail to Taos. They saw only vast and mysterious reaches of the earth's surface, endless flats, distant mountains rising in air so clear they seemed sharp-edged and near.

They reached a watered basin filled with thick grasses that didn't bend to any wind, and beheld skinny longhorned cattle there, some of them herded by children.

"Approaching San Luis," Childress said from his seat on the cart. "Nothing here. Half a dozen adobe jacals, and a defense tower. You won't find the missing ones. These peasants couldn't afford to buy a slave, much less feed and clothe one."

"We'll look anyway," Skye said, determined to miss nothing. "Where'd you learn about Mexican slavery?"

"Mister Skye, you'll spend a lifetime looking for the Cheyenne children, and get nowhere doing it that way. What you want is information. We'll get that in Taos, if it is to be gotten anywhere, Sah. We'll buy it or steal it, but we'll fetch it some fashion or other, and thereby find the string that will lead us to the children."

Skye knew it was so, and yet wanted to ride to every rancho for a look. Childress's strange enthusiasm piqued him.

They reached San Luis late in the afternoon of another quiet day, and their arrival drew everyone in the village into a rude plaza. They knew this trader and his monkey, and jabbered about him, with bright smiles. Skye rode through clay streets between brown buildings while a small crowd followed the horses and cart. Skye could scarcely see a difference between these dark, wiry people and the Indians, except for the dress. Older women wore black rebozos; younger ones wore lighter cottons, and most of the men wore only pantalones. All were barefoot.

Childress began to banter with them in Spanish, and again Skye could fathom none of it.

"I'm going to look at that tower," the Colonel said, sliding off his cart. "Always interested in blood and death." Several young men eagerly escorted him to the two-story adobe structure.

The monkey stayed on the cart, entertaining the Mexicans, who laughed at him much as the Utes had. Shine shook hands, pilfered anything he could, and chittered at them.

Skye watched the trader vanish into the shadowed interior of the tower, curious as to why the man chose to see that rather than to trade. But maybe these people had no coin, nothing to trade. Still, they would have grains, and that would be worth some dickering. The travelers had fed themselves almost entirely on the few provisions Skye had brought along.

As usual, Standing Alone was surveying the young people in the village, and finding no sign of her own.

When the colonel returned, he pulled back the canvas covering his wares, and set a few out. The women crowded about, but the men held back.

"Won't sell a dime's worth," Childress said. "They've nothing to trade."

"We could use some wheat or maize," Skye said.

"Well, I won't trade for that. Mister Skye, that tower's never been used. Built to defend against Utes and Apaches, but it never was put to a test. There's only two escopetas in town anyway. That's blunderbuses, if you don't know the word. And no powder for the lot. All the tower's good for is to store grains."

Skye dismounted, dug into his packs, and found a couple of knives he had been given for trade.

"Tell 'em I'll trade knives for grain," he said.

"But, Sah, why?"

"Because we're about starved."

A few minutes later, Skye had surrendered two knives but had a sack of rough-ground flour that Skye knew would have sand and bits of husk in it. He'd eaten plenty in his day.

They trotted out of San Luis in midafternoon heat, but suddenly Childress seemed to be in a hurry and snapped a whip over his Clydesdale.

"You learn something there?" Skye asked.

"Only that there's nothing here. These are all peasants, Skye, with their kitchen gardens and a few kine. We won't find any big ranches, the kind that might use Indian herders, until we approach Taos."

"Did you ask about workers or slaves?"

"Sah, the only thing I inquired about was that tower."

Skye puzzled that, and could not explain the man's interest in defenses.

"Trust me, Skye, when we approach a great ranch, you will find me a bloodhound on a trail. I do so yearn, Sah, yearn to find those little red gnats."

Skye stared.

"I'm a sucker for any good cause, Mistah Skye. Wherever there's injustice, cruelty, lives ruined, death, and misery, there's old Childress trying to make things right."

That afternoon they struck an icy creek that tumbled out of the Sangre de Cristos, hurrying toward the Rio Grande off to the west somewhere. Beside it was a faint road. They paused where these merry waters laughed their way west, and refreshed themselves and their horses.

Skye thought that the Clydesdale was looking gaunt, and perhaps they should all recruit for a day on the lush grasses that grew along the banks.

"Behold the trace, my English friend," said Childress. "I take it that we're near a hacienda, and we can begin our quest for the Holy Grail hereabouts."

"Where's the ranch?"

"Oh, I take it that one or two leagues will suffice."

"One or two leagues!"

"Sah, you are in country so large that it dwarfs the Republic of Texas, God spare me for saying it."

"I thought you were aiming to get information first."

"My dear Mistah Skye, here we are; a road leads westward to someplace that might harbor vile slavery and cruel servitude. As for me, I will not only search for the lost tribe of Israel there, but also reconnoiter."

"Reconnoiter?"

"A filibuster, my dear Sah, needs a map of the territory and its armed men burnt into his gray matter."

Skye laughed. "Your purposes grow clearer with every mile, Emperor. All right. We will use one another. I'm cover for you and your schemes, and you're my translator and guide in old Mexico. I'm beginning to understand the Jolly Roger painted upon the sides of your bloodred cart."

Childress grinned. "You are a man to reckon with, Sah. Let us examine this rancho, if such it be."

The Colonel took it upon himself to explain this to Standing Alone, who brightened. At last, she would be going to a place where her children might be snared.

They turned westward along the two-rut trail that paralleled the creek, and soon found themselves in a broad, grassy valley that could only be paradise for cattle.

Even Victoria brightened. Skye had never seen her so dour, so distrustful, and judging from her glare at the spider monkey, she probably had slaughtered him a hundred times in her mind.

Shine himself sensed that they were piercing toward some nearby objective, and began doing handsprings on the sweated brown back of the patient Clydesdale. The brook babbled, relieving at last the oppressive silence Skye had felt ever since he entered Mexico.

Thus they continued, under an azure sky, until near sundown they beheld an adobe settlement, a rural fortress situated on a vast meadow that was sheltered by a long arid bluff to the north. This place, too, had an earthen tower high enough to command the surrounding fields. A great black bell hung on a frame above it; a bell that might be heard for miles.

"Well done," Childress said. "See that brass poking out of the tower? A field piece. Stuff it with grape and see the carnage."

"What might threaten them, Colonel?"

"Utes and Comanches and Jicarillas," the Colonel replied. "Every one of them capable of slaughtering the occupants, ravishing their women, and roasting the males over a fire until they are cooked alive."

By then their imminent arrival had attracted attention, and assorted Mexicans, mostly male, flooded out of the placita, and stood waiting.

"Oh, one thing, Skye," the Colonel said. "These hacendados play God. If they don't like us, they can bind us up and ship us to Mexico City for a decade in a dungeon."

"For what?"

"For anything, Sah. For trespassing, for trading without permission, for breathing, for being Protestant, for failure to pay import duties. Or for warring upon the Republic of Mexico."

"Thanks for the warning," Skye said.

fourteen

The patron of this great hacienda was not the sort of man Skye expected to see. He stood quietly at the tower awaiting his guests, intelligent eyes shelved under a pale dome of forehead that surrendered reluctantly to kinked coppery hair. He was accoutered in a fine frock coat of royal blue velvet with white knee breeches. At his arm was a raven-haired beauty in white cotton.

The hacendado's gaze took in everything there was to see about Skye's party, resting on the red cart with its strange insignia, then upon the trader in his broad-rimmed Panama and open white shirt, and then upon Skye, and finally, briefly, the Indian women.

"Gentlemen?" he said, in English.

"At your service, Sah," Childress said, with a sweep of his Panama. "Traders. Perhaps we can supply your necessaries?"

"Americans?"

"I am a Texan, Jean Lafitte Childress of Galveston Bay."

"A rebel."

"Why, Sah, Lone Star Texan and proud of it, and if I give offense, it's because I mean to. You'll not find a more loyal Texan than the gent you see before you. We defended certain sacred and holy rights promised all Texans by the Republic of Mexico and wantonly abandoned by that scoundrel Santa Anna. If we distress you, we shall depart at once. With whom do we speak?"

The hacendado nodded, and then focused on Skye.

"And you, sir?"

"I am Mister Skye, London born but a man without a country."

"Are you from Australia, then, or Van Dieman's Land?"

"No, sir, seven years in the Royal Navy."

"Ah, a surprise! And what do you do?"

"I am in the fur trade."

"And why are you without a country?"

"That is my choice, sir."

"And why are you here in Mexico?"

"I am looking for two young Indians we believe are in northern Mexico."

"And who are these?" the man asked, waving languidly at the two women.

"One is Victoria, my wife, of the Crow people, and the other is Standing Alone, of the Cheyenne people."

"And why are you stopping here, so far off the Taos Camino?"

Childress replied: "To trade, Sah. We have a small but select number of items for your consideration."

"Have you the permiso from Santa Fe?"

"We're en route, to obtain just such a license."

"Then it is very indiscreet of you to offer merchandise in a nation where you have no right to do business."

This man with the blue velvet frock coat exuded some strange force of will that was belied by his soft attire. Skye sensed that a word from the man could decide their fate. There was the slightest pause, while the master of this fortified rancho, almost a village, came to some conclusions.

"You will forgive me if I prefer to do business here rather

than within," he said. "I don't know that I've ever seen a conveyance with a skull and crossbones enameled on the side of it; pray thee, what means it?"

Childress's response astonished Skye. "I'm a privateer, Sah, once employed by the Republic of Texas to prey on Mexican shipping. Now I prey on Mexicans in another fashion. The Jolly Roger is my whimsy, and the mark of my passage. I shall extract the highest possible price for anything I part with, having piracy in my bones."

The response plainly nonplussed the hacendado.

Shine leaped and chittered and danced on the back of the Clydesdale. The gathered peons, sun-stained and worn, stared at the little creature.

The hacendado laughed gently. "I like candor. You're probably here for some other reason. Admit to one sin to hide a larger one."

This time it was Childress's turn to laugh. The monkey chittered and jumped to the ground. Children squealed.

"I am Gabor Rakoczi," the master of the place said, "and this is my wife, Maria Elena Salvador y Rakoczi. I have never had the pleasure of commerce with self-confessed pirates before."

"You speak English fluently, Mister Rakoczi," Skye said.

"Three years at Cambridge does that, doesn't it? I speak the Spanish better. Love does that. Anyone who serves the Hapsburgs, as I did for years, would know Spanish." He smiled at his wife. "Mrs. Rakoczi is well advanced with Hungarian, which is the language of domesticity in the home." He paused. "Well, are you going to display your wares or is there some other purpose for which you honor us with your sterling company?"

Again, Skye sensed the iron willfulness of the man who ruled over this empire in the wilderness.

Childress hastened off his seat on the red cart and drew back his canvas. His wares suddenly looked to be few and poor.

Rakoczi dismissed them at a glance. "It is not even a good show, Mister Childress." He grinned, displaying even white teeth. "And that brings us to purposes. What does a handful of tinker's items conceal? A filibuster, perhaps? What a word! A coinage of Washington, District of Columbia, I think. Are you examining northern Mexico as a plum to be plucked? Are you here to assess my strength? Ah, I will show you if you wish. Behold the tower. There's a six-pounder in it, and plenty of grapeshot and ball, and my muchachos are experienced cannoneers. Arms? I can put thirty men into the field on horse, all with good Prague steel in hand. Lances, pikes, muskets. We are a cavalry troop, in case you wonder. Good Spanish Barb stock I brought up from Vera Cruz, Toledo sabres, pikes and pistolas. Say, would you sell me your Clydesdale there? I saw them in England and thought them dumb and docile, just like the English. Yes, a sturdy animal, useful here, but not a thrifty eater. We would have to fatten him. He's rather gaunted, wouldn't you say? I'll give you a piratical offer for it, or maybe just take it from you if you protest too much at the few pesos in my palm."

Skye stared at this hacendado who was toying with them before the gates of his rural fortress, and enjoying every moment of it. The man could do anything he threatened to do.

Childress laughed politely.

"The monkey's a good touch," Rakoczi said. "Yes! See how he entertains while you conduct your reconnaissance. Your insignia's a fine touch, too. It starts conversations all by itself. Yes, and how much information you can fetch in a hurry, with a monkey and a crossbones." He turned suddenly to Skye. "Now tell me about these Indians you seek."

Skye scarcely knew how to approach this man, but candor had always served him best. "Two Cheyenne children were abducted by the Utes four years ago and sold here in Mexico, as far as we know. This is their mother. We hope to free them."

"Sold? Sold? Free them, Skye? You are suggesting they are not free?"

"It's Mister Skye, mate."

"Mister Skye, is it?" Rakoczi's teeth were showing again. "This is the Mexican Republic, and there's not a soul here who is held in bondage, unlike the American South, or the misnamed and alleged Republic of Texas."

Skye ignored him. "We're prepared to purchase the two Indian children. They'd be almost adult now, about sixteen and thirteen."

"Purchase, Mister Skye? Are you suggesting that mortals are bought and sold here? Are you telling me that you're talking about slavery?"

"Peonage, Señor Rakoczi. Binding laborers to the land with debt. Indenture. Do you have peons?"

Rakoczi laughed softly. "Slavery! I have never heard of it. I shall tell the bishop of Durango. The church would be distressed. Come, let us talk to these slaves."

He drifted toward a young couple who stood nearby. "I shall translate the Spanish, and Mr. Childress can correct me if he detects the slightest flaw in my translation, yes? I take it you speak Spanish, yes?"

He didn't wait for a response, but questioned the couple intently, while Childress listened.

"They say, Mister Skye, that they are glad to work for me, and are proud to be under the protection of so great a master as the owner of the Hacienda de Las Delicias, which is very like heaven to them, and the master is very like a saint who will sit at the right hand of God."

Skye nodded.

Standing Alone was sitting her horse, restlessly studying the fifty or sixty people clustered there.

"Are there any Indians here?" Skye asked, abruptly.

"We always employ some, Mister Skye."

"If any of them are the children of this woman, we wish to reunite them with their mother, who grieves for them."

"They drift in, and who knows, sir. Some are domestics, and some are herders. Shall we seek them out?"

Skye thought he might do just that. "They are free to leave, then?"

"Oh, it might not be quite that simple. Perhaps they owe something. Often they have to be equipped with clothing, and tools, and of course we add their room and board."

Skye nodded.

"But come in, my English friend, and see. Tell the Cheyenne woman she is free to examine my whole placita."

Childress translated.

"And if the Cheyennes are hers, sir, and wish to leave your employ, then what?"

"I am a Christian gentleman, the nephew of a cardinal bishop of Hungary, Mister Skye, and you will find me utterly opposed to your effort to surrender them to their heathen mother when I can provide them with all the civilizing virtues, as well as the True Faith, all of which is to their benefit.

"Shall I send a young man on the brink of accepting Our Lord back to the pagan life from which he came? Never. It would be a sin. But such as you describe aren't here; let her look among us." He glanced at the low sun. "Come to vespers and see for yourself. And freshen yourselves with us for the night. You are guests here at the estancia of Don Gabor. I've never entertained a pirate before, nor a monkey, nor a rebel Texan, nor men who drown beavers for a living, and I look forward to it. Maria Elena is eager to welcome such exotic company, men of callings beyond her experience. She will be especially interested in pirates."

He beckoned them to enter the placita, which they did. But Skye wondered whether they would freely leave it.

fifteen

The adobe chapel filled slowly at sundown, while Standing Alone posted herself at its rough-planked door to observe every soul who entered there. The man who called himself Childress had advised her to examine those who came, and assured her that everyone in the hacienda would be present because the master required it. He could scarcely fathom what it was like to search in such a fashion for a lost daughter or son. She stood at the portal, resolute and silent, her gaze flicking from one to another of the Mexicans.

He stood beside her, ready to assist. One by one the peons drifted in, their faces shy and meek and sun-stained, their cottons virtually rags of faded blue and soiled white. Most were barefoot. The women looked weathered from work in the fields, bent from scrubbing clothing in the sun, worn from herding.

The narrow earthen chapel exuded gloom, save for a single candle upon a waxed hardwood altar. The men and women of Las Delicias settled silently on cottonwood benches to thank God for this day. A baby whimpered, but Childress felt himself wrapped in a peaceful and solemn celebration of a good day. He remembered his other mission, and counted sixty-two souls, datum to file away against the conquest of northern Mexico by Lamar's army.

Standing Alone saw no one who resembled her daughter or son, and when the crowd had settled she and Childress and Shine sat down at the very rear, beside Skye and Victoria.

Don Gabor Rakoczi, attired in black, recited the vespers rite in Latin, and at certain ringing of an altar bell his flock responded by rote. The air was so still that the candle never guttered, and not even the mumbling of the congregation shook the flame.

Both Victoria and Standing Alone beheld all this with un-alloyed curiosity, and Childress wondered what, exactly, was passing through their minds. Here was the white men's God. The trader had a more commercial view of things, and eyed the carved and enameled wood bultos, and the gilded altar crucifix, and found no worth in them. Shine liked the occasional summons of the bell in Rakoczi's sure hand, and bounced happily on the bench. Childress supposed that the monkey knew about as much of what was being said in Latin as Don Gabor's flock.

This evening rite concluded swiftly, and the peons filed out, their gaze quick and curious upon the strangers and the monkey. The smell of mesquite woodsmoke hovered in the air.

"We will summon you," Rakoczi said, while escorting his wife toward their rambling adobe house. She looked particularly striking this twilit moment, with a mother-of-pearl comb pinning her raven tresses back from her aquiline face. She lifted the black mantilla from her head as she and her husband traced their way across the placita.

That proved to be the last time the Colonel saw her. He whiled away the hour by settling himself in the barren adobe room adjacent to the stables where he had been posted by a whipcord-thin aged servant. Next to it was another, with the Skyes and Standing Alone in it.

A bell clanged sourly, and at that time, the venerable servant collected the guests and took them to a dining commons, with two trestle tables in it. There they were served rice and beans and some beef stew by silent bronze Indian women; later the women fed themselves at a separate bench. There was no sign of the master of the Hacienda de Las Delicias or his lady.

The majordomo arrived just when the Colonel was wondering what might happen next, and escorted the women back to their quarters. The men proceeded to the great house, where Don Gabor, now attired in a burgundy silk smoking jacket, led them into a shadowed parlor, lit by a pair of candles, and furnished mission-style, with upright chairs that would put backbone into the most slovenly posture.

"Gentlemen," he said, offering each a cigarro. "A little smoke and talk. I am curious about you. And you are curious about me and life in Mexico. I mean to inform you." He poured ruby wine into cut-glass goblets and handed one to Skye and the Colonel.

"But first a toast." He lifted his glass. "To Mexico, forever, glorious and untrammeled, and to our Holy Faith."

The don's gaze had settled upon Childress.

"Hear, hear," the Colonel said.

Skye nodded and sipped. Skye looked odd without his battered top hat. He had washed himself, and slicked his hair, and scraped his face, so that he seemed almost civilized. But not entirely. Not ever civilized in any true sense of the word, yet not a ruffian either. The man was unlike any other.

"You have seen," Don Gabor continued, "that we maintain a certain gentility here, even in a place as remote from the heart of Mexico as this. We are a bastion of the border and the Faith; indeed, that was how this grant of a hundred square leagues came to me; anyone willing to anchor the north for the republic and the church might receive the land. So here I am, among pieces of furniture and linens and china and glass and books and arms brought by ox-team from the

Sea of Cortez, or up the Rio Grande. Do you approve, Mister Childress, or do you think all this should fall to, say, the United States?"

"Sah, my esteem for your nation and its industries and arts is boundless."

Rakoczi cocked a brow and grinned, baring those white teeth again. He turned to Skye. "And you, sir. I understand you were with the Royal Navy, but I am not clear about the rest."

Skye settled into a stiff-backed chair that was plainly tormenting him. "I deserted, sir."

The candid response caught Rakoczi by surprise. "Really?"

"I was pressed into the navy off the streets of East End, when I was a boy of twelve. That was the last I saw of my mother and father and sisters. My father had an import and export business and I was much around the Thames docks. They made me a powder monkey.

"The harder I struggled to escape this—this involuntary servitude—the harder it went for me. Seven years, sir, was I held aboard ships of war, the hulls my prisons, rarely seeing land, my pittance fined away or stolen from me, my gruel stolen by older and harder men until I learned to defend myself, with the only thing I had, my fists and my rage. I came to love the sea, but I loved liberty more. I gained my freedom at Fort Vancouver in 'twenty-three, penetrated into the mountains, and have been a man without a country ever since."

"Many good men are grateful to serve the crown."

"I might have gladly, if I had not been kidnapped bodily. English are subjects, sir, not citizens, and subjects are still at the disposal of the throne in spite of the Magna Carta. I prefer the new world, and a republic, where a man is a citizen rather than a subject."

Rakoczi listened intently. The colonel was amused. At last, he had an inkling of what inspired Skye.

"So we have a self-confessed privateer and a self-confessed deserter for guests," the don said, fires building in his eyes. "And no man of honor."

Bear baiting, the Colonel thought.

Smoothly, Rakoczi refilled Skye's wineglass, and Skye downed the wine in one gulp. His face had darkened and he was about to explode, but Childress interrupted.

"Sah, I am no man of honor whatsoever, and find the very word repugnant," Childress said, cheerfully. "I come from a long line of brigands."

Skye had turned red. Obviously, the border ruffian didn't know what the smooth-talking don was up to. If the powerful lord of this estate could provoke an explosion, they would all be shipped to Mexico City in chains.

Somehow, Skye subsided. "Until you know what servitude is, sir, until you know endless months and years when your life is not your own, until you know what it is to be summoned only to obey, until you know a time when you cannot dream or hope, until you know what it is to walk the earth as a free man, you know nothing of my circumstance or of honor."

Skye was eloquent, Childress had to admit that of him.

The hacendado didn't seem very impressed, though. He chuckled politely. "I'm sure every prisoner in every jail thinks quite the same way, Skye."

"Mister Skye, sir. *Mister.*"

"Yes, yes, of course, forgive me my lack of delicacy." The hacendado was toying with Skye. He filled the glass again.

Skye downed the entire glass of wine, and rocked gently in his torture-backed chair. "There are various species of slavery, sir, but they all involve the capture of another mortal and ownership of his services. In the American South is a terrible form of it, in which a mortal is pure property, the same as a cow or a dog; in which a slave has no rights, can be tortured or even killed for any infraction.

"The Indians of the plains have a gentle form of it. They

acquire slaves mostly in war raids, and these are usually women and children, and often they become members of the tribe in time, and marry into it. . . . And then there's your country's system of slavery, sir, called peonage."

Skye was heated now by wine and anger, and the more Skye's face reddened, the more the don was amused. But he shouldn't be, Childress thought. Skye was a brawler, and the don would find his teeth stuffed down his throat before he knew what hit him.

"We have no slavery in Mexico, Skye. The peons are Mexican citizens, with rights guaranteed by the constitution. We take care of them because they can't take care of themselves. These walls offer protection against the savages. My fields offer them employment. My wealth supplies them with all they need, even when they are old or sick and have no economic value to me. The church would condemn us if we treated them badly. We have an excellent system, humane and productive. Did even one of my peons voice one word of sorrow? Would one leave, even if he could?"

"Slaves," Skye said, his voice half strangled with his own heat. "The Indians are slaves. I know their story. They live short and brutal lives in the mines, where they starve on gruel and suffer exhaustion and injury and disease, and not much better lives in the fields, where they hoe until they drop. They last five years or ten and then they die, all used up. They aren't paid and they aren't free, and if they try to escape, they are whipped to death. But we'll find two of them—if they live."

Rakoczi finally realized the sort of man he was dealing with, and moved quickly backward.

"I think, my friend Skye, it's time for us to retire," Childress said, fearing mayhem and City of Mexico dungeons. "We'll leave honor to our host."

Slowly, almost as if he were returning from another planet, Skye quieted.

Don Gabor Rakoczi, whose hand had been in a desk drawer, slowly withdrew it. A ball would not even have slowed down Barnaby Skye. At last Colonel Childress knew, as epiphany, the sort of man he traveled with.

sixteen

F ar to the west, a half dozen riders were tracking Skye's little caravan, ghosts lost in haze. He saw and noted them, though no one else did. He would have missed them but for the sheer beauty of Mexico, the etched blue ridges, the blinding sun-bleached flats, the mysterious brooding silence, all under a cobalt heaven such as Skye had never before seen. He had never penetrated a land of such aching beauty and mystery, and felt this strange sweetness of the countryside in his bones.

The riders were not angling closer, but neither did they depart. They were stalking.

Skye kept an eye on them, and an eye on natural defenses, but there wasn't much he could do. His mind was on other matters. Colonel Childress's conduct at the Hacienda de Las Delicias had all but clamped irons on their ankles and chains on their legs. The man had made a great point of announcing he was a rebel and a pirate and a scoundrel. And all this he had proclaimed to an autocrat of the wilderness who had the men and arms to throw Childress and Skye into an eternal hell. Just why the hacendado had seen them off the following morning with a white-toothed smile and a languid wave of his arm was more than Skye could understand. But they were free and had been for two silent days.

Skye intended to do something about it before he and his wife and Standing Alone were enmeshed in even greater peril. Just what, he wasn't sure. He had spent the quiet hours of travel pondering it.

This silent morning, he had made up his mind: he and the crazy Childress were about to part company. The only question was whether to wait until they reached Taos, or whether it would be right now, period.

Victoria, who knew his moods, had fathomed what he was thinking. "He's no damn good," she had said, out of the blue.

Childress rolled along in his carmine cart with the Jolly Roger emblazoned on its flanks, his draft horse clopping its way to Santa Fe, his face shaded by his straw planter's hat, and his gaze restless, his attention flicking from person to person.

All that day the riders far off to the west tracked them, but never approached. Skye guessed they would attempt something at night if they were not friendly, and as the day waned he began looking for a place to fort up, maybe even a dry camp.

Late that soft spring day they struck a creek burbling out of the Sangre de Cristos, and a much-used campsite. The creek rolled out of a canyon half a mile east, and Skye decided to retreat there.

He pointed.

"Camp in there tonight," he said.

"But Mister Skye, Sah, that's a piece, and there's no road."

"In there."

Victoria nodded, and steered her horse and packhorses eastward. Standing Alone followed. Childress looked like he might not, but surrendered with an angry shrug and steered his cart overland.

A while later they were unpacking in a secluded flat hidden from the great plain they had been traversing.

"At least the grass is good," Childress muttered, as he

slipped to earth and unharnessed the Clydesdale. For a fat man, he was nimble.

It was a good place. The grass rose lush and tender. The fragrance of piñon pine drifted across the creek-carved hollow, a demiparadise of live oak, juniper, and pines. Skye thought they could risk a cook fire, but not after dark. He hadn't seen the stalkers for some while but he was ready for them, and this was a place with a narrow mouth that could be watched.

The monkey watered the Clydesdale, and then, as usual, began gathering dry wood, upon Childress's command. But the monkey and his master would have to go, Skye thought.

They had nothing but parched corn to eat, so the women started water heating. With a little salt, the mush wasn't bad, and it put energy into a man. In Taos, they would replenish.

Skye scarcely knew how to do what he had to do, but he was a man and he would do it, and that would end his alliance with this bizarre fool from Texas.

He waited until they had all scooped the mush into their mouths, including Shine, whose portion was tenderly dished out by Childress. While the women were scouring the blackened cookpot, Skye studied the canyon where the creek burst out of the foothills. He saw nothing in the violet twilight.

"Mr. Childress," he said harshly. "In Taos we'll go our separate ways."

The fat Texan looked surprised. He lifted his fine planter's hat, and pursed his lips. "It's a mistake," he said.

"No, it's what I want. It's necessary. Sorry."

Childress sighed. "I feared it would come to this, and I know why you're doing it."

"Then I don't have to say any more."

Childress laughed softly. "No, but I will. You're a man of honor, pursuing an honorable cause that rests heavily upon you. You've allied yourself with a privateer and God only knows what else." He was enjoying himself. "Scoundrel, reckless fool who endangered the whole party at Las Delicias calling himself a rebel and adventurer and privateer and pirate. Yes, Sah, and a man who's got the Jolly Roger painted on his cart for good measure." He chuckled softly, enjoying himself. "I knew it would come to this, Sah."

"Then that's how it'll be."

"I trust you'll pay me for my horses."

"Take them. We'll walk if we have to."

"Over a thousand miles of northern Mexico."

"Yes, ten thousand miles if that's what it takes."

The Colonel sighed. "Admire your determination, Skye."

"It's—"

"Yes, yes, yes, and with good reason. You'd make a fine Texan, Sah."

"We've had company all day," Skye said.

The trader's gaze steadied on Skye.

"That's why we're here. Good concealment, and we can defend."

"Who?"

"Half dozen riders far west, tracking us."

"Rakoczi's?"

"Don't know."

"Utes, Apaches, Federales, Rakoczi."

Skye nodded.

"My friend Skye, you're a man of honor, and you make uneasy alliance with a man like me. I know that. But I beg to advise you that the problem isn't me, it's you. The Mexicans enjoy a scoundrel, in particular, a fat scoundrel with a spider monkey. I'm the sideshow, Sah. I'm your diversion, and you proceed unmolested."

He lowered his voice almost to a whisper. "It would not be like that if you proceed without me. They fear an earnest man pursuing a good cause. It upsets them. Don Gabor Rakoczi, for instance. You he baited, me he ignored. You he drove to the brink, not me. And it was a deliberate act, I assure you. I know the Mexicans. Their entire way of life rests on the backs of peons, cheap labor, slaves in all but name, indebted and forced to stay on the land for protection. In a trice, they could turn you into a peon, my friend."

"No, they couldn't. Because no one will ever take my liberty from me again."

It was the way he said it that made Childress blanch. A breeze tucked sparks into the sky. Skye motioned to Victoria, who brought a leather camp bucket and doused the fire. It hissed, and sour smoke stained the air. But then the velvet purple twilight settled over their camp. Standing Alone headed downstream, toward some brush. She was largely left out of these conversations because of the barriers of tongue and tradition.

Skye wasn't done.

"Colonel, who are you?" he asked. "And why are you here?"

"A filibuster, Skye, a man looking for pots of gold at the end of rainbows."

"Neither of us will leave this camp until you tell me the entire truth."

"Why, Sah, what more is there to say?"

"There's plenty more."

"You've gone sour on me, I'm afraid. Can't be helped. Some men don't take to society."

"You didn't answer my question. This outfit doesn't move until you do. And that goes for you and your cart."

"I've responded to the best of my ability, and I'm sorely tested and offended, Mister Skye."

"We're not moving."

"I'm exactly what I say I am."

"And what else?"

"Sah, if you could only know how much I am a sucker for good causes. Your quest to free two hapless Cheyenne touched my very heart, my core, my soul, the center of my bosom. You have the whole of me there. Give me a great cause, liberty, justice, honor, the relief of oppression—save for religion, Sah, I don't get fired up for the Faith, but all else, I am a guerrilla and a reformer, ready to walk beside you to the southern tip of Mexico to find these children and restore them to their blessed mother. I'd have run the guillotine in France. I'd be dumping tea into Boston Harbor. I'd have fired one of those shots heard round the world at Concord. I'd be following Simón Bolívar across South America, holding his flag. And that, Sah, is how I swear and uphold the holy and unpolluted truth, my conscience, my heart, so help me God."

Skye grinned. "Guess we'll just stay here until you're ready to level with us," he said.

The fat man peered off into the gloom, fidgeted, leaned forward, and whispered: "I'm doing advance reconnaissance for President Mirabeau Buonaparte Lamar. He has it in his thick head, affixed somewhere just behind his receding forehead, that the Republic of Texas ought to reach to the Western Sea, and he set me onto it like a fat dawg sniffing trees. And you, poor old Skye, are an unwitting conspirator."

Skye hiccuped, fell to the grasses laughing, roared like a lunatic grizzly, and Victoria wanted to know what was so damned funny; all white men were crazy.

seventeen

The chittering of the monkey awakened Skye but it was already too late. Above him, as he peered into the gray predawn, were half a dozen skeletal faces. These materialized into Indians standing over him, one with a nocked bow but the others were simply watching. Skye felt for his rifle and found that it was gone.

He scarcely dared move. Victoria was stirring beside him, and then he heard her soft cussing in the quietness.

"We've been had," said Childress from under his cart.

Very carefully, Skye sat up. The Indians let him. They wore loincloths and little else. Some had shirts, many wore a red bandanna or headband that pinned their black straight hair, most had light moccasins. Skye didn't have the faintest idea who they might be or what they intended to do.

"Jicarilla Apaches," Childress muttered. "Not tame, no Sah."

The monkey leaped about, mesmerizing the Apaches.

Off in the gloom, Skye saw a dozen others collecting the horses. They had been hobbled except for the Clydesdale, which had grazed freely, as usual, dragging a halter rope with him. Maybe this was only a horse raid. Maybe he would live a few more minutes. Maybe not.

Slowly Skye lifted his hands, showing that they contained no weapon, and then signed, Friend.

An older Apache laughed.

That was a good joke. Skye eyed the steel arrowhead aimed straight at his chest and subsided into utter quietness. But his gaze searched restlessly for anything, any clue as to what might happen, any means of escape. He saw nothing. These could be his last moments, then. He helped Victoria sit up and held her hand.

The monkey mesmerized the Apaches. They tried to grab the little creature but he was much too agile for them. A young warrior raised his bow but an older one stayed him with a guttural bark.

Some of the Apaches began opening the packs and extracted various items: cookpots, knives, a powderhorn, spare clothes. Others gathered around the red cart, yanked the canvas off, and plunged into the heaps of trade items and robes and pelts in it.

"Bloody thieves. I'll flay the hide off your backs," Childress proclaimed from under the cart, rising up in wrath. A foot on his chest flattened him. One young warrior discovered the skeins of blue beads, and exclaimed. He held one up and howled. In moments, the beads were parceled out, along with awls, flints and steels, knives, ladles, cookpots, sacks of sugar, jugs of molasses, bolts of calico, bed ticking, and two pairs of four-point blankets.

Skye observed Standing Alone, imprisoned between two of the Jicarillas and not resisting. She looked grimly at Skye and the trader, but said nothing. She looked disheveled.

Skye dared to hope. This was a looting party, but maybe not a murderous one—at least so far. But he knew the reputation of all Apaches and knew how lucky he would be to see the sun set on this day, or a sunrise tomorrow. He did not know whether these were the ones who had ridden parallel all the previous day, but it seemed likely.

The Apaches seemed to be looking for spirits. They

opened the molasses and sampled it. But as far as Skye knew, Childress wasn't carrying any ardent spirits, and that was a stroke of luck. They'd all die, and fast, once the Apaches began working on some Indian whiskey.

It was not yet dawn. He adjudged their number at thirty. They had the horses in hand, bridled and saddled, except for the Clydesdale. Shine, ever helpful, snatched the halter rope of the big animal, and led it to the rest of the horses, while the Apaches watched, amazed. Then with one graceful bound, Shine leaped up to the Clydesdale's neck, halter rope in hand, and sat there over the mane, chattering and babbling.

Most of these Apaches were on foot. Maybe they had a horse-holder down the creek somewhere, or maybe not. The Apaches wouldn't have many horses. These would be enormously valuable to them.

"I think if we're quiet, they might leave us," Skye said softly to Victoria.

The older Apache, probably a war leader, kicked him and waved his knife. The meaning was not lost on Skye.

Skye made the sign for water, but the chieftain just stared. So far, they hadn't even let Skye or Victoria stand up, and Childress was a captive under his cart.

As the day quickened, one of the younger Apaches discovered the skull and crossbones enameled on Childress's cart, and drew the rest to it. This occasioned much talk among them. They fingered it, examined the identical insignia on the other side, and studied Childress.

Skye tried a finger message: "Big man makes death."

The chieftain muttered something, and some of the warriors prodded Childress to his feet. They marveled at his girth, poking fingers into him to see what all that fat felt like. The Texan fetched his straw hat, stood quietly while they absorbed his stature, and then he launched into a soft, conversational, almost delicate address:

"I've thrown better men than you to the sharks," he said blandly. "I've strung up your kind by your thumbs and delivered a hundred lashes, and I'll do the same to you. Let me have that whip, the one you have in hand there, you miserable cur, and I'll flail your skin right off your back and take your nose off and snap your eyes out for good measure, and while you're poking arrows into me I'll cut your chief over there to pieces and feed him to the wolves. Then I'll pull out your arrows and stuff them down your gullets, you bloody buggers."

All this Childress delivered with such aplomb that Skye marveled. Had the privateer no fear? Skye's own fear caught the spittle in his throat and silenced him and set his heart to racing, but here was the fat man blaspheming everything about the Apaches. The mad Texan was about to get them all massacred.

"You miserable dogs, you curs who sniff your own vomit, give me that whip and I'll show you a thing or two," he said, never raising his voice, and yet the power of his words reached every one of the Jicarillas.

Childress walked slowly with his hand outstretched toward the Apache boy with the whip in hand, and surprisingly, the boy surrendered it. Childress plucked it up, and suddenly the whip turned into a live, whirring thing, rattlesnaking here and there, snapping and popping, while the Apaches stood spellbound.

"Put everything back in that cart or I'll cut your heart out," he said, never raising his voice. But he did point at the cart, and at the loot the warriors had lifted. Some of it now adorned them.

Skye had never seen anything like it. Not in all his years in the Royal Navy, or all his years in the mountains, had he seen a man as vulnerable as Childress rake a hostile crowd with sheer force of will. The stern commands issued out of him with the precision of a metronome, and the plaited whip whirred and cracked, but no one moved.

It was not enough. The chieftain said something.

Half a dozen warriors circled Childress just outside of

whip range, then rushed in and subdued him. Only one felt the lash. At another wave of the hand, other warriors caught Skye and Victoria and Standing Alone, and began stripping away their clothing, relentlessly, methodically, until they had it all.

Victoria snarled but she was helpless against such brute force, and so was Standing Alone. Childress had been reduced to the buff, and then it was Skye's turn. By the time the Apaches were done, Skye's party didn't own a stitch of clothing except for Childress's hat. For some reason, they awarded him his hat, which perched on his head majestically, as he stood in huge white array. His gargantuan white belly and piano legs rose like a mountain under his Panama.

Skye could not even describe his feelings, standing there before them all with every last shred yanked off of him, and now adorning the Apaches. The chieftain had commandeered his black top hat along with his rifle, powderhorn, and knives. A subchief had his bear-claw necklace. But they did not take his medicine bundle. Victoria cringed and covered herself, but Standing Alone seemed resigned to her fate, and stood calmly, her slim beauty astonishing. Then, with innate Cheyenne modesty, she turned her back upon them, and stood quietly, all the more galvanizing for having turned her back to them.

At a word from the chieftain, the Apaches swiftly loaded their booty onto the backs of the horses and their own backs, and vanished as silently as they had come, padding out of the secluded bottoms. Skye watched his horses head downriver, along with the Clydesdale with the monkey riding the mane.

Dawn had scarcely penetrated this canyon on the west slope of the Sangre de Cristos. Skye watched the Apaches vanish around a bend in the creek, and waited a moment more for surprises, but nothing else happened. He felt helpless, more so than ever in his life because he was naked.

He turned, wanting to inventory what was left, and found

that nothing was left. Only the cart, and the useless harness for the Clydesdale, which was lying beyond the cart. The cart was empty. Every bit of merchandise and every pelt was gone. The canvas that covered it was gone.

The Colonel approached. His Panama stayed proudly atop his vast acreage of flesh.

"We've walked the plank, and now we're bobbing in the sea," said Childress. "A plague on their bloody bodies. Where's Shine?"

"He rode the Clydesdale."

Something vital seemed to bleed from the Colonel. "Lost him, too, then."

"The Clydesdale was last; he can't keep up with those lighter horses."

"Then the Apaches'll kill him. They won't let him return here."

"You got any ideas?"

The Colonel brightened. "I will perform my ablutions and then we can sit down under the cart and wait. None of us can walk more than a hundred yards in this cactus."

Skye thought it would be a long wait.

eighteen

*N*othing for food. Nothing to keep the sun from frying them or the wind from chafing them or the chill of night from numbing them. Nothing for their feet. Nothing to hunt with, or to defend themselves with.

Skye well knew what the odds were. The Colonel was right: they had walked the plank and now bobbed in the empty ocean. It was only a matter of time. Yet he had been in tight corners before and he was not a man to surrender.

"Let's look around," he said to Victoria.

She nodded. Slowly they patrolled the area looking for anything useful. A forgotten knife, edible roots, a rag. The others were doing the same. But the Jicarillas had been thorough, and had left nothing.

"We'll find someone on the Taos road," Skye said.

"That's a half mile of cactus, Skye," the Colonel said.

"I'll get you there without stepping on one cactus," Skye replied.

He motioned to Victoria to bring along Standing Alone.

"Let her walk behind us," he said, respecting her needs.

"Skye, I'm staying right here under the cart," Childress said. "I've water and shade, and I'll wait for help."

"Colonel, you'll have water and some shade with me. We'll walk the creek."

"I'm staying."

The Colonel sat down under his cart.

The man was determined not to move, so Skye didn't argue. "We'll send help if we can," he said.

"Skye, Sah—good to know you."

"And you, Colonel." He turned to the women. "All right, then. The sooner we reach the Taos road, the better chance we have."

He stepped into the creek and found the water numbing, the rocks slippery, and the footing treacherous. He lurched forward, tumbled, and landed splat in the icewater.

He roared, bolted to his feet, and began shivering. But there wasn't so much as a rag to dry himself.

Victoria laughed.

He turned to roar at her, but she just stood there up to her calves in water, grinning at him.

They started down the creek, one miserable step at a time, often in rocks, sometimes in sand, occasionally in muck. Skye stubbed his toes and wondered whether this was any better than walking the faint trail beside the creek. He wanted sunshine but there wasn't any; the sun lay low behind the towering Sangre de Cristos in the east.

Still . . . they walked, step by step by step, for a half hour before Skye called a halt. His feet were numb and bruised. Instantly Standing Alone turned her back to them. He sat down and rubbed his legs, which had turned blue. Victoria was cold, too, and working on her slim brown legs.

Then they started again, hiking down the river, plunging into hidden holes, teetering along until Skye's feet gave out and they rested again, this time beside sedges.

That's when Stands Alone began waving frantically, uttering sharp cries, pointing.

They looked.

The Clydesdale was progressing toward them. No Apache was driving it.

"Bloody horse," Skye said.

"Monkeee," Standing Alone said.

She was right. Shine was patiently leading the horse by its halter rope.

Victoria scowled. "Little Person," she snapped.

Skye stepped to land, stubbed his toe, but eventually reached the horse. The women followed.

The monkey chittered, danced, and leaped up on the back of the big brown horse.

"We've been rescued. Don't know how he did it," Skye said. "You ladies ride it back, harness him to the cart, put the Colonel in, and return. I'll wait."

Victoria grinned malevolently. She helped Standing Alone clamber onto that big animal, and Skye helped her, and then he watched the Clydesdale trot smartly upstream.

Skye sat in the bullrushes, wanting some clothing and some moccasins and feeling vulnerable. Hunger caught him, too. They had eaten nothing. The sun was burning in, and he lowered himself into the shade of the bankside brush, fighting off insects. Adam and Eve, he thought, could not have enjoyed Eden.

It took an hour, but Skye barely noticed. His feet still hurt. But at last, midday, he heard the clopping of the draft horse, stood, and beheld the horse and red cart approaching swiftly, driven by that great white whale, Colonel Childress, still wearing his Panama. Shine had resumed his usual perch on the Clydesdale.

"Sorry, Skye, I'm out of fig leafs," Childress said as he pulled up.

The women, both of them sprawled in the bed of the cart, grinned at him. With what little dignity he could muster, Skye clambered in, and immediately the Colonel snapped the lines over the croup of the draft horse and took off at a swift trot.

"Colonel, how far to Taos?" Skye asked.

"I reckon forty or fifty miles—three days."

"We'll be burnt. Maybe we should travel at night."

"Well, aren't you the modest one. Once you're in the drink, Skye, you have to swim for the nearest shore."

"Maybe we should pull up some grasses to cover ourselves."

"Skye, you're naked as Adam. Enjoy it. Admire the scenery. What you need is a good Mexican cigarro."

"Are there any villages closer?"

"Maybe some ranchos."

"What'll we tell people?"

"Why, Skye, that we're a pack of libertines and lechers en route to scandalize the pueblo."

"What is this word, lecher?" Victoria asked, anticipation in her voice.

Skye grunted. It was all he could do to sit naked in a bouncing cart with two bouncing naked women, both beautiful.

Victoria was enjoying it. Standing Alone mostly turned her back, but once she flashed her warm, knowing smile at Skye. Then, unaccountably, the two Indian women began giggling.

"Look for food," Skye grumbled.

They reached the Taos Camino and paused there for one last drink from the creek before turning south. The sun had climbed well into the firmament and soon would be scorching their flesh.

Skye, disturbed by his proximity to the women, offered to drive the cart, but the Colonel declined, perhaps for the same reason. The trail traversed an empty waste, and they saw nothing. Thirst built again in Skye, along with hunger and the sensation that the sun was going to destroy him.

"We'd better hole up if you can find shade," he said.

"Mister Skye, Sah, tell me where that might be."

Skye examined a bright arid plain devoid of trees. But there was brush, and an occasional arroyo.

"Find an arroyo, Colonel. We'll perish in this sun, if we haven't already." At least the two white men would, he thought.

"The sooner we reach succor, the sooner we will be preserved, Sah. The shore is still beyond sight, but we'll make landfall soon."

There was no stopping the man. Beyond the turning wheels of the cart lay white clay, dust, small waxy plants that could endure in such a climate, rock, and boundless blue skies.

Skye turned himself on the cart bed, figuring to roast all sides evenly, but he knew he would be in trouble by nightfall.

Skye's world reduced to the walls of the cart, and he closed his eyes. There was little he could do. The heat built, sucking moisture out of him. His stomach rumbled. He felt the first pangs of dehydration; a dry mouth, a fearsome thirst.

"You all right?" he asked Victoria.

"Damn hot," she said.

The women were doing better than he was. He closed his eyes against the midday glare.

Some while later, the Colonel whooped.

"Succor, assistance, help," he bawled, and the passengers peered out to see a carreta coming their way, far ahead, with three people walking beside it.

Skye squinted at the apparition. It was a rude cart with stakes holding a tottering load of crooked firewood on it, drawn by a gaunt burro. Three young men in peasant cottons and sandals walked beside it, axes over their shoulders. They were so swart they could have been Indians themselves.

"Ah, amigos!" bawled Colonel Childress, waving a white arm at them as the parties closed.

They stared.

The Colonel rattled on in Spanish, and all Skye fathomed

was that he was talking about the Jicarilla Apaches. The young men's gaze roved between Childress, huge and white and naked, and the occupants of the cart, resting at last on the women. They gaped, unable to look elsewhere. Standing Alone turned from their stare.

"Agua, agua," Childress was saying.

The young men conferred and then produced a goatskin water bag that had been hanging from the back of their cart, which they handed to Childress, who lifted it and ran a trickle down his gullet while Skye watched enviously, afraid the fat man would drink it all. But Childress took only a swallow and handed it to Skye, who handed it to the women. There was enough for them all to get a few swallows. Childress handed it to the monkey, who drank expertly while the woodcutters stared dumbfounded.

But they had no food and no clothing to spare; not even a rag. Childress talked with them while Skye and the women waited.

At last the Colonel turned to his passengers. "Arroyo Hondo, a village, is an hour or two ahead. We are saved!"

Just barely, Skye thought.

nineteen

rroyo Hondo lay before them, a scatter of adobes nestled in a steep-walled canyon cut by a creek. The man styled Jean Lafitte Childress saw his salvation, but knew it would come only at the price of his mortification. He sat nakedly upon the cart, with a cargo of naked people. It would not be easy.

He spotted an adobe church or chapel, and two hundred yards behind it, through trees, a black-clad crowd that plainly was burying someone. Probably most of this rural village was there.

"We're close," he said to those huddled miserably behind him. "A long plunge downslope first."

He steered his Clydesdale down a steep incline, trusting the heavy horse to brake the cart, and when the land leveled he found himself among cultivated fields. And coming toward him was a bent old woman in black, supporting herself with a staff.

He wished he had encountered a male, but there was no help for it. He slid his Panama off and onto his lap, not that it would help much.

She tottered forward, paused at the amazing sight of the red cart driven by a naked man, and waited.

"Señora," he began in Spanish, "we have been waylaid

by the Apaches, and they took everything from us, even our clothes."

"Yes, it is true," she replied. "Dios! I have never seen a man in such condition in sunlight."

"We need help, señora. Por favor, could you find something for us to wear?"

She peered up at him, shaking her head. "Señor, finding something for you is a task beyond my poor ability. The amount of fabric! It would take a month to weave it and another to sew it. And what of the others?"

She hobbled slowly toward the rear of the cart, paused, peered in at the cringing occupants, who presented their backs to her. "Yes, they need covering also. The pale man looks burnt. The women endure the sun. It has been a long time since I have seen such nakedness."

"You are our salvation, señora!"

"I wish I were thirty years younger," she said. "I would have a body like those women. Then I would attract the smiles of men. I have not been smiled upon for longer than I can remember, now that my paps are withered. Ah, to be young and smooth!"

"We are all suffering from the sun, señora."

She leaned on her staff, pondering. "Let us go to the church, and there will I find something for you. But you cannot let that monkey in. It would be a sacrilege."

"The church! Where that crowd is burying someone?"

She nodded. "They are burying Manuel, my son-in-law."

"Your son-in-law? Why aren't you there?"

"Because he is my son-in-law."

The last place Childress wanted to drive was the church.

"But that crowd—"

"Naked man, that crowd has only begun to bury him and they are on the other side and will not see you. He was a prominent man, so they will take their time hating him and wishing perdition upon him. They want to make sure he is good and buried, so that his bones will not escape and haunt us."

"Ah . . . What will we find there? A sheet? Altar linen? I don't think—"

"Come," she said, and hastened toward the long adobe edifice, rapping her staff on the clay. Colonel Childress followed, grateful that the adobe walls and trees hid the graveyard beyond, and the reproachful eyes of that crowd.

At last they pulled up before the dark doors.

"I'm not going in there, mate," Skye said slowly, peering over the top of the cart.

"Me neither, Skye, but she says it's the place to get help."

She paused at the hand-sawed plank door. "I have the honor of sweeping this holy place each day," she said. "I know everything. Come with me."

The women peered out of the cart but didn't move. Childress felt glued to his bench. Finally Skye eased to the ground, and crabbed his way toward the door, hunched over with whatever modesty he could summon. He had found courage that eluded the colonel of the militia of the Republic of Texas.

Childress sighed, lowered himself to earth, and followed, his mind swarming with disasters and shame.

They watched the old woman enter, curtsey, then trot along the shadowed wall of the nave toward the sacristy, pass a bulto in its niche, and vanish around a corner.

"I can't go in there, Skye. Not without a stitch."

Skye grunted, plunged into the gloom, and knelt suddenly at the back of the nave.

Childress could scarcely imagine such an act.

"Forgive us this trespass, Lord, and we thank you for our salvation," Skye said. "We mean no affront to you. We are desperate, and you have promised to help the naked and the poor."

Skye was speaking for both, and Childress was comforted.

The privateer knew suddenly that Skye had inner resources that were quite beyond his own. Skye stood, with quiet dignity, and walked through cool shade, no longer crouching in desperate modesty. The chapel was a simple place, with pine benches. No candle flickered. A small dark cross stood upon the altar.

The old woman in black beckoned from the door of the sacristy, so Skye and Childress padded there. Not even Skye's desperate prayer made it right to be naked in such a place.

The woman headed straight toward a closet where robes hung.

"See, señor," she said. "He is a Franciscan who is the priest here, and fat like you." She squinted at him, and pulled a brown-dyed woolen habit from the closet. "Though I doubt that his parts equal yours, but with a priest, who cares?"

It was a generous one, a monk's attire, with a hood and a soft white rope at the waist.

Childress had a fit of conscience. "Is this right, señora?"

She sniffed. "Would you prefer to offend little girls?"

That did it. He pulled the brown habit over him and knotted the rope at the waist. The presence of that cloth over him was as comforting as a keg of rum, he thought. She gave another to Skye, who gratefully slipped it on and sighed. It was a little long for Skye, and trailed in the dust.

"I have never appreciated what clothing means," Skye said. "It is more than warmth and protection. It is dignity and safety. It keeps us from offending."

Childress turned to the woman. "We cannot pay. We have nothing. The Jicarillas left us in a wilderness to perish. Is there something for the women?"

He eyed the embroidered vestments, chasubles and surplices, albs and stoles, but she shook her head. "Those belong to God," she said. "God forbid that I surrender them. But these that you wear belong to our padre, and I will confess this to him."

He hunted for sandals, and she saw his intent.

"The feet of Franciscans are bare," she said. "It is a mortification of the flesh."

Childress wanted to get out of there before the burial crowd broke up. "Señora, let us find something for our women."

She nodded, led them through the nave and into the sunlight. Standing Alone and Victoria stared at the brown-robed men.

The old woman walked to the rear of the cart and clambered in. "I will show you, señores," she said.

Childress steered the horse away from the little church and followed the woman's instructions. They headed down a lane, and finally stopped at a flower-decked patio enclosed by a low adobe wall. Even in this raw frontier place, these people had fashioned serenity and beauty.

"A few things of my daughter will suffice," she said, sliding off the red cart. The women followed her shyly, while Childress and Skye settled themselves in the courtyard.

"Do you realize, Brother Skye, that I was more famished for cloth over my carcass than for food?" he said.

"Brother Childress, that will pass," Skye replied. "I am ready to eat lizards again."

"Do you suppose we can find a begging bowl? If I beg in my bastard Spanish and you keep silent, we might be taken for a pair of mendicant monks."

"With concubines," Skye said.

"And a red cart with a Jolly Roger upon it."

"Are your bare feet fit for walking, Brother Childress?"

"Alas, we will have to master the ways of this country."

The monkey had fled the back of the nag, and was swinging through a peach tree.

"There is nothing there, Shine. It is much too early and they are green," Childress said.

The monkey chittered and swung toward a string of red chiles. He bit into the end of one chile, spat out the vile contents, and scolded the monks.

When the women emerged into that courtyard, each wore a simple shift of unbleached linen, modest and plain. The dresses fit loosely, and the women looked pleased to be shielded once again. The covering would suffice. The women, too, had been transformed from crouching creatures to dignified persons.

The old woman appeared, this time with two round loaves of bread. "Take this, my friends. It is warm still," she said, thrusting the loaves toward Childress.

Bread never tasted so fine.

"Señora, to whom shall we give thanks for this?" Childress asked, wanting a name.

"I was christened Milagro," she said.

twenty

Skye marveled. That very morning they had found themselves naked and bereft, a deadly circumstance that should have destroyed them all. But they did not perish. He could thank a monkey for that, and this old woman whose name, he gathered, was Milagro.

He looked at his brown habit and smiled; and Brother Childress was even more the fat monk. The women sat quietly, masticating chunks of fresh bread. The monkey was swinging everywhere, his tail wrapped around branches as he explored this little green courtyard of the most gracious house and garden in Arroyo Hondo.

The old woman sat on a split-log bench, watching them, her eyes bright. The monkey vanished inside the building, and when it emerged it carried something that looked like an earthen jug.

Skye leaped up. The monkey was stealing something and Skye would not abuse this woman's kindness by letting that happen. But when Skye approached, it swung upward and sat on an eave, scolding Skye and waving the crockery jug.

The old woman laughed.

He turned to Childress. "Tell her I will get it, whatever it is. We'll not be stealing this old woman's food."

The old woman nodded and said something.

"It's molasses," Childress said. "Very precious, the only molasses in Arroyo Hondo."

The monkey dodged Skye's every effort until Skye began shouting at it. And then Shine leaped meekly to Skye's feet and left the jug there. Skye carried it to the woman, who nodded and set it in her lap.

"Ask her how far it is to Taos," he said.

Childress queried the woman, and learned that Taos could be reached in a day if one left at dawn and the weather was dry and the horse didn't go lame.

"We should go," Skye said, restlessly. He really didn't want that funeral party to return and discover him in a monk's habit and his women wearing someone's dresses with nothing under them. There could be trouble.

Childress caught his urgency, and thanked Milagro profusely, and listened to her lengthy reply, whispered in a throaty, soft voice, punctuated with small smiles, and finally a giggle and a euphoric grin.

"What was that?" Skye asked.

Childress flashed one of his buccaneer smiles. "I told her I could not repay her, for we have nothing, and she said she was already repaid. I said, yes, you're repaid by God, and by our gratitude. She said that wasn't it at all. She'll get another sort of payment from it.

"She said that when the family and neighbors return, she will tell them that she saw a red cart drawn by a huge horse with a monkey on its mane, and everyone in the cart was naked, and a skull and crossbones was painted on its side, and so she took the naked ones to the chapel.

"She says she will recite that with relish to young and old and that the family will stare at her as if she is daft, and pat her on the shoulder and tell her that she's getting old and seeing things and listening to the devil, and saying things she has invented, and maybe she should say her beads more often.

"She says they would rather believe that Jesus Christ

Himself had visited her than believe a red cart with naked people in it had arrived in Arroyo Hondo. And then she would giggle and laugh, and they would never know the truth, and she would have her secret the rest of her days, and it is an old lady's joke."

Skye laughed. He saw the old woman grinning primly, a finger at her mouth, anticipating the big joke she would play on her family, and how they would all think she was a loco old lady, and that was just fine with her.

They drove off with clothing covering their bodies, fed and comforted. At the last moment, Shine leaped aboard the Clydesdale, unhappy to abandon such a paradise. Skye sat on the bench beside Childress as the horse dragged the cart up the long grade and out upon the open plains once again.

"Now we're monks," Childress said. "Maybe that's best."

"No, mate, we're not monks and if we pretend, we'll be found out."

"I don't know how we can get into worse trouble than we're in, Skye. We haven't so much as a knife or a cookpot, no money, food, shelter, horses, boots or sandals, and I'm the only one who speaks the language. At least, as monks, we could beg a meal."

"We could always hire out."

"I've never worked a day in my life, Skye. I take what I want, but that requires an evil heart, a cutlass, some grapeshot, a few pistols, a dirk, and assorted instruments of terror. I'm not fitted out to be a monk or a laboring man. I've been a buccaneer for as long as I can remember, and it's a family tradition. Skye, there isn't a thing in my Galveston digs that I purchased. I take great pride in it. Everything's stolen."

"We can work."

"Work! You can; I won't."

"First thing is to get to Taos and keep ourselves and the horse fed," Skye said, not wanting an argument just then. "We have two Cheyenne children to find."

"You still thinking about that?"

"I've never stopped thinking about it."

"With nothing but the clothing on our backs, and that borrowed? And not an ounce of food?"

"Yes," Skye said.

Victoria, who was listening, laughed. "When he sets his mind to something, it gets done," she said. "That's how he gets drunk."

Dusk found them in an open flat. The mountains to the east caught the setting sun and glowed gold. They were far from water, and would have to make a dry camp. But Taos was not far away. At least there was bunch grass for the horse, and the last of the bread. They found a shallow arroyo that offered some protection from the rattling wind, and settled there in the twilight. Skye divided the bread, reserving a piece for Shine, who snatched it happily. He eyed the skies, worried about the clouds building up in the east over the great black mountains.

He and Victoria settled against the warm slope. They were without blankets, and Victoria's thin linen dress would not ward off the chill. He put an arm over her shoulder and drew her into his coarse brown robe. Childress vanished into the juniper brush for a while, while Standing Alone chose solitude. For her, a modest Cheyenne woman, the dress she wore meant everything, and especially an end to her suffering and the endless violations of her person by other eyes. The monkey was steering the Clydesdale from place to place, sometimes tugging on the lines when the horse lingered.

"You glad you came?" Victoria asked.

"Yes."

"You think we'll get out of here?"

"We're in trouble."

"I don't know much about these Mexicans. But that Milagro, I like her. She helped us."

"Yes, she did. But from now on, we're going to depend on the Mexicans for everything—food, shelter, warmth, clothing, sandals, and . . . liberty. I hear they don't take kindly to strangers."

"What is liberty?"

The question startled Skye. Victoria had never known anything but liberty, subject only to the traditions of her people.

"The children we're looking for don't have it. They can't live their life as they choose. They're slaves. We may not have it if we run into trouble. I think we'll be all right."

"Some Apache has your rifle."

"That's one of the ways I'm feeling naked. But there's this about it. Now we're no threat to anyone. No alcalde—that's a mayor, sort of—of any town here is going to worry about us."

He wasn't sure he believed that, especially with Childress obviously collecting military information. For all he knew, the Mexicans might have an exact understanding of Colonel Childress and his mission. But he wanted to hearten her.

Standing Alone approached, and after some hesitation, settled down beside Victoria in the lee of the arroyo.

"She says it's cold and this is better," Victoria said.

The women conversed softly, often using their hands, and Skye listened patiently, understanding very little of it.

"She says the old woman was kind, and the Mexicans are good people," Victoria said. "Food and clothing for us all. The old woman shared what she had. She likes Mexico. Standing Alone thinks maybe her children are comfortable here."

Skye had no answer for that. If her son had been taken to the mines in the south, he had been subjected to a life of unremitting toil. He would be fed barely enough to keep life in him, and he would be naked, because the masters spared their slave labor nothing beyond what kept body and soul together.

"Yes," Skye said, "tell her the Mexicans are good people,

most of them. They have a beautiful spirit. They would help anyone in trouble. They have a great faith that teaches them good things, but sometimes they ignore the teaching of their church. Sometimes they treat their own people badly and sometimes they treat Indians badly too."

Victoria did, and Standing Alone absorbed that bleakly.

"If her son was sent to the mines where they dig the metal, he is suffering and in danger. If he's working on a plantation, hoeing and weeding, or herding cattle, he would be better off. If her daughter's working in a household, she may be well off. But they aren't free. They are either peons, held to the land by perpetual debt, or slaves."

Victoria translated as best she could, and listened to the reply.

"Then they are savages, she says. The Cheyenne would never do such a thing. We must hurry, before it is too late."

Skye pressed Victoria's hand in the dusk. "We will, and it may take months," he said. "But there will be a way."

twenty-one

They rode into Taos so starved that Skye barely saw the bold beauty around him. Even the monkey had turned cross with an empty stomach, and clacked angrily. But in the midst of Skye's suffering he beheld an adobe town snugged close to piñon-clad foothills under a bold blue heaven. Here were more earthen dwellings, wizened old women in black, warm-fleshed men in faded unbleached cottons, some wearing peaked hats of straw.

But he barely saw them. His stomach howled; a dizziness possessed him. The women were enduring their famine better than he, and even Colonel Childress was weathering the terrible hunger better than Skye. But Childress could somehow live on his fat, while Skye grew fainter with each passing hour as the horse and cart clopped slowly into the village.

Taos amazed him. Bursts of green, the leaves of towering cottonwoods, startled the pervasive earthen tones. Water spilled here and there, its sources unknown to him. The town looked somnolent, but when they reached the plaza and were caught in the middle of commerce, he knew that Taos was a lively place. Maybe someone could spare him a crust of bread.

Not only hunger was tormenting him. He was appalled to be wearing the habit of a Franciscan, and didn't want to be taken for one. Even worse was Childress, wearing the holy robes that concealed his vast torso, but also his broad-brimmed planter's hat. This duplicitous dress concealed a pirate and opportunist, who even then was examining assets with a grasping gaze.

They had argued all the way into town. Skye wanted to head straight for the alcalde, or whoever was in authority, and explain their circumstances. Skye hated false pretenses and deception. They would surely be found out soon enough; he couldn't even speak Spanish, and knew nothing of the rites and customs of the Franciscans, and it would go badly for them to be exposed as impostors. But Childress had forcefully argued that the Mexicans were likely to throw them into jail if they told the truth; they never believed a story, even of hardship and loss, and their impulse was to throw irons on anyone arousing their suspicions.

Slowly, the red cart negotiated the narrow alleys leading into the plaza, and then Childress drove around the perimeter of that heart of the city, his huge horse attracting a crowd. The monkey soon added to the mass of people pacing beside the cart, pointing to the skull and crossbones, and shouting questions at Childress, who smiled, lifted his Panama, and proceeded to show off. Victoria and Standing Alone gazed at this lively village from the bed, whispering to each other.

They passed a vendor of some sort of Mexican treats, and that was when Shine abandoned the mane of the Clydesdale and leaped toward the vendor, his heart set on pilferage.

People shouted, and then laughed. The monkey won himself some morsel Skye couldn't identify, covered with a thin dough and contained in husks of corn. Shine returned to his perch on the horse in one bound, and began peeling off the husks and nipping at whatever lay within. Skye envied the little rascal.

"Shine's got a tamale. Here we are, Brother Skye. Food and succor everywhere. Just let Brother Childress collect some food."

Skye nodded sourly. He was too dizzy with hunger to

resist. The women watched from the bed of the red cart, even as strangers gathered around it, pointing to the emblem on the side, and to the giant Clydesdale and the monkey. Shine soon abandoned his perch and was looting everyone in sight of food, springing hither and yon, sometimes even to the vigas, the projecting beams, of the buildings, where he chattered. The people of Taos gladly fed the little fellow, laughing at his thievery.

They certainly were curious about this strange assemblage in a bright red cart, and whispered among themselves. Children studied them shyly, and then giggled at the monkey, who sat masticating his loot and scolding the crowd.

"Ah, amigos, amigas," Childress said, standing in his seat, sweeping that grand hat off his head. "Socorro, por favor. Donativos, help some poor brothers in distress, foster the faith, feed the hungry, share your food with those in holy servitude to God."

No one moved. No one believes him, Skye thought.

But then the monkey began some gymnastic whirls, ending in the theft of a sweet from the vendor, accompanied by shouts and bawling, and suddenly the crowd laughed and dug into their purses for a coin or a bit of grubby paper. Childress passed his hat, which collected not only some coin, but also the corn husk–wrapped things Childress called tamales. The Colonel was not shy about thrusting his Panama toward anyone who looked like he might have a coin, and occasionally a brown hand would snake out and drop something into the hat, whether from charity or because of Shine, who was a born showman, Skye could not know.

"Mil gracias, a thousand thanks for serving God and the brothers and sisters," Childress cried. "You have fed two humble brothers, and their, ah, helpers." He turned to Skye. "The women. What'll I say?"

Skye hadn't any idea.

"Ah, succor for the concubines," Childress roared in English.

Skye, already faint from hunger, suddenly got a lot fainter.

His eye was upon various burly Mexican males standing quietly about who did not seem so amused and whose gazes were not friendly. The law? Store keeps? Politicians? Powerful ranchers? Skye could not know. He was in a foreign nation, broke, hungry, dizzy, and in bizarre company.

But Childress was not idle. Nimbly, he handed a corn-wrapped tamale to the women, and another to Skye, who didn't bother to be polite. He wolfed the food, and found it filling.

"Ah, Brother Skye, a delectable repast, a faith offering from the humble to the exalted brothers of Saint Francis," Childress said. "You see? In Mexico, religion gets you everywhere. Now, brother Skye, make the sign of the cross."

"I will not commit sacrilege," Skye replied. "We're impostors, that's what, not friars."

Childress beamed, faced the cheerful multitude, and made an elaborate sign for all to see.

"There now. I've turned us both into holy men, Skye. Consider me a master of the revels."

Skye's stomach howled for more, but Childress had distributed every scrap of food that had fallen into his hat. There remained in the Panama some sort of specie, both paper and silver, and Skye eyed it eagerly. His scruples had all but vanished in the face of rank desperation, and he even felt a glow of thanksgiving. The pirate and his little simian had put a little food in his belly.

"Where do they hide the slaves?" Victoria whispered. "I don't see none."

Skye didn't either, and wondered whether these smiling people had been maligned by Yanks and Texans with avarice in their craniums. Many of the spectators in that clay plaza looked as though they might be part-Indian, but that was the essence of Mexico, that admixture of bloods. Standing Alone slowly unfolded, slipped off the end of the cart, the thin covering of her dress barely concealing her form, and catching fevered glances from warm-eyed males, and then began quietly walking through this cheerful multitude. Skye knew she was looking. She would never stop looking for the boy and the girl ripped from her so suddenly, long ago.

A frowning rail-thin Anglo man in a black suit approached from the door of a mercantile, and stood staring.

"Who are you? You're no more friars than I'm a Chinaman," he said in English. "If you're trying to pull the wool over the eyes of these people, you're making fools of yourselves. You're already in trouble."

"I am Barnaby Skye, and this is Mr. Childress, a trader," Skye said before Childress could stop him.

"And what brings you here in monks' habits? With two Indian women, the first Clydesdale ever seen here, a monkey, and a red cart?"

"We can discuss that later, in private. With whom do I speak?"

Skye's old English reserve and correctness was asserting itself. Childress glared. It was apparent to everyone watching the exchange that Skye was speaking English to this merchant. Childress's game was up.

The merchant curtly motioned Skye off the cart. Skye slid to earth, feeling the weight of that unfamiliar habit slow him.

"William Larrimer," the man said in a low voice that didn't carry more than a yard. "Merchant here. Now tell me what you're doing, and be fast about it. Your time is running out."

Skye glanced at Childress, who was studiously ignoring all this.

"He's a trader. I'm with the two Indian women. We're looking for the children of one. We think they're here, in trouble."

"What? Say that again? No, don't. Godalmighty. Why are you wearing disguises that any half-baked idiot can see through?"

Skye choked back his temper. "We had trouble with the Jicarillas thirty or forty miles north of here. They left us with nothing but the cart. Naked. Not a stitch of clothing, not a scrap of food, not a riding horse or saddle, not a knife or weapon or a pot. Childress's horse escaped, and that saved our lives. We got the habits in Arroyo Hondo."

"Let me get this straight. Childress is a trader with a monkey, a red cart, and a goddamned Clydesdale and you're along for the ride."

Skye nodded.

The man's skepticism oozed out of his corded face and fired his sapphire eyes. "This doesn't add up. Now I want the truth, Skye, and fast, because if you're not telling it true, you'll endanger every Yank trading here. Childress knows better than to wander in here and trade without a license from Santa Fe. Especially in some damned Franciscan habit. This isn't the United States. What did you say his company is?"

"Childress and McIntyre. They've put up a store north of here, on the Yank side of the Arkansas."

"Where's he from?"

"Galveston Bay, he says."

"A Texan?" Larrimer's face turned hard.

Skye nodded.

"One damned mess," the merchant said. "You're trouble and you'll be lucky to walk away."

twenty-two

Skye watched an odd-looking priest start across the plaza with a lumbering gait.

"You're too late," Larrimer said. "That's the Calf."

"The what?"

"Padre Martinez. His head, see it? They call him the Calf. He hates Yanks."

"I'm not a Yank."

"Lot of good that'll do you. I shouldn't even be seen with you."

"Mr. Larrimer, we're destitute and we need help. Anything you can do—"

"What you've done, Skye, if that's your name, is start trouble for every citizen of the United States living here."

Colonel Childress, who had been bantering with the people of Taos, paused as he watched the ponderous progress of the priest, who parted the frightened peons as if he were Moses.

"Why does he worry you?" Skye asked Larrimer.

"He's more powerful than the alcalde, and an alcalde is not just a mayor; he's police chief and judge, too. The Calf's agitating to put all us heathen out of the territory, or march us off to the City of Mexico. The Calf's a law unto himself. Not even the governor rules this priest."

The Calf was indeed a strange-looking priest, his huge walleyed head perched heavily on a stocky frame covered with a dusty black cassock.

At last the priest stopped before them, as the crowd fell back. He peered at each man from bright and penetrating brown eyes, then the cart, monkey, and Indian women, and finally at Larrimer.

"Que pasa?" he asked Larrimer.

But Childress replied in a burst of Spanish that Skye couldn't follow. The fat privateer gesticulated grandly, foam at the lips, pointed at his empty cart and the two women, at himself, and at Skye.

"What's he saying?" Skye whispered.

"That you're a pair of Franciscans from St. Louis that got robbed by the Jicarillas."

Skye barely contained his rage. This was worse trouble because it was a lie, and preposterous.

The Calf peered, skeptically, as if nearsighted, wetting his lips and pondering. He turned to Larrimer, and said something.

"I'm translating. Who are you; what are you doing here?"

Skye was damned if he would lie. "I'm a man without a country, Barnaby Skye, and I'm helping this grieving Cheyenne woman find her son and daughter. We think they were brought here by the Utes. We came to obtain their liberty."

"Are you a friar?" Larrimer translated.

"No, I am in the fur trade, working for Bent, St. Vrain. We were left without clothing, or a weapon or a pot thirty miles north by marauding Jicarillas. A merciful woman in Arroyo Hondo lent us these garments, fed us, and sent us on our way. She took us to the church there, put these habits over our nakedness, and urged us to leave swiftly."

"A likely story. Where are you from?" Larrimer translated.

"London."

"Where's the fat one from?"

"He says Galveston Bay."

"Tejas! Who owns that monkey?"

Skye gestured toward Childress.

"What is his name? The Texas one. What is he doing here?"

"Jean Lafitte Childress. He started with a wagon of trading goods. We lost them all to the Apaches, and our horses except for this. We came with him, with our own horses and gear."

The Calf stared at the Clydesdale. "The great horse looks like the Calf," he said, and Larrimer translated. "Why are these symbols of piracy and death painted on the side of this cart?"

Skye shook his head. There were facets of Childress that were beyond fathoming.

"He wants to know who she is," Larrimer said, pointing at Victoria.

"She is my Crow wife, Victoria."

The Calf laughed heartily. "Concubina," he said.

Skye didn't need the translation. "Wife," he said, heat building in him.

The Calf chuckled nastily, and spoke again.

"You will be of great interest to the authorities," Larrimer translated. "One says he's a monk from St. Louis. The other says he's a man from London looking for Cheyenne children. Monks with two sluts, a bloodred wagon, and a monkey." He beckoned. Skye thought the priest's finger was an inch in diameter.

"Do we have to go with him?"

"Skye, if you don't, you're likely to get yourself killed. See that?"

Standing on the periphery of this crowd stood three young men bearing lances. Skye thought all of Taos had collected there, twenty deep. These were no longer warm and friendly faces.

"What's going to happen to us?"

"I don't second-guess Mexican officials. But the last few illegal traders or . . . filibusters, is that it, Skye? . . . got sent off to Mexico City in chains, and the few that survived the long walk in irons are still there and won't be leaving there. Not unless they leave feet first."

All this Colonel Childress absorbed angrily, glaring at Skye as if his truth-telling were a criminal act in its own right. Skye didn't care. Childress's lies had gotten them into this.

Skye saw that they had little choice. He nodded to Larrimer. Did he see some pity in the man's corded face? Then the huge, ominous crowd began to seethe along, carrying Skye, Childress, Victoria, and Standing Alone with it. Shine leaped up to Childress's thick shoulder, and even he looked subdued and afraid. Someone was leading away the Clydesdale and the wagon, and Skye doubted he would ever see the rig again.

Skye glanced at Standing Alone, who bore all this with her innate dignity, enduring the stares, keeping her thoughts private. Victoria, always the observant one, was studying the clothing and weapons of these people, looking at faces one by one, as she was harried along with the throng. Where were they going? Did this earthen village have a jail?

They were escorted across the dusty plaza and through an alley to a massive building with walls as blank as the future, and there pushed through the thick doors and into the sharp coolness within. Skye had no inkling of the purpose of this structure; only that it contained chairs of rawhide, benches, and a beehive fireplace in a corner. The sole window could swiftly be shuttered; the heavy slab-wood door could be barred. As a jail it would do just fine. The women in their thin shifts would soon be chilled in such a place.

This was some private residence. The massive door creaked shut behind them, and Skye felt the claustrophobia he had experienced deep in the bowels of men-o'-war. The room wasn't large. Skye headed for the high window, and could see one of the men with a lance standing beside it.

"Skye, why didn't you keep your trap shut?" Childress asked. "I could've talked my way out of it."

"Lied your way out of it," Skye retorted.

The monkey abandoned the Colonel's shoulders and explored the room with swift bounds, hunting food but settling at last in the patch of sun on the sill of the high window.

"Skye, get this straight. I'm a privateer. I will do what I will do."

There was no sense arguing with the man. Skye turned his back on him and looked to see how Victoria and Standing Alone were faring. The Cheyenne woman had settled into a chair.

"Victoria, tell her we came here without the permission of the governor—the chief. I'll get her out some way, but I don't know when or how."

Childress started laughing. "That's what they all think before they walk the plank."

Skye boiled. He started toward that fat pirate, but the door opened again, shooting bright sunlight into the room and half blinding him. Shine started chittering.

This time a hawkish black-bearded man appeared and surveyed them all with imperious eyes. Four soldiers backed him, this time armed with broadswords.

"I am prefect, Juan Andres Archuleta. I make a, a . . . disposition of your case," he said. "I speak little English."

"We're hungry," Skye said.

"That is of no consequence. We are much entertained by your party, but we have learned many lessons from our past."

He nodded, and two of the guards caught the women by the arm and escorted them out. The last view Skye got of Victoria, she was being dragged into the sunlight but she was looking back to him, and her eyes told him of love, and desperation and determination. Standing Alone didn't require dragging. She walked willingly, but paused at the bright door frame, looked back at Skye with sorrow. Then they were gone.

"We'll deal with your concubines separately."

"My wife is not a concubine!" Skye snapped.

"She is what I choose to call her, a puta."

Skye lurched at him, only to be constrained by Childress, who clamped an arm over him. The grip was hard. Bright steel blades gleamed just ahead of him.

"Very gallant, Americano."

"I'm not an American. And that was my wife."

"Si, si, you have say that. You're a man without a nation, and therefore, all the easier for us to deal with." He turned to Childress. "A Tejano rebel. A privateer. Maybe a spy. Maybe doing some little task for el Presidente Lamar."

"I'm an ordinary privateer, señor, at the service of whoever has the biggest purse. And when no one has a purse, I engage in my own violations of the laws of the sea."

Archuleta contemplated that. "Ah! I am glad to have your . . . confesión before witnesses, and that of your friend Skye," he said. "That is all I need."

twenty-three

Standing Alone found herself in a chill adobe room along with Victoria Skye. A guard with a lance and lust had taken them to this place east of the plaza.

Through a small window she could see the dark mountains, the fierce blue of the sky, and the buildings of the village. Outside was freedom, a place to walk unimpeded across sunny fields. Never had she been without her freedom. This place called Mexico had a strange way of welcoming people, putting them in earthen boxes.

She had come a great distance. She had long since ceased to grieve her boy and girl, who were like the dead now, phantoms, fading spirits in her mind. This quest had become something else, and she didn't know exactly what. If her children still lived—and she sensed that one of them did—she would find them and give them as a gift to the People, who needed understanding of where their flesh and blood were taken, and how they were used, for the loss of a child was a loss to the whole People.

This was new to the Cheyenne, this slavery, this using of children. Somehow she knew, and it was spirit-knowledge, that if she brought her children, or surviving child, back to the People, then the Cheyenne would triumph over the Ute thieves, and over these strange Mexicans who lived inside buildings of mud.

She knew, too, that if she could find and free her son, Grasshopper, he would become a great leader of the Cheyenne, a tower of strength for his people. She burned to free him, not just for herself and her clan, but for the People themselves. He would take a new name and leave the boy's name behind. Out of his captivity and suffering would come a man of such strength and spirit and holiness that his blessings would last for generations.

All this she had been given in four visions and dreams; all this she kept to herself, locking it in her bosom until the time might come to reveal it. This was her secret as well as her passion, and she would willingly die to fulfill the things she had seen in her dreams.

For years she had sat quietly at the gate of Bent's Fort, listening to Americans and Mexicans. It was the Mexicans she studied the most because they might reveal the whereabouts of her children. Gradually, during those four years, she learned to fathom the words spoken by these people though she never uttered a single one. But there were many words still unknown to her. They had called her a concubina, which she had never heard, but she knew what a puta was, and because they said that of her she despised them right down to the marrow of her bones.

At least she despised the men. The old woman who had succored them and given her the shift she now wore she did not despise. She knew how thin was the loose-woven cloth, how revealing it was in sunlight, the shadows of her body always visible, and she had not missed the stares that pierced right through that thin shroud to her bosom and belly.

The Mexican women wore several layers and thus armored themselves from the stares of men. But she and Victoria had only the thinnest cover of this loose fabric they called linen. For this had the holy man, the Calf, stared at them both and the look in his eyes was unmistakable.

They were prisoners for the moment, but she did not intend to remain one. Neither did Victoria. They were not sheep to be herded by shepherds. They were women of the People, not Mexican women, and women of the People knew the arts of war. Victoria Skye was merely an Absaroka dog, and without the powers any Cheyenne woman possessed, but it didn't matter. They would help each other. She had not come this far, looking for her children, to surrender.

She peered about her: this was a small storeroom. In the dim brown light she saw coarse sacks of beans, some dried red fruits strung on a cord and hanging. A closed door stained the color of the sky led to some other part of the building.

Then that door opened, and a voluptuous full-breasted Mexican woman appeared, looked them over, smiled, and closed the door again. This woman looked to be not more than twenty winters.

"We could go out that door," Victoria said in the polyglot tongue they had evolved, half signs, half words.

Standing Alone shook her head. She had learned patience.

"Let's eat," Victoria said. There was food if only they could prepare it. "I will even eat what these people eat."

They converged on the sacks and earthen jugs looking for something to wolf down. But they found nothing like that. Grains in great crocks, oils in jars, beans in sacks. The thought of food made her salivate, and then ache for something, anything to assuage her hunger.

But she was a woman of the People and sternly contained herself. Her captors would not know of her desperation. She drew herself proudly, and stood still, while Victoria hunted relentlessly for anything she could eat, poking a hard bean into her mouth and trying, without luck, to masticate it.

"I will find a way to take some of this to Skye," Victoria said, hunting for a cloth or a sack or a pouch she might conceal on her person. "I will help my man."

Standing Alone was not sure Victoria would ever see her

man again. But they both hunted, and finally settled on tearing a piece of burlap out of a sack, using their teeth for the want of a knife. They realized that every scoop and ladle had been removed; there was no iron to turn into a weapon.

That's when the door of the storeroom swung open on its leather hinges, creaking noisily. The walleyed holy man, Father Martinez, peered into the gloom, and motioned them out into a kitchen room with a beehive fireplace, tables, and benches to sit upon. The pretty young woman hovered behind him. The scent of meat stewing in a pot hung over the fire dizzied Standing Alone.

"Come, come," he said in Spanish, motioning them out of the cramped dark storage room. "Do you understand my tongue?"

Standing Alone did not acknowledge that she understood him perfectly well. He stared a moment, his gaze roving over her.

"The sluts don't understand," he said to his young companion. "Very well, Juanita, I'll show them things more ancient than words."

The young woman laughed, baring an even row of white teeth that contrasted to her lush brown lips. Standing Alone looked closely at this woman and thought she might be pregnant. Was this holy man the sire? She had heard that the priests of these people never embraced a woman, but here was this young one living so familiarly with him.

"I will see what they understand," he said, surveying them with some amusement.

What a strange man he was, with his huge head shaped by its bones into the face of a calf, with malice in his eyes and a certain slyness visible because he did not guard his spirit.

He turned to his captives.

"Is it that you speak Spanish?" he asked.

Standing Alone wondered whether to respond. Maybe it was best not to admit to it. But maybe it was better to find out what was in store. She nodded, slowly.

"Ah! It is good, bien. You have been the sluts of these Texas spies I caught, and that is a grave offense, and worthy of death. But I will spare you. A good, obedient savage, willing to work and sew and cook, willing to hoe the fields, weed, harvest, do whatever is required, can redeem her life."

Standing Alone nodded. Soon she would translate for Victoria, but not yet.

"Ah, I see you understand. Now, first, to prepare you for your new life, I will baptize you, for this is required of all who live in Mexico. This will seal you in your new faith, and you will become Christians and your souls will be saved."

Saved from what? She would find out. And she would find out what this baptism meant, too.

She nodded, and searched her mind for the words she needed to ask a question. "What of the hombres?" she asked, not able to summon more words.

The priest laughed. "The men? They will be taken to Santa Fe to plead before our governor. He will decide whether to execute them or send them to the City of Mexico to be tried."

"Why?" she asked.

"Don't trouble your head about it. They are gone. You will never see them again."

He reached for a small bowl, which had the emblem of a cross upon it.

"Ah, what is your name, woman?"

"Call me what you will."

"And her name?"

"That is for her to say."

"No, it is for me to say, for the name your people gave you is gone, and you will receive a new one from the church and the civilized world, so that you can partake of the gifts of God. You will be Maria, and she will be Juana. It is so, yes?"

She fumbled for words. "So it is you name us."

Victoria asked what was being said. Swiftly, with the fingers and hands, and with their patois, she explained.

"Sonofabitch," Victoria said.

Standing Alone wished she might know what that meant. The Crow woman said it all the time. It was some holy invocation of the speakers of English.

The priest, meanwhile, lifted a lid from the vessel in his hands, and summoned them to him. He gestured that they should kneel before him. Standing Alone and Victoria both understood, and both refused.

"You must bow before God," said the Calf.

Standing Alone stared.

The priest pushed her downward, but she refused to kneel.

"It will go hard for you, then, concubina," he said, and she registered the word she did not understand.

The priest's woman watched, her gaze somber for a change.

Then this padre, Martinez, she remembered, decided it didn't matter: he dipped his fingers into that water and pressed his moist fingers upon her head, firmly, until she felt wetness. "I baptize you in the name of the Father, the Son, and the Holy Ghost," he said in his tongue.

He performed the same rite upon Victoria.

"Now you will know what sin is," he said.

Standing Alone did not feel any different, but wondered whether she was cursed or blessed.

twenty-four

Skye's fury exceeded even his hunger. He paced his adobe prison, brimming with bitterness. There were guards outside, each armed with a lance and two with swords. They would be taking him somewhere, probably Santa Fe, for some purpose. Maybe it wouldn't end there: he had heard talk of being taken to the City of Mexico, there to rot in some dank prison.

He glared at Childress, who sat quietly. Skye wished he had never met the man. He should have seen through the fat trader, if that is what he was, instead of making common cause with him. Childress had not hesitated to lie to the Mexicans and that got them into grave trouble.

It would have been hard enough to win a sympathetic ear just telling the truth; but Childress had attempted to fob the pair of them off as monks, which had won him a horselaugh and a spell in prison, if not something much worse.

Skye rued the day he had stumbled upon the man and his phony trading company and his bloodred cart and draft horse and monkey, all guaranteed to call attention to the man. And if that weren't enough, Childress had painted piratical emblems on his cart and boasted of his years as a privateer. Any sensible man would have kept silent about his nefarious life.

He slowed his pacing and paused before the Texan, who was still bulging out of his monk's habit.

"Get one thing straight, Childress. We're through. If we get out of here, we're going our separate ways. You understand?"

"I do, but I don't suppose Shine does."

"And that goes double for the monkey."

"Skye, we work well together."

"No man who lies to anyone works well with me."

"I salute a man of honor," Childress said. "I myself impose no constraints on my conduct. I do what's necessary."

"And get us into trouble," Skye snapped.

"Yes, a pity, isn't it? Here you are, stuck with Jean Lafitte Childress, born without a scruple. I've sent innocents off a plank into the briny sea, robbed merchant ships, pillaged coastal towns, beheaded assorted women and children . . ."

Skye didn't know what to make of the imbecile. He only knew that if and when he got free, he would go in the opposite direction of wherever Childress and his damned monkey, if he still had his monkey, were heading.

If he hadn't hooked up with the flamboyant fool he and Standing Alone and Victoria would have arrived in Taos without disturbing anyone and would have been perfectly free to make inquiries about the children. They probably would have had their horses and packs, too. That cart had attracted the attention of the Jicarillas, and that was the beginning of their downfall.

Skye paced, the only defense he had against the howling of his empty stomach. It had been the better part of two days since he had eaten. Childress didn't seem to mind; he dined on his own fat. But Skye knew if he didn't get fed soon, he would take on those guards if he had to and head for the plaza and the markets he saw there. He would eat.

The door creaked open, and this time a sturdy raven-haired man with vast mustachios entered, flanked by guards.

The man surveyed his prisoners, obviously enjoying himself.

"Juan Andres Archuleta, prefect of the northern province," he said.

So he spoke a little English.

"I'm hungry. Haven't eaten."

Archuleta turned to Skye, studying him blandly, and then smiled. "Monks are succored on spiritual food," he said. "You eat the Bread of Life."

Skye forced himself not to do what he was about to do, which was to land on the man and throttle him.

"I am not a monk. And I haven't eaten today and most of yesterday."

"A pity." Archuleta looked the prisoners over, and yawned. "You will proceed at dawn toward Santa Fe. It is a matter for our gobernador, Armijo. Si, he will settle your fate. He enjoys such proceedings. He's very fond of foreigners. If he finds you guilty, he will give you a quick and merciful death against the wall."

"What are we charged with?"

Archuleta shrugged. "Just now, nothing, Brother Skye. There is nothing against you. But there is much testimony, which I have written down and will send along to Santa Fe."

"I am not a monk."

"So you keep saying. A pity, for if you were, I might set you free. Your *boca grande* puts you farther and farther into the trouble, no?"

"I am here with my wife and our friend, a Cheyenne woman, to find her children."

Archuleta yawned. "Si, si, a pity, Reverend Brother Skye. How cold is the rule of justice, and how it crushes the unfortunate. But your sweet piety, it will you see you through, a martyr of the Holy Faith. Maybe they will canonize you someday, and make you a saint."

"Where is my wife?" he said.

"Your wife? You are married, Brother?"

"Where is she? And our friend?"

"You'll be pleased to know she is with our padre, Martinez, si?"

"And what is she doing there?"

Archuleta smiled softly. "Ah! I am told she has received the baptism. Soon she will be a daughter of the faith."

Baptism? Victoria? She who lived within the soul of her people?

"You imprison not only bodies, but souls, señor," he said. "You capture souls for Christ at the point of a lance. Do you think the Lord would approve?"

Archuleta smiled, obviously amused at the thought. "We leave at dawn," he said.

With that, he withdrew. The door creaked shut. Skye heard the thud of a bar locking it. He knew he would spend the hungriest night of his life unless succor arrived. At least there was an olla of water available to the prisoners.

He drank of the cup, bitterly.

He did not sleep that night. There was no bed, but that was not what caught him in fits of wakefulness. Neither was it his hunger, which bit cruelly at him. It was an ancient anguish. Other mortals now controlled his destiny by force of arms; the food and water and clothing he needed depended not on his efforts, but on their whim.

He felt at one with all the world's most helpless people, those whose fate, whose tomorrows were unknown to them. He felt at one with those Indian children, abducted years earlier, whose fate was not their own; deprived of hope, of caring, of love, of comfort, but simply bodies to be used by masters and then discarded.

On the floor in the far corner, Childress lay curled up on his side, apparently asleep, and far less concerned by this twist of the noose of life than Skye was. Skye stared, knowing he had learned a lesson: never again would he willingly ally himself with anyone he didn't trust.

He would never trust anyone who deliberately called attention to himself with bizarre stories, or conduct. He would never trust anyone with a loose mouth and a lack of ordinary honesty. For the rest of his days, if he escaped this hell, he would let caution govern him.

He didn't know where the monkey was; it could easily leap to the high window and out. Skye amended his views: never trust a man with a monkey. He peered around in the gloom, trying to see the little simian by whatever light was given him by the stars, but he saw nothing. Maybe the guard had run his lance through the little monster, a prospect that did not displease Skye. A chill settled upon the already cold room, but Skye had little to cover himself, so he pressed his body into another corner and waited for dawn.

The stars sailed through their orbits, and Skye sat rigidly, his heart with Victoria, his mind unsettled. And then he heard a scrambling up on the sill above, and felt the faint rush of movement. The monkey had returned to the master. It sprang over to Childress, who muttered something, and then back to Skye, and chittered softly. There in his hands was some object, but Skye could not make it out at first. Then his nostrils did, and he felt himself holding a chunk of bread. Half a loaf of bread.

He felt its springy hardness in his hands, and smelled the yeasty aroma. He sighed, grateful for this mercy, but ashamed of his harsh thoughts. Only minutes earlier he was entertaining the hope that a lancer had run the monkey through. It was another lesson, he thought, bitterly.

He tried to pet Shine, but the monkey seemed a blur of motion, and Skye saw the shadow up on the sill once again.

"Well, thanks anyway," he muttered.

"You can have mine," Childress said.

Skye refused to reply, even if the offer was kind.

He ate slowly, savoring the moist and textured bread, the humblest but greatest of blessings. He could have eaten two loaves, but this would do. A spider monkey with an uncanny way of being helpful had rescued him, at least for the moment.

A few merchant seamen had monkeys, kept as mementos of some tropical port. Some merchant ships had monkeys aboard, mostly for amusement. But they were the rarest of domestic animals and served no useful purpose. He wondered where Childress had found this one, and how Childress had trained him to be so useful.

Skye settled himself against a cold wall, and tried to think: How would he escape both the Mexicans, and the flamboyant Childress, alleged privateer and trader, and rescue the women?

But no answer came to him.

twenty-five

The prefect, Archuleta, entered, flanked by two soldiers. Jean Lafitte Childress eyed them from the floor, where he had curled in his monk's habit, staving off the sharp chill. Skye sat against an earthen wall watching, his gaze sharp in the soft dawn light. The monkey leaped for the high window and sat there studying the intruders.

The prefect pointed at Childress, and then beckoned him.

Slowly, his bones aching from cold, Childress stood and walked through the door, followed by the soldiers and the man who would decide his fate.

"Buenos dias, amigos," Childress said expansively. "I respect your persons, but your hospitality leaves something to be desired."

They marched him into the plaza, hushed now as the villagers of Taos slumbered into the dawn. The sweet smoke of piñon pine drifted from chimneys. Where were they taking him?

They left the plaza, turned up an alley, scattered two cats, and the prefect opened a door of a substantial building. Childress could see that its interior was better furnished than most in this rude town; massive mission-style chairs and a settee filled a room. A small fire wavered in a beehive fireplace.

The prefect waved Childress to a chair. "Sit yourself," he said in Spanish.

A hefty woman with her hair in a tight black bun immediately brought a steaming cup of coffee.

"Ah! Nurture for the body! Perhaps I will soon enjoy the famous hospitality of the Mexicans," he said, hopefully.

But the prefect said nothing, drew up a straight-backed dining chair directly opposite Childress, and sat in it.

"Who are you?" he asked abruptly.

"You have my name, sir."

"What are you doing here?"

"I am engaged in the pursuit of empire, Sah."

"What the Americanos call a filibuster?"

Childress stared, scornfully. "They lack imagination. My purpose is much more noble, Señor Archuleta. I am going to sever the northern reaches of Mexico from the mother country and found my own nation, the Republic of Childress."

Archuleta smiled slightly. "Yesterday you were a monk. The day before, you were a trader operating as Childress and McIntyre. The day before that, so to speak, you were a Texas privateer preying on Mejico!"

"I am all that and more, Sah."

"Now let me see, señor. A monk in a Franciscan habit with a monkey, a red cart, a draft horse, and the ensigns of piracy on the side of your cart. Two beautiful savages accompanied you, indecently attired. You entertained us with a fine story: the Apaches took everything, except of course your horse and cart and harness. So you drove to Arroyo Hondo stark naked, baking in the sun, where you wished to be succored. And an elderly woman came to your assistance, si?"

"Ah, señor, it is all true, as true as the gospel."

Archuleta laughed softly. "Tejas, you are from Tejas," he said.

"Indeed, sir, sired in the bosom of piracy, Galveston, the

home of the most black-hearted of all mariners."

"And what are you going to do next?"

The question surprised Childress. "Why, Sah, outfit my-self on credit, recruit an army of peons and mestizos and indios to overthrow Mexico, and establish my capital up on the Rio Arkansas."

Archuleta smiled. "A noble enterprise, señor. A large task for a man of great girth. What else have you done?"

"Sah, I have sent Mexican women and children off the plank and into the sea; I have plundered Mexican galleons and barques. I have run the Jolly Roger up my masts and flown it from the pinnacle. I have financed wars and excur-sions against Mexico, widowed Mexican women, orphaned children, stolen casks of gold doubloons, driven men mad, schemed against Santa Anna . . ."

Archuleta yawned. "The missioner up at Arroyo Hondo wants his cassocks back. I've gone to great expense, from the public purse, to put raiment on you. I shall have to levy a tax to pay for all the cloth. I regret that it's rather like a tent; at least it covers your vast white belly. There. Shirt, pantalones, sandals, and you already have a Panama."

He gestured toward some clothing hanging on a peg.

"I will shed this disguise, Sah, and encase myself in your rags. They look to be utterly beneath my standards. Clothing makes the man. You have dressed an emperor like a peon."

Archuleta lifted a blue-veined hand. "Not yet. Not until you tell me about Skye, if that is his name. Everything. Leave out nothing. Your life depends on it."

"Skye? Why, amigo, there's the meat you want. I never beheld the man until a few weeks ago, when he rode in with his concubines. I questioned him closely, of course. Amigo, I can tell you, in all privacy, that he is a Protestant revolution-ary, intending to overthrow all that is sacred in Mexico and turn it over to Puritans."

"Ah! It is so?"

"He is such Calvinist that he does not touch his savage

women; they are servants, there to comfort him only, and help him in his designs to transform Mexico."

"Why should I believe this, señor?"

"Have you seen him laugh?"

Archuleta nodded. "He is a serious man."

"Beware Skye. He confessed things to me, as we came along the trail. He is a burning man. He is a man brimming with wild ideas. He is a man to ignite gunpowder. He is a man to hand out pamphlets, recruit armies, sow discontent. Sah, beware the smoldering revolutionary, who outwardly seems calm, but inwardly is a raving wolf."

Archuleta nodded. "A likely story. Why should I believe you, when everything you have told me is absurd?"

"Ask him. He never lies, which is most unfortunate. He could go far if he knew how to invent."

"I have. He says he is looking for the children of one of his savage women. That is his story. How do you make that to be a crime against Mejico?"

"Ah! Wake up, amigo. He will enter each estancia, each hacienda, looking for the children, or so he says. And he will be actually collecting information: how many hombres, how well is the place fortified? Dios! His story is perfect for his purposes. . . . Ah, what are you going to do with him?"

Archuleta exhaled slowly. "Send him away."

"And his women?"

Archuleta smiled. "They have already been taken care of."

"How?"

"Labor is scarce; they will be valuable."

"They are slaves, then?"

"No, we have no slaves in Mejico. They will be taught the faith, and employed in the province."

"By whom?"

"Padre Martinez is looking into it. Perhaps he will keep one, give one to his brothers."

"Will they be free to return to their people?"

"*Basta*. Put on those clothes. Leave the habit. I will return it to the church, as a favor."

Archuleta slipped outside, and Childress found himself alone. He cast his glance about, looking for useful items such as a knife or spoon or bit of food or flint and steel, but he found little of immediate value in the room.

He lifted the heavy brown robe over his head, and sorted out the clothing left for him: a pair of cotton drawers, a great shirt of unbleached muslin, and some baggy pantalones of heavy material that he thought might be duckcloth or canvas.

There were two pairs of leather sandals, large and smaller. The large ones were too large, but were the only choice. He settled his Panama on his majestic locks, and looked once again rather like himself.

When at last Archuleta reappeared, he motioned Childress out the door and into the sunny alley. And there was his shining red cart, hitched to the Clydesdale, and Shine perched upon the Clydesdale's back, licking his fingers.

"You are free. I have no reason to hold you, señor."

"But I have given you a dozen."

"Indeed. They were entertaining."

"How shall I make my way? I haven't a peso."

"You have a monkey."

"Ah, yes, Shine. But he is a thief. You would set a thief loose among your people?"

"It is an entertainment, señor. They give him whatever he wants. And so you will fill your belly."

"This is disappointing. I thought I would at least have the honor of facing the firing squad before the wall. Mexico has shed the blood of thousands, si?"

"I cannot give you that great honor, Señor Childress, even if you should find it fitting and glorious."

"And what of Skye?"

Archuleta shook his head. "Do not pity him, señor."

"Ah, the wall, then?"

"He will have a chance to confess, first. But that is a trifle. Maybe I will send him down to Santa Fe, so that his fate will be well known and a lesson to the army of Tejas."

"Ah! Most fitting, señor. He has no country and is alone."

Archuleta smiled.

twenty-six

The helplessness that engulfed Skye that morning was familiar. He had spent a large part of his life unable to shape his own destiny or choose his fate or seek his own happiness. He spent a bad night, famished, his only sustenance the bread he had miraculously received, his body aching from being propped against an earthen wall through the endless dark, and his senses offended by the foul odor rising from a pit in a corner where many before him had relieved themselves.

But there was a certain solace in familiarity. Through all the terrible years as a slave boy on a frigate, he had waited for his chance and eventually fashioned it at Fort Vancouver. The odds here were even worse. He possessed nothing, not even the monk's cowl that clothed his body. His feet were naked in a land of cactus. He didn't know the tongue, had no weapons, could not even ask directions. He could not explain himself, seek help, seek comfort, seek to free Victoria and Standing Alone. And yet he would watch and wait and look for his opportunity. Someone, somewhere, would help him. These were a cheerful and generous people; someone would help.

When Childress returned, accompanied by the prefect, Archuleta, and two soldiers, the Texan had startling news: the Galveston privateer was being freed.

"They're letting me go, soon as I translate for them."

"You free? No charges?"

"Free as a lark, and they're giving me my horse and rig, too."

"And me?"

"Sorry, Skye."

Skye stared first at Archuleta, and then at Childress, waiting for reasons. Why not himself? What had he done?

Archuleta began whispering in sibilant Spanish, and Childress translated.

"You're a Texas spy, he says, and they're keeping you, sending you down to Santa Fe. Your fate will be decided by the governor, Armijo."

"Fate?"

"They shot a couple of Texans poking around there, collecting information for Lamar, pretending to be traders. There's a Texas army crawling west, Skye. Over three hundred armed men, determined to expand Texas at least to the Rio Grande, if not more. Naturally, the Mexicans are a little jumpy."

Skye absorbed that bleakly. "Why are you free?"

Childress didn't reply, shrugged, smiled blandly. Archuleta started in again, this time in harsh tones.

"He says you're spying for Texas, and he has a witness to prove it, and if you confess it might go easier for you. You know the fate of spies in time of war."

"Witness?"

"Archuleta says he wants the entire story; what Lamar is paying you, what your purposes are, who you report to, how many Texans are coming, where they will come, who leads them, how they are equipped, and how long you have been snooping in Mexico."

Skye stared warily at Childress, suspicion mounting up like lava in a volcano.

"He says you are a self-confessed man without a country, so there is no help for you, no international rules to observe.

You are alone. You do not claim Texas. You do not claim the United States. So you are without hope. You will be entitled to a priest before the end. But if you talk, and give them intelligence, you might be kept alive . . . They are not opposed to mercy, for the truly repentant."

"Mercy?"

"A quick death rather than a slow one; firing squad rather than noose."

Skye stared at Childress, suddenly knowing where Archuleta got all this. The fat man had betrayed him to save his own miserable hide. There was no sense in talking further; not one word, that could be twisted or ignored. He doubted that one word he might say would be accurately conveyed to the prefect.

Archuleta continued to cajole him: talk, and there would be a good meal, beans and some brandy. Talk and he would have sandals, and see some daylight.

But Skye had nothing to say. He would not lie, would not invent stories, would not alter the story he had already given Archuleta and Father Martinez. Archuleta badgered him, but Skye's mouth was sealed. He stared at Childress, the fat man who had called himself a friend, who was now dressed in pantalones and a shirt and sandals, and whose Panama covered his head. The fat man who had betrayed him for a few rags and some food and a chance to save his hide.

Eventually, Childress stopped translating altogether. Skye's silence rebuffed them. Archuleta shrugged, glared at Skye, and herded Childress out the door. Skye was suddenly alone, never so alone, and suddenly without much hope. He raised himself on his toes and could just see out the high window to the enameled red cart, hitched to the Clydesdale, awaiting the Judas from Galveston Bay.

Archuleta and Childress shook hands; the prefect bowed slightly. Skye's erstwhile partner clambered up and drove away in the bright sun, beneath the bold blue of the heavens, heading for the plaza. The monkey would no doubt feed him there, entertaining the Taos people, stealing whatever Childress needed to keep body and soul together.

Skye exhaled slowly, feeling that foreboding and sinister knowledge that his life was swiftly draining away. He had felt it before, this special loneliness. But this time he was not alone; he had Victoria to think of, and Standing Alone.

He had no idea what had happened to his women, but he knew they were not free, that they had been forcibly baptized into a faith they didn't understand, and that the padre, Martinez, had commandeered them. He hoped desperately that they might be free; that Victoria would somehow learn of his whereabouts, slip along this narrow alley, letting him know she was there and seeking means to free him. But the alley was silent.

He had to do something. He might not be able to save himself, but perhaps he could save her. Did they want information about Texas? He had none, but maybe he could conjure up some, if it would save his beloved woman and their Cheyenne friend. The thought stabbed him; he never lied. He had always been a man of honor, whose word was true. But now he was tempted. If the prefect would free those two and start them back to Bent's Fort, he could conjure up whole armies of Texans, enough Texans to satisfy every civil and military officer of the Republic of Mexico. And die for it.

But he loathed that very idea. He would sacrifice himself to save her; that was the nature of love. There had to be a way. Yet he could think of none. He scarcely even knew how to begin. There was no option except to wait, look for chances, and strike hard and fast if he could.

He cased the plain room, which made do for a jail, with its high windows with iron bars planted in them. Given time, he could escape, even if he had to claw apart the adobe with his fingernails. There was nothing. An empty box. A bench of clay to sit or lie upon. An earthen olla and earthen cup. He could crack that over the head of a soldier, maybe.

They still had not fed him.

A while later the door creaked open again, and this time the merchant, Larrimer, entered, with the prefect and two soldiers. One soldier brought a bowl of stew to Skye, who wolfed it down. It was not enough.

"Mr. Skye, there are rules to this engagement," Larrimer said. "Any question you ask, I must translate exactly and wait until Señor Archuleta decides whether I should answer."

Skye nodded. Larrimer looked worried.

"I myself am suspect, Mr. Skye. Every foreigner is, especially those who speak English."

Skye nodded. "Why am I held?"

Larrimer translated and Archuleta answered: "You are a spy for Texas."

"Who says?"

"Childress the trader has told everything."

"Childress! Is that how he freed himself?"

"Archuleta believes the information given him is accurate."

"It's a pack of lies!"

"Careful, Mr. Skye."

"Where is my wife?"

"You have no wife."

"Where?"

"She is under the loving care of Padre Martinez. And the other squaw."

"Is she a prisoner?"

"She is being succored, so that she might become a woman of the faith."

"What will come of me?"

This time, Archuleta spoke at length, while Larrimer nodded.

"The prefect says that soon you will be paraded naked three times around the plaza, so all who see you can revile you and spit upon you, who invade our homeland. Then you will be put in chains, and will walk with a squad of soldiers to Santa Fe, where you will be subject to a trial. Governor

Armijo has taken to holding trials for Texans and provocateurs just like General Santa Anna's trials. You will reach into
an earthen jar where there are many beans, half white and
half black. If you draw out a black bean, you, ah, stand at the
wall while the snare drums rattle. If you draw a white bean,
your life is spared, but not your liberty. You will be in Mexico
all the rest of your days."

Skye sagged into the wall.

The prefect had one further instruction.

"You will please to pull off that habit of the Franciscan,
which so fraudulently covers you."

Skye could not bring himself to do it, or to face what was
to come, so he stared.

But the sharp scrape of a sword pulled from its scabbard
changed his mind, and moments later he stood naked.

twenty-seven

His camouflage had never failed him. The world saw a giant gaudy grandee telling impossible stories, calling attention to himself in every possible way, and dismissed him as a man demented.

And so it was this time: he had spun stories, each more improbable than the one before, some of them even true, and he and his monkey and bloodred cart had caught the eye of everyone, and soon these people had taken the measure of him and dismissed him, just as he intended.

The man called Childress settled in the sunny plaza, and soon enough a crowd collected around him to watch Shine, who was even then swinging from the vigas, dropping to the clay, pilfering everything in sight, much to the delight of grinning children and smiling adults and nervous mothers. Shine was an accomplished thief and considered theft to be his mission in life.

He sprang toward the cart of a tamale vendor, scooped up two of the corn-husked meals, and retreated to a rooftop, where he chittered happily. The vendor pretended to be vexed, but was laughing at all this. Shine pitched one tamale to Childress, who discreetly hid it in his wagon. In time that heap would grow and include whatever the little monkey could lay his hands on. He was especially adept at collecting small tools, such as knives and spoons, right before the very eyes of the victims, who actually enjoyed the broad daylight robbery.

Shine pulled corn husks away and wolfed down the tamale, smacked his hairy dark lips, and then vanished into a mercantile, while the Mexicans strained to see inside and discover what act of piracy the little monkey would commit next. They were not disappointed. Shine emerged with a remnant of blue fabric, and dropped it into the cart, while the owner fumed and smiled, uncertain whether to laugh or wax indignant. Childress wisely returned the merchandise.

Next, Shine plucked Childress's Panama from his head and wandered through the crowd, holding it by its rim and collecting reales and pesos and candy. If anyone failed to donate, he scolded angrily, dancing from one foot to the other, his tail lashing dangerously, until the victim surrendered. People were delighted. All of Taos was seeing not merely a monkey, but a piratical, demanding, crafty one was well.

When had Taos received such an entertainment? A great sigh of appreciation went through them, children squealed, mothers clucked and herded the children away from such a hairy menace to good order, and meanwhile, the heap in the red cart grew.

Shine returned, handed the Panama to Childress, whose quick and furtive glance suggested to him that he had acquired a dollar or two of Mexican coin, a great deal, actually, coming out of an impoverished frontier town. It would buy food.

Shine rested a while on Childress's ample shoulder, and then plunged anew into the crowd, entertaining them as a trapeze artist might, swinging from roof to roof, viga to viga, while the crowd craned its necks to watch this novelty. Childress furtively counted: he now had somewhere around three American dollars, mostly in reales and centavos. Not enough to outfit, but it would spare him immediate embarrassments.

There would not be more. Shine had pushed these people to the limits of their tolerance.

Childress enjoyed Taos, which baked in a morning sun, its people bright and happy, its views majestic, its air cool and sweet. It would soon become a part of the Republic of Texas; everything east of the Rio Grande would become a part of Texas. He might be a mercenary, but he was other things as well, and this foray had acquainted him with certain things that he would include in his reports.

In any case, he was temporarily Texan also, though he had no great loyalty to the new nation. Lamar had sent him, the eyes and ears of the strong army advancing behind him. Houston had been elected but did not recall this robust corps of Texas filibusters rolling west, all of whom bragged they could lick any ten Mexicans they encountered. Childress's price had been a thousand Republic of Texas dollars—in gold. He had brought none of that with him. He eyed the happy crowd, counting men of military age while the good burghers of Taos gawked.

But he was also looking for slaves, and found none.

All this sunny sport was interrupted by the rattle of a drum from the shadowed northeast corner of the plaza, and there Childress beheld an awful spectacle. The drummer, a soldier dressed in the blue and white of the republic, snare-drummed his way through the sunlight, calling attention to what followed, and that turned out to be poor Skye, his flesh white and naked and hairy, his arms tied behind him so he could not even supply himself the modesty of his hands. Prodding him along were two more blue-coated soldados, and finally the prefect.

A sudden hush descended, and this martial party emerged from the deep shade into bright sun. Women gasped. Who had ever seen such a thing? Most of them intuitively gathered their children and turned away, or fled into the alleys. Some girls stared; old women in black calmly settled in to watch, licensed by age. And men drew to attention.

Now the awful parade marched slowly around the plaza. Skye's efforts to hasten his ordeal to its end were thwarted by a rope that stretched around his neck and back to one of the soldiers.

Skye knew not where to look, and stared rigidly ahead, his mortification apparent in his stiff posture. But then he saw Childress and stared, his gaze so relentless that not even a lifetime devoted to persiflage could help. Childress averted his eyes, knowing he could never meet Skye's piercing stare. Closer Skye came, the rattle of the drum shattering composure.

The Mexicans whispered: what was this? Who was this? A man from Tejas! Ah, see what happens to spies and provocateurs! A few spat. Skye passed; around the plaza he went, and passed again, and still he stared at Childress. But what did Skye know? Childress could do or say nothing. Not yet. In time, Skye's stare might be altogether different from what it was just then.

At last, after three times around the plaza, they stopped Skye and Archuleta read a proclamation: Be it known to the good citizens of Taos, that this man of Tejas, a spy and enemy of the republic, would be marched to Santa Fe to meet his fate, in the company of soldiers. Let it be a lesson to all.

An impressive display, Childress thought. He examined the equipment of the soldiers. They lacked muskets, but had broadswords and lances, and he didn't doubt they knew well how to use them. Skye had never stopped staring at Childress, and the last he saw of Skye, the naked man was still staring at him.

Childress felt momentary discomfort, but set it aside. He rarely felt any emotion and considered it a liability to his professional conduct. His storefront operation on the Arkansas gave him all the cover he would ever need.

They were hauling Skye away now; he watched sharply, intending to find out whether Skye would be marched, barefoot and naked, to Santa Fe, or whether they would toss him in a cart, a veritable tumbril. If they did not protect him from the sun he would surely die of burn.

He had little time. He summoned Shine, who had been bounding along beside Skye for a few moments, and the monkey landed on the seat beside him. The crowd was slowly dispersing; there would be no more shenanigans to entertain them this bright day.

"Señor," he said to an older man, "por favor, could you direct me to the residence of Padre Martinez?"

"Si, Señor Monkey Hombre, it is thus," the old man said, gesticulating. "He has a young woman who helps him keep house," the man said, with a certain wryness.

The Calf had a mistress. That intelligence was not new to Childress, and no remonstrations from the bishop had compelled the priest to surrender his woman. On the contrary, the priest openly declared that celibacy was unnatural and ought not to be required of any clergyman.

Childress found the Calle Rondo and proceeded up it, until he reached the place, a blank-walled adobe structure with only a door to signify a dwelling. It was not a rectory. Within, he knew, there would be a small, richly planted patio with the house opening around it. The wall looked to be eight or nine feet, nothing he could look over. From his vantage point on the street, he could see nothing of what transpired within.

Victoria Skye and her friend, Standing Alone, would be somewhere within, probably doing domestic chores. Padre Martinez maintained no small establishment. Childress doffed his Panama, handed it to Shine, and pointed. The monkey peered at him, uncertain of his intent, but then leaped gracefully to the parapet, and vanished. The few people on this shady lane eyed him curiously but did not question him. They had all seen him in the plaza; perhaps he would be visiting the padre.

Childress sat and sweated, the sun being high now, but all he encountered was profound silence. He feared that his monkey might have been captured, though no mortal could hold it for long by ordinary means. But at last he saw the familiar little body perched high above, still carrying the Panama. Then Shine leaped gracefully into the cart, and in one more bound, onto the seat beside Childress. Within the hat lay some round loaves, a little succor for the hard times ahead.

Victoria Skye's medicine bundle, which always hung from her neck, lay on top.

They were waiting.

twenty-eight

*N*othing in Skye's previous life had prepared him for the mortification of being marched naked through a public place. To strip away his clothes was to strip away his mortality, reduce him to an animal.

Some of those who first saw him turned away, and he was grateful to them. But others stared, rapt, at the sight of him, and he had no defense against it. He finally stared back, eye for eye, one by one, and many of those who watched found themselves facing an intense stare, until they too fell away, embarrassed.

But then he had come to Childress, perched on his red cart, the author of his troubles, and so he stared at Childress too, a gaze so relentless that not even that fat fraud could endure it. And so it had passed, and the harm that came to him was not to his body, but to his spirit. The guard took him back to the room from whence he had emerged, and they untied his hands. His aching arms fell to his side and he massaged them.

Larrimer was still there, compelled to translate, and Archuleta stood by, a certain amused look in his dark eyes.

"You're to put on the duds," Larrimer said.

They handed Skye some pantalones of coarse hard cloth,

and a shirt of the same material. He donned them gratefully, feeling himself a human being once again.

Archuleta murmured other things, and Larrimer translated.

"You're going to Santa Fe now for a trial. Governor Armijo will preside."

"I want my wife with me."

Larrimer consulted. "He says that's not possible."

"A man on trial is entitled to see his family."

"He says fate has decreed otherwise. Spies do not receive such blessings."

Skye started to protest his innocence, recite his intentions in coming here, but he held his peace. That litany would get him nowhere.

"Where is she now?" he asked.

This time Archuleta was more specific. "In the care of Padre Martinez," Larrimer said. "She will be employed, and her friend as well, in peaceful labor suitable for an Indian woman."

"What if she wants to go home?"

That produced a long exchange, and then Larrimer said, "She cannot, for her own good. The republic and the church must look after her body and soul, and put her to productive labor, so that she might see God."

"Slavery."

Larrimer did not translate, and Archuleta did not ask what was said. But he knew, anyway. "Slavery is forbidden in Mexico, by the republic, by the church," he said. Larrimer translated.

"Will she be in service at the padre's house?"

"No," Larrimer said at last, "she will be placed with a hacendado as soon as she shows evidence that she accepts her new life. And the same for the other woman. They will be separated, to avoid small difficulties."

"And does she have a choice?"

"No, she's in debt for her food and shelter and some clothing that was given her. So is the Cheyenne woman. He says that in Mexico these things must be paid with labor, and it is a criminal act to run from creditors. Mexican law is strict and just and virtuous, protecting all. The alcalde says that these things will all be decided for the good of the women."

"Are they going to feed me?"

Archuleta shrugged. He seemed to have understood more English than he admitted to understanding.

"How many days to Santa Fe?" Skye asked.

"Quatro, cinco," the prefect said, not waiting for translation. He turned to the three soldiers, addressed them at length, in curt tones, obviously admonishing them to be on guard with this dangerous man, and then sent them off.

They marched him south along smooth clay streets that did his feet no harm, perhaps because many hundreds of bare feet tramped them each day. Four or five days along unpaved and stony trails. Skye wondered how long his bare feet would last. Three of the soldiers were on foot, one ahead, two lancers behind. But then another, a corporal, appeared on a horse. He wore a cutlass. There would be no chance of outrunning that one. They all wore the blue and white of the republic, but not shoes or boots. These men wore sandals, as did so many in Mexico. But at least they had thick cowhide under their feet.

The countryside immediately south of Taos took his breath away. He had not expected beauty, but there it was: the dark reaches of the Sangre de Cristos to the east, the golden plain, the bright green vegetation below, the pastures of lime-colored grasses, sheep, cattle, burros.

They passed a few peasants, cheerful and sunny people who stared at him and whispered. Many carried enormous burdens on their backs. One lashed at a burro drawing a creaky carreta full of fragrant green hay.

A great adobe church loomed to the southeast, its twin towers golden in the sun, its beauty utterly amazing to Skye.

This lovely building had been lovingly fashioned from the very earth by these people, and Skye found himself admiring these Mexicans for their artistry and industry.

A great peace seemed to radiate from the church, and he sensed its holiness and sacredness. Not a soul entered through its massive doors, and it seemed to slumber there in the strong light of the noonday.

The smooth path and the church lifted him for the first time, and he began to think about things: how might he free Victoria and Standing Alone? He knew where they were—for the moment. How might he escape this escort? And if he did, how might he avoid swift recapture? The odds were terrible, and even worse for finding his wife and Cheyenne friend and spiriting them all out of Mexico, barefoot.

Whatever else he needed to survive, shoes or sandals would be high on the list. He began to observe what lay alongside the trail, something, anything that might spare a barefooted man anguish. But there was only rock and cactus and sticks.

The terrain changed; the soft dusty clay of the path yielded to sharp-edged rock patched with prickly pear, and his feet knew it at once. He stubbed a toe, and limped. Then he cut a sole on a tiny shard of rock projecting upward invisibly, and left blood in his steps. His left foot hurt, and he began to limp. A soldier prodded him along with the lance, enraging him. And yet . . . he knew he had a weapon now; his own blood.

They saw the blood, spoke among themselves, and as they did he slowed. His first and sole defense was to slow to a crawl, go as little as possible. He winced as he walked; he didn't need to exaggerate the pain; feet unused to being bare are easily bruised. They prodded him again, the tip of the lance poking hard into his kidney, and he hurried for a moment, and then slowed again.

Thus by degrees he slowed them, only an hour out of

Taos. The longer this walk took, the better were his chances of coming up with something, anything.

Then they prodded him again, this time angrily, and he limped forward until he stepped on a thorn, which jabbed deep into the ball of his left foot, and he bellowed. He sat down, ignoring the threats. The thorn had broken off, and was not easily removed, especially without so much as a knife.

This time the corporal shot a string of invective at him. The other two lifted him to his feet and force-marched him forward. Skye no longer had any plan at all; the pain began to rake his feet and ankles and calves, and he could scarcely imagine going through five days of this.

Two of his wounds leaked droplets of blood; no great flow of it, but enough to speckle the trail behind him. He walked as slowly and carefully as he could, ignoring the sharpness of the soldiers, who began to harry him. He had experienced much worse pain in his life, but this was repetitive, the stabs coming again and again, each step of his left foot a torment.

He sat down, and the prodding of the lances failed to budge him. They wouldn't kill him; he was certain of it. They fell into a discussion that became an argument, and though he couldn't grasp the words, he understood the gestures. The two foot soldiers wanted the corporal to dismount and put Skye on the horse, and the corporal was not about to surrender his comfortable seat and emolument.

Skye listened to the clash of wills, rubbed his sore foot, dabbed away the blood oozing from the broken thorn, and waited, all the while wondering if he could escape once he had the horse and the soldiers were on foot.

It was, in fact, a plan, but whether it was utterly foolhardy he didn't really know. What would a barefoot fugitive do with a posse of the Mexican army hot on his trail?

Then, suddenly, the argument subsided. The corporal did

not dismount. One of the privates turned to Skye, talking heatedly, but Skye could grasp none of it. The man pointed at the wounded foot, unsheathed a small knife, and sent fear rocketing through Skye. But the man pantomimed what he intended: there would be some minor surgery on the trail. Reluctantly, Skye extended his leg, and the private placed the foot in his lap, with surprising gentleness. He ran a hand softly over the wounds, grinned at Skye, and held his knife ready.

Skye clenched his teeth, waited. The soldier's deft plucking with the tip of his knife extracted the stub of the thorn, which had run deep into Skye's sole. He held it where Skye could see it. It looked like something off a cactus. Blood oozed. The other private rummaged through his field kit for a bandage, and wrapped Skye's foot tightly. He wished they would have cleaned it first. The bandage would help, but wouldn't last long, not in this flinty rock. They helped Skye to his feet, a definite kindness in them, even though the corporal stared darkly at the whole process.

And so once again they began, pacing themselves to Skye's limping. Santa Fe looked even farther away than before, but maybe there was hope in that.

twenty-nine

*V*ictoria listened carefully but could not understand a word. That didn't faze the pretty young Mexican woman though; she obviously expected Victoria to understand everything, and if she wasn't understood, then she would talk louder and faster and wag her hands and flail her arms.

Instructions, orders, explanations, sweeping gestures. All Victoria got out of it was the sense that she and Standing Alone were expected to do things. Then the sweet-voiced young woman tried talking very slowly, as if to an infant, but that did not yield understanding.

Meanings did pervade that flood of Spanish words and gestures helped. The young padre's woman was expecting help in the kitchen. Victoria and Standing Alone were supposed to toil there, peeling vegetables, cooking meat in the kettle hanging in the fireplace, shelling peas, fetching kindling, scraping pots, and in between, scrubbing clothing and hanging it to dry.

The padre had been gone all afternoon, for what reasons Victoria did not know. But that was all right: it gave her a chance to survey this place. She had swiftly learned that it was a very private and peaceful place, with a high-walled garden, and only a few small windows on the second floor.

It seemed grand; much larger and better than most of the houses of Taos. No wonder the padre wanted women to care for it.

That morning, the young woman had admitted a stiff older one dressed in black and summoned Victoria and Standing Alone. Then the dour older woman did a strange thing with a string. She took measurements; that was plain. The older woman wrapped the string around their waists, and made some marks on paper; then she did the same at the bosom and the hips, and finally she measured from the neck to the floor, and then she vanished out the barred patio door, which had a mysterious locking mechanism.

That afternoon, the stiff-backed old woman reappeared, this time with a bundle of clothing, some of it well worn and mended, some new. Now they made Victoria and Standing Alone pull off the shifts they wore and don this new clothing: drawers, a light and very full underskirt, a sort of tight blouse. The two Mexican women nodded, and with gestures told Victoria and Standing Alone to put their shifts on over all this other clothing. And so they were dressed very like the Mexican women, in layers of clothes, except that they were barefoot. The two Mexicans talked back and forth, nodding, looking pleased with what they had wrought, and then the older woman was let out into the narrow street.

As the afternoon unfolded, the Mexican woman set them to work in the kitchen, building up the fire, kneading dough, peeling carrots and potatoes, and finally slicing up pieces of beef the woman had produced from some cool place. All these went into a black cast-iron pot along with some salt. Ah! Victoria knew all of these things, and so did Standing Alone, so the work went easily. But it was irritating not to know how to talk to this woman of the padre, or learn anything. And the woman was not interested in learning Victoria's tongue, either.

But the padre's woman didn't press them hard, and there

was time to explore. Victoria wandered into a large room in which the smooth walls had been coated with white, and found little niches in the walls, and carved wooden statues in each niche, each carefully and brightly painted.

"Ah! The gods of the Mexicans," she said, surveying each one. The males had black beards. One beautiful woman was larger, dressed in blue, and had a sunburst of gold behind her, and before her were two candles. She smiled into the room and blessed it with her serenity.

"The mother god of the Mexicans," Victoria said, even as she beckoned Standing Alone along. "See how they honor her. I like that one better than the one on the cross." But then she remembered the words given to her by Skye once, about this god who willingly sacrificed himself so that others might be welcomed and made whole by the Above One, and she felt a strange respect flow through her. She wished Skye could be there to explain all these mysteries.

On the wall was the hanging god, the one dying on a cross, but there were no candles before him anywhere. He was everywhere, in each room. She had seen this god before, too, and thought him very strange.

There was a table and a chair where one could make the marks on paper, and a woven basket with the money of these people lying in it. There were many coins, and some paper too, but Victoria had no idea whether this was much or little money. She had seen such things in Saint Louis, but not these coins or this paper. They explored the other rooms, believing that this holy man had great wealth, and then the patio.

In the garden, she discovered Shine sitting on the high wall with the fat man's hat in hand. Shine chittered his greeting, swung down, and Victoria knew instantly what to do. When the young Mexican woman was not looking, she plucked up two little round loaves and dropped them into the hat. Then she pulled her medicine bundle from her neck and put it into the hat as a sign. Someday it would come back;

she didn't doubt that. Standing Alone stared, alarmed, but Victoria laughed. In moments, the monkey was gone, two graceful bounds from a tree to the wall.

Now Childress knew where Victoria and Standing Alone were. Aiee! It was good. Skye and Childress would come. Maybe they would have rifles and food and moccasins, and maybe fleet horses and saddles and a cooking pot and flint and steel and blankets. She thought of Skye, and ached for him, and ached to know where he was. He would come for her, or she would come for him, and they would escape. But for now, she needed to plan: to know how to get food to take with them, to learn how to escape, to learn a few words of these people.

She did not see Skye or Childress during that long day, and as evening approached, the Mexican woman kept them busy in the kitchen. Then the padre, this Martinez, appeared, looked the Indian women over carefully, nodded, said things to his woman.

The women put things on a table for him, savory meat and vegetables, some hot-baked bread, which Victoria liked, and a porcelain bottle of amber liquid. She wondered what that was, sneaked a sniff and discovered a sharp tang, but she dared not drink it. Then the padre sat down alone, and poured the amber liquid from the bottle into a cup and drank.

He sighed, sipped more.

She knew what it was! Firewater! Whiskey! She could see him relax and enjoy the hour. He swept one cup and then another into him, drinking as prodigiously as he ate. She and Standing Alone peeked from the cooking room until the Mexican woman hustled them away. The holy man and the Mexican woman talked much, but Victoria couldn't grasp a word of it. She sensed the talk was about herself and Standing Alone.

The padre Martinez disappeared up a stair, and the Mexican woman watched as the dishes were cleared off. But all that interested Victoria was where that brown bottle of the firewater was going. The Mexican woman put it into a cupboard. Ah! Victoria saw the place.

At the last, the Indian women were shown to a small room where things were stored. With gestures, they were made to understand that they should sleep there. But there were no blankets, nothing but a clay floor, and it was a cold place, the chill of the evening radiating through the earthen walls. Victoria sighed; she had slept in worse places, and this one would keep the wind and rain away.

The Mexican woman padded away, and Victoria furtively watched her progress through darkened rooms and up a stairway. So she would sleep up above, like the padre. Good!

Victoria waited, but not long, and then collected the brown bottle and a cup, and made her way back to the storage place.

"See what I have," she said.

Standing Alone looked doubtful.

"Whiskey!" Victoria unstopped the bottle, poured some of the amber fluid into a cup, and tasted it.

"Aiee!" Pure fire smoked down her throat. She had never tasted anything so awful.

"Have some of this medicine," she said. "Big medicine!"

But Standing Alone shook her head, and made signs with her fingers that Victoria could barely interpret because it was so shadowed. But the Cheyenne woman was telling her that she never had tasted white men's whiskey because it destroyed her people, and she wouldn't start now.

"Take a little just to warm you. It is cold," Victoria replied.

But Standing Alone shook her head.

Victoria sighed. Ah, if only Skye were there to share this bonanza with her! She tried again, another sip of that fierce and wild amber liquid that inflamed her tongue and mauled her throat. It slid down with a heated rush, and she gasped. The Mexican firewater was ten times more violent than the American firewater.

But, ah! What a good hot pleasant feeling was building in her belly! She sipped again. And again. Finally, she fell into rhythmic sipping, letting the firewater shoot joy through her veins, and letting herself relax after a taut and terrible day. She was a prisoner, stuck inside a place from which she could not escape, but this was a solace.

"Take this," she said, thrusting the cup at Standing Alone, but the woman pushed it away.

"It is good. I am not cold now."

Victoria started laughing for no reason at all. She drank much more, for several hours, as sleep overtook her, but the good feelings gave way to dizziness and nausea, and she did not feel well at all. She tried to stand, but could not. She needed to find the place where she could relieve herself, but could not remember it.

Finally, she lay on the cold clay ground, which whirled around and around, and she could not sleep well because her head hurt and her body was rebelling against the Mexican firewater. She had consumed half of what was in the bottle.

Beside her, Standing Alone slumbered peacefully.

Aiee! She would pay for it in the morning!

thirty

olonel Childress hastened back to the plaza. There was so much to do, so little time. He circled it until he discovered a tailor wedged into a southside corner, and then tugged the reins.

"Fetch," he told Shine. "I'm going inside."

The monkey plucked Childress's Panama from his master's noggin and began scouting the deserted plaza for easy marks, while Childress barged into the small, cool shop, where a horsey-faced young man, pale as a winter moon, was sewing.

"Ah, my good man," Childress began in Spanish, "I shall want you to put all that aside and perform a great service for humanity, God, and the universe. And what is your name, señor?"

"Laroccha."

"Ah, Señor Laroccha, the finest tailor, I am told, in all of Mexico, am I not correct?"

Laroccha scarcely nodded.

"I am Governor, Sir Arthur Childress, British administrator of Barbados, the Lower Antilles, British Guiana, and the Windward Islands. I was set upon by savages, as you can see, and need proper raiment at once. A black worsted suit, two white shirts, a cravat, stockings, smallclothes, and you will please direct me to a cobbler. Important! Official business. Have it all mañana."

"Mañana! But, señor! Sir Arthur!"

"Mañana!"

"I cannot do such a thing."

"Hire help. Hire every seamstress in Taos."

"But the cost!"

"Damn the cost. It's all to be charged to the government."

"The government?"

"Yes, Government House, Office of Administrator, Trinidad and Tobago. Post it the day you complete my order. I'll sign. Charge what you must! Levy extra! But set to work, man."

"But . . . I can't wait so long for payment. It will be half a year. I am a poor man."

"My friend, how well I understand all that. The queen of England will vouch for my purposes. I'm here on the most delicate of international missions, one that will benefit the Republic of Mexico, and I need a set of clothing pronto!"

"Ah . . . could you not give me a surety, say half?"

"My old friend, go to your prefect, Juan Andres Archuleta, and see about me. He will vouch for me, you can count on it."

Laroccha sighed. "I will take your measure, señor, and think upon it."

"Do that! I'm a busy man; negotiating for a large estate."

Laroccha pulled out a tape, and began measuring, mumbling to himself, penciling figures.

"Gobernador Childress, you are a hombre of heroic dimension, and you will consume a veritable shipment of fabric . . . you will forgive your poor clothier for adding something for your noble size, as well? I will require the toil of eight or ten others."

"Why, I would not want you to deprive yourself of a suitable and fitting reward, my friend."

Laroccha sighed. "Tomorrow at dusk? For the fitting?"

"Bueno, consider it an agreement," Childress said. "Be sure to check with the prefect. He will put you at ease, viejo."

Laroccha nodded tentatively.

"Now I must acquire some duds for my ladies, who were set upon by the Apaches as well. Who would you recommend?"

"Ah, Madame Vollers, wife of the late French consul, señor. Just across the plaza, and up the narrow stairs."

"Bueno. Mil gracias. You shall have your reward."

Childress hurried out into the morning sun, and cut straight across the clay to the upstairs shop of madame.

He saw Shine, hat in paw, jabbing it at people who were taking their paseo this bright new day.

"Soak 'em good," he muttered.

He hastened up the stairs, scarcely noticing the effort to hoist his bulk one story, and entered a salon with a great jangle of bells. Within were half a dozen elegant gowns, all on dressmaking dummies, all completed as far as he could see.

A birdlike woman emerged from behind a curtain, patting her graying bun of hair with feathery hands.

"Señor?" she said.

"My dear duchess," he said, "I have come to purchase two of your finest gowns, your most noble creations, for two ladies in distress, who were put upon by the Jicarillas a few days ago."

"Ah, poor dears! I trust they are brave?"

"Very brave, señora. Now I don't have their dimensions, but they are small and slender, and come up about to here." He pointed at his chin.

She smiled. "I have just the dresses," she said. "See, I have several that are ready but for the hems. Now, how shall we proceed?"

"Señora, I am Governor Sir Joshua Childress, administrator of Barbados and Bermuda and Corpus Christi, here on important diplomatic business."

"But aren't you the hombre with the red cart and monkey?"

"Why, señora, that is no ordinary monkey. It is a Frangipangi Ape, the only such creature in captivity, a rarity that your eyes will never behold again. Admire it with all your heart and soul, for you have seen one of the miracles of God."

"Well, yes . . ."

"Bill the British Government, señora. Government House, the Province of the Caribbean, Barbados."

"Ah . . ."

"And those hats! Yes, the ones with the broad brims and fruit about them, I shall require two. And slippers. Half a dozen small, medium, and large."

"But gobernador, I require cash. I will not accept any other. I am a recent widow, much abused by people of little kindness or courtesy, and therefore careful."

"But, señora, the circumstances are temporarily difficult."

She stared, stonily, and Childress knew defeat. "Very well, I shall return. What is the price of all that?"

She sighed. "For you, I will add ten percent."

"Add! You mean deduct."

"Add."

"Never mind. I shall find a seamstress with a kinder heart."

She stared. "It is an ordinary spider monkey found in Central America."

Childress retreated, and hunted down Shine, who was temporarily occupied somewhere. There was so little time.

"Shine, blast you," he bellowed.

The little monkey appeared at once, lazily swinging from roof to roof, carrying the Panama delicately, and then he dropped down to the cart. Within the Panama were several coins, some glistening gold. Two were double eagles.

"Ah! I see you have been engaged in criminal activity! I shall have you arrested someday," he said, scooping up the coins. A swift count revealed sixty-odd Yank dollars. He handed a silver real to the monkey. "Here, buy yourself some tamales."

Shine chittered and chattered, and swung away.

Colonel Childress once again negotiated the formidable stairway, and burst in upon the frowning proprietress.

"A price! I shall pay you in advance, señora."

"In what?"

"Gold and silver."

"Ill-gotten, I imagine. I am only a poor widow, and here I am, accepting tainted money. How much have you?"

"Ah, I can't quite calculate in pesos. It appears to be sixty-three American."

"The two dresses are seventeen and eleven in Yankee dollars, and the hats three apiece, the slippers twelve, coming to forty-six in all, but I will accept sixty-three." She held out her hand.

"Señora!"

"Or I can summon the prefect."

"But, señora!"

The steely look in her eyes told him he was skunked. Dolefully he metered out the gold pieces and then the silver into her small patient hand.

"Very well," she said. "I must give half to the church for accepting your dirty money."

She plucked the dresses from dummies, folded them, added the hats and slippers, and thrust the bundle at him.

"You are a princess, a queen, and a saint," he said, backing out the door.

She stared at the coins, and as he left she was biting the gold ones.

Shine was sitting on the red cart, wiping his hairy lips.

"Well, my little pirate, you have done me a service," Childress said. "But we have more to do. This cart will never do. It is too well known."

He drove slowly through Taos, looking for a wagon-yard or livery barn, but found nothing that filled that bill. Taos was still too rude. Then, on the southeastern reaches of Taos, parked behind a sprawling house with Chinese lanterns dangling in the breezes, he beheld an ebony calash, or maybe it was a victoria. It was a thing of beauty, a don's vehicle, with facing quilted leather seats, a fold-up hood, and a raised bench for the driver. Two restless trotters flicked their tails at flies.

"Ah! Shine, we have success!"

He parked his red cart at the door of the stately adobe home, and knocked.

A young woman dressed head to heel in black opened to him.

"Are you the mistress of this establishment?" he asked.

"No, she's attending Don Amelio, señor."

"Is that his calash?"

She looked outside. "He always drives it."

"I should like to see him, if I may."

"He's indisposed, señor."

"Oh, he won't mind. I wish to offer him a favorable trade."

"But, señor, that is not possible until late in the day."

"You don't say! What is the nature of his indisposition?"

"Ah, sir, it ill behooves me to say." She smiled. "This is the residencia of the Señora Aguirre y Canales, who lost her husband to the beastly Tupamaro Indians not long ago."

"And Don Amelio?"

"He comes once a fortnight to console her, señor. She needs much consoling." She laughed merrily.

"Ah! My sweet little chickadee, I don't mean to invade paradise, but there is profit in it for you and me."

"There is? What?"

"Ah, your name is what?"

"Carmelita."

"Well, my dear, beautiful, holy, and faithful and blessed Carmelita, I am going to offer this charitable hidalgo my new red cart in exchange for his worn-out calash, and if he agrees,

I will reward you handsomely. All you have to do is present the agreement to him."

"I will?"

Childress pointed. "You see that monkey? He's rare and famous. He's yours if you can keep him."

"A monkey?"

"He will help you in all your endeavors if he decides to live with you."

"I've always wanted a monkey, señor."

"Good! Now fetch me a pen and ink and two sheets of paper, so I may draw up an agreement for him to sign, and then you may present it to him for signature."

"A monkey," she said, her face ecstatic.

"Yes, and he will get a splendid red cart, and will bless me for it," Childress said. "Lead me to a writing table, señorita, and I will draft the arrangement."

thirty-one

Skye limped, stumbled and fell. The trail turned precipitous as it wound through a giant defile toward the Rio Grande. It was soft clay one moment, razored rocks the next, and laden with sticks and prickly pear. His bandaged foot turned bloody, his right foot began to bleed also, leaving speckles of red in the dust behind him.

He willed himself forward, his legs punching pain at the base of each step, hot pain that shot up to his thighs, dull pain that eddied through his whole body; stinging pain as his abused naked feet hit sharp rock or debris. It was hard going, but he refused to quit. He thought of Victoria. He would keep going because of her. He thought of Standing Alone and her lost children, the reason he had ventured here. He had to keep on walking.

The soldiers, actually, were sympathetic. He had expected sadism, but found them to be gentle with him, and the more his feet were abused, the more they let him rest. He had expected the lances to prod him, but these were amiable Mexican boys, not hardened professionals, and they eyed him kindly, and perhaps condescendingly.

Any Indian could manage barefooted; most mestizos could too. But this tender-footed Anglo could not; he had lived his life inside of shoes and boots and the soles of his feet were without callus or thickness or hardening. They joked between them, and while Skye couldn't grasp the words, he knew the meaning: this tough white hombre had feet as soft as a baby's.

His struggles slowed them to a crawl, but he couldn't help it. He dreaded to put each foot down, knowing the flare of pain that would strike as his foot settled on the ground.

But they made some progress, and Skye did the best he could. He would always do his best, even if he were headed for a trial in which his fate would rest on a liar's testimony. One could live with all the courage he could muster, or not, and Skye chose to live in hope.

By late afternoon they had pierced to the shadowed bottoms of the river, and here they met small settlements, little farms, large cemeteries, and skinny cattle. And here, at last, a peon driving a creaking carreta overtook them. The vehicle was drawn by a pair of burros tugging from within a homemade rope harness, and carried within it two squealing hogs caught inside a wall of stakes rising from the cart-bed. The squeaking wheels had been fashioned from a large tree, and rimmed with iron.

The corporal halted the wizened old farmer, who was clad in rags, and addressed him harshly. The peon eyed Skye and shrugged.

The burros began nipping stray grasses and weeds as the debate ensued.

But then the old man walked around to the rear of the cart and pulled up one of the stakes imprisoning the hogs, and motioned to Skye. Within was a carpet of urine-soaked straw and pig manure, but it looked like heaven. Skye limped to the little cart, crawled through the opening, and was smacked by the sheer stink. But he settled between the snorting hogs with his back resting on the front of the cart.

"Vamos!" cried the corporal.

The privates were grinning and making jokes. Skye would have liked to know the jokes, but he could guess well enough.

He stared at his bloody feet, and suddenly the pig droppings didn't seem so bad. The howling pain that had ripped breath out of his lungs settled into a dull ache, but his ears were soon battered by the squeaking of the wheels. One soldier walked at either side of the cart, while the corporal rode behind, his purpose to find anything out of order.

"Pig dung is worse than any other," Skye said to no one, since none could understand him. "This is the worst offense to my nostrils since the fo'castle where I rotted for years."

They eyed him blandly. The little old peon kept glancing at him, as if this exotic gringo would get him into terrible trouble.

The carreta creaked and groaned, the burros tugged, and the pigs pressed him restlessly, but at least he was off his bloody feet. His hunger returned and he eyed his pink and gray traveling companions, thinking of bacon and chops. The entourage proceeded peacefully until the next village, where the old peon began to argue vehemently, his gestures hot and troubled. Skye understood not a word, and yet understood everything. This had been the old man's destination. He did not wish to go further. But the soldiers were pressing him.

Muttering, he finally surrendered to the corporal, and the party creaked south again through the bottoms of the Rio Grande. Skye's porcine companions shrieked and pawed and wet the straw; they were all going to the butcher and they knew it.

By dusk of that day, Skye was as starved as he had ever been.

"Comida," he said, remembering a word.

The corporal nodded. None of these men was unkind to him; perhaps they knew he was doomed, and doomed men required the utmost courtesy.

They turned into yet another settlement, two or three adobes surrounded by crops and pastures, and the usual flower-decked cemetery because the Mexicans were so good at dying and so eager to celebrate the dead.

The corporal rode ahead to evict the tenants of one of the adobes, and soon enough a half dozen brown people, ranging from great age to infancy, hurried out of the casa with covert glances at Skye and the little swine caged behind the stakes of the carreta. Skye watched them hasten toward a neighbor's casa, laughing and chattering as if this were a normal thing. He felt embarrassed, as if he were the cause of this dislocation of a simple country family, but it was not his doing: the corporal had commandeered the farm.

They directed him inside, and he slid to the ground while the old peon held on to the hogs. He discovered a warm and bright room, with a meal of some sort boiling in a pot and some bowls upon a rude table. He sank onto a bench, aware of how much he stank, while outside the peon and soldiers were transferring the hogs into some safe place or other, and seeing to their needs.

Skye found an olla, poured some water over his soiled pantalones, and tried to wipe away the filth, to little avail. Every step was hell, but he kept at it, wanting to cleanse himself, both body and soul.

They fed him some mutton from the black iron pot, and he took a second and a third helping, feeling the ache in his belly slowly dissolve. He wondered if the soldiers would pay the family whose casa they had appropriated or if this was simply the luck of the draw in Mexico.

The old man appeared, having secured his hogs somewhere, and with him came an odor of the barnyard. He helped himself to the last of the boiled mutton as the soldiers watched. The meat rested uneasily in Skye's stomach, and he knew he was unwell.

Skye wanted to wash himself, but couldn't fashion the word, but he remembered his school Latin. "Lava," he said, experimentally.

That sufficed. The corporal nodded, led him outside alertly, in fading light, to a battered watering trough for the animals, where Skye shed his filthy shirt, washed it, scraped offal off his stained pants, and tried to cleanse his body as well. But it was futile. His toilet done, Skye limped back inside, thoroughly chilled, to the casa lit only by the coals of the dying kitchen fire. They would all be sleeping on the clay floor.

He studied the room for anything of value: a weapon or food or clothing, but then subsided. It was bad enough that the soldiers had commandeered this family's food and shelter; he would not add to the offense by taking things not his. Oddly, he found himself wishing he could leave something for them: if he was going to die in Santa Fe, he wanted to die without debts. But there was nothing he could do: the soldiers may have been kind to a limping man, but they were no less wary of him, and alert to anything he did.

He did not sleep, but lay restlessly. The soldiers knew he could not escape, not when he could barely hobble, so they slept peacefully. The chill of the floor rose through his wet shirt, but there was no help for it. He lay taut, feeling a weariness in his body that matched the weariness of his mind. He was worn out. He had come all this way to find two abducted children, but here he was, under arrest and being taken to Santa Fe for a mock trial and probable death or certain imprisonment, his women were bound into slavery he knew not where, the man he had trusted had betrayed him, and everything had fallen apart.

He felt a turmoil in his bowels, and knew he was getting sick. He tried to ignore that torments of his body, but could not. He lay sweating and cold at the same time, feeling fever build in him and steal through his limbs. He could no longer lie quietly. Time ticked slowly, and he knew only that his body was burning, he was thirsty, his breathing was labored, and that he was gravely ill.

A convulsion twisted him, and then a rush of nausea, and he could no longer fight the violence of his belly. He crawled onto all fours, crawled away from the rest, and heaved up everything within him, a sour, vile rush of noxious vomit that swiftly stank up the dark room, and left him in tears.

He lacked the strength even to find his way to the olla and some fresh water, but fell back onto the clay, scarcely caring whether he lived or died.

And that is how he spent the night, his limbs cold, brow burning, and his spirits wavering like a guttering candle. Finally he sensed the presence of light, and opened his eyes, and stared up at solemn faces above him. There was a woman, and she was applying compresses to his forehead, and then he slid back into oblivion again.

thirty-two

Colonel Childress drafted a bill of sale in duplicate: a used calash and team for a red cart and draft horse. He waved it in the air to dry the ink.

"Now, child, I want you to take this to him. Awaken him from his slumbers, do you understand?"

"I shouldn't do that, señor."

"Why not, Carmelita?"

"He is not himself. He will peer at me with big eyes, black holes, as if all color has left them, and he will frown, groan, and fall back into his bed."

"And where is the señora? Does she sleep into the afternoons like the don?"

The girl shrugged. "Sometimes."

"My little Carmelita, chickadee, listen carefully. Tell Don Amelio that the British Viceroy of Grenadine, Grand Bahama, Great Inagua, and Rum Cay requires the calash on urgent business for Her Majesty, the queen, and in return he will receive the Order of the Garter and a handsome red cart."

"I can't remember all that, señor, and I'm afraid . . ."

"Write it down."

"I can't read, señor."

"Then remember it. Queen Victoria's viceroy. Quick now, and don't forget the pen and ink!"

She looked ready to bolt. "Remember the monkey," he said. "It's yours if you can keep it."

"Don Amelio doesn't like to be awakened after he has been smoking the pipe, señor. I might lose my position."

"It's a national crisis. I am saving Mexico from conquest."

She stared long and solemnly at him, sighed, plucked up the papers and the ink bottle and quill, and slowly headed for the stairway leading upward to—who knows what?

He hoped the señora would not appear.

It took an infernally long time, and he paced the room, oblivious of its colonial charm, the whitewashed adobe, the mission-style furniture, the bultos, and the Navajo rugs scattered about.

Then at last she slipped down the stairs, looking rumpled.

"Let me see it, child!" He snatched the papers from her.

There, in a shaky hand, was a signature, barely legible. And another, on the other sheet.

"Ah! He agrees! Take this! He gets one copy, I keep the other. Now, my child, you must tell me what happened."

She dimpled up. "He was fast asleep, señor, so I shook him gently, and he said, 'not again, witch,' and I said there is a nobleman from England who wants your calash, and he said, 'bother,' and rolled over, and I said it was a national crisis and you were the viceroy of . . . all that. And he said some cruel things to me, reached for the quill and bottle, and made the signs, señor viceroy. Do I get my monkey?"

"Of course, of course, if you can keep him."

He walked to the great front door. "Shine, fetch!"

The little beast leapt off the Clydesdale, bounded inside, evoking a squeal, and began ransacking the establishment. He fastened upon a silver salt cellar, and leaped up to a mantel to shake it.

Carmelita trailed him, twittering and laughing.

"See now, child, it is better than having a niño. Catch him if you can."

Childress hurried outside, led the Clydesdale to a nearby

pen and unharnessed it, and then returned to the calash and its weary team, studying the powerful black horses and the ebony carriage with its yellow wheels. Yes, perfect. The black calfskin leather was new and soft, the shining lacquer showed no scuffs or chips, and the hood raised and folded easily.

He wondered how long the poor horses had been standing there, decided to do something about it, unhitched them, led them to a watering trough, where they sipped water furiously. When he judged that they were again in good fettle, he hooked the chains to the doubletree.

"Shine," he bellowed.

Nothing happened, and at once he was worried.

But then the hairy little rascal flew out of an open window, hung on a shutter as it swung, and landed on the ground, clutching something shiny.

But now it was confused. It eyed the ebony carriage and two sleek black trotters, hunted for the red cart, and discovered the Clydesdale unharnessed.

"Shine!" he bawled, but the monkey leaped up to the Clydesdale's broad back, patted his friend, chittered softly in the ear of the giant horse, rubbed his eyes with his free hand, combed the mane, and reluctantly swung to the ground, not happy.

The big horse nickered affectionately, and clacked its teeth.

But what did it matter? "Shine, we are the masters of our fate," Childress said. "I am Lord Childress, viceroy of the universe."

The spider monkey glared at him, and pitched the shiny object to the dirt. It was a salt cellar.

"I always have sat above the salt," Childress said, cheerfully.

He discovered Carmelita at the great door, oozing tears down honey-colored cheeks, weeping sadly. That innocent child did want a monkey and was tricked, but all that could not be avoided. He snapped the lines over the backs of the two trotters and was rewarded by a swift tug and the soft sway of the calash as it rounded the long circular drive out to the dusty road. He had things to do, and little time. Within days, his friend Skye would be drawing a black bean or a white bean.

Childress drove his fine calash back to the plaza, while his monkey sat on the seat beside him, studying his new conveyance and sucking his fingers. It knew better than to jump onto the backs of the trotters.

Slowly, the Colonel drove around the plaza looking for a cobbler. He eyed the windows, and cased the few second-floor quarters, but he could not find a maker of boots. He tried each side street, wheeling up clay alleys, stirring up the floury clay, looking for anyone who might have footwear. Finally he asked an old woman, and she pointed back at the plaza. He parked his calash and undertook to survey the plaza on his bare feet, but could find no bootmaker. The Mexicans mostly wore sandals or slippers that looked very similar to Indian moccasins. The few caballeros who had boots probably had them custom made in Santa Fe. Childress sighed. Very well, it would be Larrimer, then.

He entered the cool store, enjoying the redolence of leather and fabric and coffee beans.

Larrimer approached. "They let you out, Brother Childress, eh?" he said, coldly.

"Mr. Larrimer, I am in dire need of some boots, or at least shoes, and you have some ready-mades, I believe?"

"Show me some cash and I'll show you some boots."

"I haven't a cent. The Apaches made off with everything."

"Even your habit, I see. Unless you've renounced your orders and taken up with some woman." Larrimer's thick eyebrow shot upward.

"I regret announcing that I was a monk; I was desperate," Childress said.

"You might have won some sympathy by saying so. But not now, Childress. Not ever."

The Colonel knew he wasn't getting anywhere, so he tried a new tack. "Mr. Larrimer, I have a fine trading outfit on the Arkansas River, just across the international boundary. We do a business with the Utes especially. Childress and McIntyre, sir. I only regret that whatever I say will meet with skepticism because of my previous indiscretions. But it is so. And I would most eagerly give you a chit for merchandise from our stores in exchange for boots. In fact, sir, merchandise worth ten times the price of your boots."

The odd thing was that Larrimer did not laugh.

"Well? My goods are, what, a hundred miles distant? I'll add something for transportation."

"What's there?"

"Blankets, kettles, axes, hatchets, knives, saws, a few rifles, flints and steels, bed ticking, flannels, calico, salt, molasses, pure grain spirits, tobacco in plug and leaf form, vermilion, beads, awls . . ."

"I suppose you'll want some boots for Skye, too. What's his size?"

"I don't know," Childress said, marveling at the man.

"You'll want some ready-made duds for him, too, I suppose. Shoes or sandals, and some clothing. Weapons, powder, food, gear . . ."

What was this? Childress could scarcely fathom it. "I can draft an agreement, Mr. Larrimer."

"How will I know your subordinates will honor it?"

"The monkey's paw, sir. I press it into an inkpad, and press it onto the document. It's our sign and seal, the paw of Shine."

"What is the total worth of your stock?"

"Why, Sah, given that I haven't been there for some little while, I can't say. But perhaps three thousand at wholesale."

Larrimer grinned, and not kindly. "All right. You sell me your goods and the premises, and I will outfit you and Skye up to three hundred."

"But . . . but . . ." Larrimer would profit tenfold.

"I know it's there, Childress. You don't have to persuade me. Childress and McIntyre Traders. Several travelers have reported the place to me. I even know what prices you charge, how many men you have, and what tribes are camped there. I'm willing to gamble."

"Ah, would you keep my help employed?"

"Your Texas pirates? No, I'll send my own man to operate the place. He'll take inventory . . . and if there's trouble, be warned: I have my means."

"Mr. Larrimer, Sah, done!"

Larrimer grinned sardonically.

thirty-three

The padre's young woman seemed less and less friendly as the next day wore on. She raged at Victoria and Standing Alone, which only left Victoria bewildered. She couldn't understand a word. But the woman's displeasure was plain to her.

One moment the woman would be snapping; the next moment she would pantomime what she wanted: Wash those cloths and clothing in a wooden tub of water, pound and squeeze them on a ribbed board, rinse, and hang them on a line. Fetch more water.

"Agua! Agua!" the woman cried, pointing at the water.

Victoria knew that. She knew many words of this tongue even if she could not put them together.

Make the fire hot: this involved a device new to her, a lung of leather that blew air when the handles were operated. Victoria made the air come out, and the fire began to crackle. Standing Alone watched carefully. They were both studying ways to escape, ways to defend themselves.

This day the walleyed padre wandered about in his long brown robe, gazing strangely at the Indian women, his giant head lolling this way and that to see them. Maybe he could see only things that were far away, the way many old men see. His soft brown eyes studied them, the gaze poking and

probing until Victoria thought she couldn't stand it. Sometimes the gaze seemed to lift her skirts, and then she looked
right back at him and he looked away.

She wished he would go away, do his priestly things, but
this day he hovered in the great kitchen, watching them as
they scrubbed vegetables or stirred the great black pots. He
had plans for them; that she knew. Maybe that was why his
woman was so snappish this day. She was his woman, all
right, and showing the signs of a baby, now that Victoria
studied her.

Then the padre's woman took them away from the big
kitchen and into the quiet bedchambers and made them
broom the floors, empty pots into a smelly cistern in the garden, and shake the blankets. The padre's woman was more
relaxed now that they were all away from the padre. But he
hadn't left; he was there, watching.

Victoria and Standing Alone had been given no time to
rest, and were fed very little at dawn, a thin oat gruel before
the sun brightened the morning. They hadn't been allowed
to talk, either; whenever she and Standing Alone tried to com-
municate in their own sign language and vocabulary, the
Mexican woman started bawling at them.

Was this the future? Victoria knew that if the time came,
she would fight, ferociously, no quarter, for her freedom. She
would steal a knife and hide it as soon as she knew where to
secret it, and one for Standing Alone, too. There were some
in the kitchen; big, crude ones with dull blades, but all the
better for a fight. She knew Standing Alone was thinking the
same thing: sometimes they looked at a knife or a long fork
and their gazes met. She knew!

A wave of contempt for the Mexican woman flooded
through her: what sort of petty tyrant was this person whose
strength was not her own, but the padre's? Could she not
even take care of this man's dwelling place?

Victoria found reasons to head into the walled garden,
always to look for the Little Person perched on the high adobe

wall, but she did not see him, and her spirits sagged. For some reason, that little creature, the very one she was so darkly hostile toward at first, was her salvation. But she saw nothing, and no succor offered itself. Had that animal not taken her medicine bundle to the fat man? Didn't he know she and Standing Alone were here, behind great walls?

Then, late that afternoon, a Mexican man was admitted, and this man was dressed in a black suit coat and an open shirt, and had oily straight hair that fell away from his face. He talked with the padre for a while, and then the Indian women were summoned with a languid hand.

Victoria stared at him, wondering what this rumpled brown man would do.

The man in the suit coat addressed Victoria:

"Madam, it is I speak zoom English, and it is I am bring here to tell you zum things. For we know you habla, speak, this tongue, and do no comprende what is your mistress be saying."

Mistress? Victoria nodded, not giving the man the satisfaction of a reply in Skye's language.

"Mañana, tomorrow, a carreta, wagon, it comes and it carries you to a rancho grande, the Estancia Martinez, which is owned by the hermanos, zee brothers, of zee blessed padre Martinez. Four thousand sheep. There you will be employed for the good of your souls and bodies, and the love of Jesu Cristo."

"I think we would like to stay here in Taos."

"Stay? This place? No, no, woman, that is not possible."

"Then maybe we refuse employment, eh?"

He stared solemnly, and shook his head. "No, you cannot refuse. You go."

"Why?"

"Because zis is require."

"I am married. You must not take me from my husband. So is she."

He blinked, and shook his head. "No, not married in Mejico. What parish? Where are zee records, zee sacrament? No, no, it is without force, like nada."

She pointed at Standing Alone. "She has a man. And children too."

"No, not in Mejico. It be no good, no good."

She pointed at the priest. "Is he married? He has a woman."

The oily-haired man glared at her.

"I heard the padre say there is no slavery in Mexico."

The man's big brown eyes blinked once, and again, as if he were careful with the words he was preparing. "Little woman, you owe much for your care. Zees things, the comida, food, the casa, the clothing on your backs, this is muy, very costly, yes, you are much in debt. So you must vork, eh? *Vork!*"

"So, when can we pay off our debt?"

He shook his head. "Sometime. Your vork not very valuable, si? You onnerstand, si?"

"What if we won't work?"

"Ah, pity, dolor, you taste zee whip."

"What if we go away, eh?"

He shook his head. "Do not even think of it, comprende?"

She understood and laughed at him. He seemed to puff up and withdraw into himself. Standing Alone understood little of it, and looked at her blankly.

Victoria simply laughed, the scorn in her dark features rising upward and bursting out upon the kitchen.

"Bastard," she said.

"Silencio!" bawled the padre.

She took her time. The oily man in the suit coat decided it was time to leave, and the padre showed him out. Victoria watched them at the big plank door, and she tried to understand how to work the iron mechanism that would let them out. She had seen these things before in St. Louis, but not anywhere else.

The padre's woman looked amused.

Victoria's fingers flew, and in swift gestures and their small stock of words she conveyed their fate to Standing Alone, who drew herself up proudly, unbent, unbowed, and stared at their mistress.

So she would be taken away from Skye, farther and farther, and placed into a life of grinding toil, probably worse than this light labor she had suffered this day and the day before. Tonight. Now or never. At dawn the distance between Skye and herself would stretch farther, and farther, and things would get worse, and worse . . .

Tonight.

The Mexican woman put them to work again, and set Victoria to collecting piñon wood from a large bin located at the alley wall of the patio and stacking it beside the several beehive fireplaces. She walked out there, through the serene patio with its quiet peace, past the herbs that grew in a special plot, and a lordly agave, to the place where the woodcutters stacked wood.

She plucked up a piece, and another, and then she saw the low wooden doors beyond, doors that opened on the alley, doors used by the woodcutters when they unloaded the wood from their burros and stacked the sticks within the wall for the householder. She turned and looked behind her; no, no one was watching. She stepped deep into the shadowed woodbox, and lifted a small bar. She pushed the door, and it swung a little, creaking as it did. Frightened, she peered over her shoulder, and edged the door back in place. Her heart tripped as she plucked up the sticks for the evening's dinner.

Out.

And even as she carried the load in her arms toward the kitchen, she spotted the Little Person perched quietly on the high adobe wall, watching her with bright eyes. She nodded at the fiend and continued inside, unloading her wood before the beehive fireplace.

She walked out into the garden again, and hovered around the woodbox while the little creature watched her.

Then, suddenly, it vanished, and she wondered whether it understood. As soon as this household quieted, she would lead Standing Alone to this place, and they would crawl over the stacked wood, and crawl out of the walled patio.

Oh, if only the Little Person might understand. Was there anything she had failed to understand? Any message? Any sign? She saw nothing, even as she gathered a few more pieces of piñon pine for the fireplace. Anxiously, she watched the sun dive toward the horizon. Fretfully she watched the padre eat and drink and take his leisure. In agony she listened for sounds from without. Then, as dusk settled and she and Standing Alone were cleaning dishes, she beheld the Little Person named Shine on the wall again.

Her heart hammered, but there was nothing she could do, not yet, not until this house had settled, not until a great darkness could cloak them as they slipped through the house, the garden, and the woodman's gate. Sometimes she saw the monkey, sometimes she didn't. Sometimes she heard the soft clop of horses beyond the high wall, sometimes only a terrible and lonely silence. Once, a carriage wheel groaned outside the walls.

But at last the priest vanished into the darkness, and so did his woman, and Victoria and Standing Alone lay quietly in the storage alcove that had been their refuge.

Now, as the stars lit up the sky and the last blue light faded in the west, far beyond the Rio Grande, she heard the chittering of Shine up on the wall somewhere in the murky night, and she arose, and took Standing Alone with her, and crept through the garden toward the little wood gate.

thirty-four

The woodcutter's door squawked, but Victoria paid no heed. She crawled over the stacked wood, with Standing Alone right behind, and soon they found themselves standing in a dark alley with nothing but starlight to illumine the way. She peered about, seeing nothing.

"Mrs. Skye, my dear, this way."

That voice belonged to the trader, Childress, but she could see nothing.

"I shall send Shine."

Almost before the words had escaped the man, she felt the Little Person tugging on her skirt.

"Aiee!" She didn't really trust the animal.

But she let herself be led, and soon they came upon a conveyance of some sort.

"What is this damn thing?" she asked.

"It is a carriage, a calash, to be precise. Do climb in."

"Where's Skye?"

"That's a long story. First we must make haste to escape here."

She boarded the creaking carriage, barely able to see. No light shown in the streets and no moon lit the way. But she could see that it had facing seats, and that Childress was perched on a raised front seat behind some black horses, and that a sort of hood rose at the rear, making a safe black cavern there. She settled into a soft leather seat, pulled Standing Along beside her, and instantly the faint snap of the lines over the croups of the horses started the carriage on its way.

They didn't talk and ·her mind teemed with a thousand questions. Where was the red cart? Where was Skye? Where did this come from? Whose was it? Where were they going? But she waited impatiently, knowing that silence was necessary just then, as the conveyance rumbled softly through the shrouded clay calles of Taos. They rolled around the west side of the plaza where a few lamps lit a few windows, and treacherous light caromed off the ebony carriage, and finally onto the camino leading south into open country.

"Ah, that's better," Childress said. "We'll go down as far as the church and wait for the moon. I'm told the road grows rough and dangerous beyond there, and we'll need the lamp of heavens to guide us."

They proceeded through a vast and cloistered darkness, and Victoria marveled that Childress would drive two horses at all upon such a night. But with each passing moment, they were rolling farther and farther from Taos, and the imprisonment there, and she felt light-headed with relief.

And worried about Skye.

She discovered the Little Person sitting beside Childress, and then felt the evil thing come sit between her and Standing Alone, as if to welcome them to this vehicle.

At last the towers of the great adobe church of San Francisco de Asis at Ranchos de Taos rose ghostly in the starlight, and Childress tugged his team to a halt.

"Now then, my dears, on the seat in front of you is a large package that contains some dresses, hats, and slippers. Ladies, please remove your present outer clothes and put these on. It's important."

"What is this?"

"You are about to be transformed. These are fine silk gowns, worn by ladies of the highest caste."

She explained this to Standing Alone, and they groped about, finding the package.

"I shall be looking straight forward, ladies, and in any case the hood behind you plunges you into perfect obscurity."

She pulled out slippery things, trying to fathom what all they were, and then began to struggle with her clothing, tugging and yanking to lift her dress over her head. But her mind was on other things. "Where's Skye, dammit?"

"On the way to Santa Fe, guarded by soldiers, to stand trial as a Texas spy. Perhaps they will execute him."

"What? How is this?"

"Madam, when we were both prisoners of the prefect, I took great pains to betray Skye, informing the Mexicans that they had nabbed a saboteur and operative of the rebel state of Texas. Of course they placed him under close guard, even as they released me to do as I choose."

"Sonofabitch!"

"Exactly. I refer to myself in just such terms, madam."

A terrible grief welled up in her. Skye in grave danger. This man the cause of it.

"Where are we going?" she asked, darkly, wrestling with clothing she didn't understand.

"Why, we're heading for Santa Fe to rescue him."

She had her dress off, and was rotating a slippery one she could not see, looking for a neckline. Standing Alone was having trouble too.

"We can't see a damned thing. What's the front of this dress?"

"Ladies, that is beyond my realm of competence."

Then Shine leaped gracefully back to them, and tugged at the fabric, and she surrendered to him. Damned Little Person was smart, but as long as he was on her side, maybe she could tolerate him. The monkey chittered and chattered, and then he held it out to her. She discovered buttons. She slid her arms under the fabric and pulled it over her head. Shine bounced and clacked his teeth and made disgusting noises.

She got her dress on and fumbled with the buttons that ran down her bosom. She had scarcely heard of buttons until she had seen them in the settlements.

"You'll find slippers in several sizes. Find some that fit, and make sure they match. I think you will be the queen of Zanzibar."

"The what of damned what?"

He laughed. "Madam, trust me. Yes, the queen of Zanzibar. You're exotic. That will do nicely. Just do this: in company, never speak to me in English. Only in Crow. And tell our friend to use only her own tongue. From now on, you are the queen of Zanzibar, and I am the Margrave Childress, royal governor of Trinidad and Tobago."

She grunted. This was all a mystery to her.

"The more exotic, the better. We will be whatever my imagination requires."

She was pawing the slippers, trying to sort them out, with little success. But off to the east, the sky over the black mountains had lightened, and soon there would be a moon. Maybe she should wait.

"What is this carriage? How did you get this?"

"By nefarious means, fraud and deceit, foul conduct, and criminal sleight of hand. Shine was my accomplice."

Big medicine. The fat man had powers she could barely grasp. She didn't know the half of what he was yammering about.

"This carriage, madam, assures our complete success. I am the queen's royal viceroy of British Guiana, and you are my ladies, and we are touring, looking for an estate."

"I thought you were the margrave, or something."

"Details, details. Trust me."

They sat quietly in the calash while the sky lightened, and finally the white moon rimmed the skyline of distant black peaks. She stared at him, amazed. Childress wore a black suit and silk top hat, a snowy shirt and red cravat, all of it encasing his enormous bulk, and even had shiny black boots on his feet.

"Where'd you get that stuff?"

"I defrauded a tailor, my dear."

"Where did you get *our* stuff?"

"A seamstress defrauded me, cleaned me out of all my loot. I should say that Shine was the generous provider of the means. I did not inquire too closely where he obtained his lucre. Never look a gift horse in the mouth."

She might have laughed, had not her fear for Skye clawed so hard at her.

"What does all this stuff do for us?"

"My dear, we were vagabonds, and now we are people of great rank, and there will be much fawning and bowing and scraping wherever we go. Also, it's very important never to pay for anything. That is expected. When we're hungry, we'll demand food and that will be that. They'll bring it. Royalty never pays.

"Also, you're safe. The two Indian women indentured into perpetual servitude have vanished. Practice looking haughty."

She didn't quite fathom all this, but neither did it matter.

"Now, my ladies, if you are ready, I shall turn around and we shall have a little examination of our wardrobe. By all means, step out and straighten up."

She nudged Standing Alone, and they stepped down from the carriage. Childress stepped majestically to earth, and toured around them in the soft white light of a gibbous moon.

"Ah, yes, a little large, a little long, but we'll have your dresses hemmed in Santa Fe. Tell our Cheyenne friend she has mismatched slippers."

Standing Alone corrected her mistake.

"Yes, yes, you'll do. Queen of Zanzibar, and I'll think of something for her. Mesopotamian royalty, Pharaoh's bastard daughter. But now, the hats, don't forget the hats."

She discovered a broad-brimmed one and pulled it on, and Standing Alone imitated her.

"Yes, yes, quite excellent. Very exotic. Watershot silk dresses and hats with silk flowers on them. I think I shall call her the queen of Sheba."

"What's a queen?"

"A woman chief, or a chief's wife."

"Ah! I'm a chief!" Victoria swept around in a circle, commanding the moon and stars to obey her.

"Well, mesdames, let's go find Skye and rescue him. In that compartment under the seat is all sorts of gear, including clothing for him, sandals, a brace of revolvers, blankets, some beans and a cookpot, a few knives and other fangs, and whatever else I could commandeer from Larrimer. Step in, now."

She stepped in, amazed by the fat man.

thirty-five

Skye stared up into concerned faces. The soldiers peered down at him, but so did a slender woman who knelt beside him, studying him with tenderness.

He hurt. No part of him escaped. But his bowels especially tormented him, always on the brink of convulsion, and he was always teetering into nausea. He didn't want to be moved. He closed his eyes because it hurt to look anywhere, and the morning light tormented his brain. The woman applied another cold compress, but he was already half frozen, and he couldn't comprehend it. He tried to paw her compress away, but she held it firmly to his forehead.

The soldiers were debating; he gathered that much, and wished he could grasp their sibilant, staccato language. He knew what it was all about: to stay here and wait for him to get better, or to load him in that stinking carreta and keep on going. In the midst of all this talk, he heard the old man whose cart had been commandeered, and it was not hard to guess what he had to say about it.

"Agua," he said, and moments later, the woman pressed an earthen cup to his lips. He sipped, feeling the chill liquid slide into him, and the water convulse his stomach once again.

He had been sicker than this before, but never so nauseous, or so filthy from lying among pigs. The Mexicans continued their debate, until at last the voice of the corporal silenced them all: soon enough he would know what the soldier had decided.

The woman continued her ministrations, so Skye opened his eyes to look at her. She was young and pretty and strong.

"Gracias," he whispered. At least he knew the word for gratitude.

She nodded.

He heard the squeak of the carreta, a sound that had been the counterpoint to much of yesterday's travel, and he knew that they would be leaving soon. Sure enough, in a bit they helped him to his feet, and he stepped gingerly over the clay floor of this little jacal and out into the morning sun.

It was a fresh sweet dawn, and he would have enjoyed it but for his wasted and wounded body. Every step hurt, but he made his way to the carreta, where the proprietor of the cart, burros, and the little hogs awaited him. He crawled in, assisted by the soldiers, and discovered clean bedding there. The hogs were next; carried squealing one by one into the carreta, and then the stakes were driven into the holes in the bed, and Skye was off to the meat markets of Santa Fe once again. The dispossessed family watched cheerfully as the cart creaked and squawked its way down the clay pathway. Skye closed his eyes, determined to save his strength and ward off as much pain as he could.

The pigs jostled him, and he realized they were rooting at him with their bristly snouts, snorting softly. Maybe they considered him edible. He pushed them back, but they were curious about him, this third party en route to their executions. They seemed naked as babies.

He had never been on intimate terms with hogs before, so he watched them even as they watched him, and the carreta creaked its way south. They were all watching each other, the soldiers watching him, the weathered old peon watching his pigs, the burros, the swaying cart, and the soldiers, and the corporal riding behind them keeping an eye on them all.

They squeaked and chattered through little settlements, and on each occasion the Mexicans swarmed around the cart, examining Skye and the pigs, whispering and smiling. Skye didn't need to know the tongue to know the nature of the jokes. Swine and foreigners, they were all the same to these grinning people. They even weighed about the same, were the same color, and yielded about the same amount of meat, he supposed.

Mostly he closed his eyes because light pained his head, and he ignored this rural Mexican world, except when the pigs jostled him by rooting around in the straw, or in one case, urinating. A goodly part of the day passed, and the more he traveled on his dubious bed of straw, the more the cart hammered his aching body. His fever did not go away.

Thus the day passed well into the afternoon, and then he was aware of a commotion behind him. When he struggled to his elbows to see beyond the mounted corporal, he spotted a fancy ebony carriage pulled by two sleek black trotters. Not even the light skim of dust over this rig dulled its magnificence. A bulky man in a black suit and silk top hat drove smartly, and behind were a pair of women got up in high fashion, with wide-brimmed hats shading their Mexican faces.

He settled back into the straw. There would be more jokes at his expense, but he was too tired to cope with them, too sick to care.

There was an exchange in Spanish between the corporal and the driver of the fancy rig, and some laughter. He heard the word "Inglaterra," and the corporal said "Tejas," while gesturing toward his prisoner. Texas. England. Were they talking about him? The privates marching beside, their lances over their shoulders, were enjoying the exchange, and glancing covertly at Skye. The two hogs turned and studied this new intrusion upon their lives with alarm.

He closed his eyes and focused on gaining strength. If he

was to survive, he would need to make a good case in Santa Fe, plead the truth and do it so eloquently that the cynical governor might free him. It wouldn't be easy: that miserable Childress had betrayed him so thoroughly he might not have any sort of chance.

The two-rut road wound out of a defile, passed yet another cemetery, and the country broadened into a tawny benchland above the twisting river, marked by dots of green juniper.

Here the road widened too, and the impatient driver of the black carriage eased to his right and began to pass the entourage. Skye struggled up to get a look, and discovered an apparition: driving this elegant rig was *Childress*, got up in a black suit, silk top hat, white shirt, and cravat, and sitting in the rear seat like royal princesses were his wife *Victoria* and his friend *Standing Alone.*

No! Impossible! Delusion! He fumbled into the straw, dumbfounded, and then struggled up again, disbelieving: he was sick, this was simply delusion and mirage, a trick of light. Victoria didn't look like herself; Standing Alone looked even less like herself; the fat man might have been Childress, but wasn't, and all this plainly was a cruel hoax of fate. It had to be a hoax; the women didn't so much as blink an eye, but stared blandly right through him. But yes, there was the monkey, Shine, sitting right beside Childress.

"Look at that hog going to market," Childress said in English, and a voice Skye knew well.

Skye rose and stared at him so darkly that Childress coughed, his hand politely to his lips.

"At your service, Sah. Her majesty's lord viceroy of the Lesser Antilles," he said, and the queens of Zanzibar and Sheba, en route to the capital."

The corporal eyed him suspiciously, unable to grasp English, so Childress enlightened him in Spanish: Zanzibar, Sheba, Antilles.

"Ah!" exclaimed the corporal, impressed by these people of vast importance.

The carriage had pulled alongside now, and Skye stared at the women, his own wife in some outlandish costume that made her look like some Hottentot. She nodded slightly; an eyebrow arched.

"Sick," he said softly. He lifted his bloodstained feet.

She made no sign.

"Love you," he said desolately, something thick and painful filling his chest. Were the women prisoners of that betrayer Childress? Was the Texan relishing every moment of this encounter? Somehow, Skye thought not: this was a rescue effort. "Thank you, whatever you are doing," he muttered.

She pointed at the carriage floor with her toe, and he saw something blue-black lying there; a weapon. And wrapped parcels of provisions. How had this happened? Who had helped them? Had they really come to help him? Where did this rig and equipment come from? How was it paid for? Who was Childress now pretending to be? What would happen?

Dizzily, he sunk back to the straw.

"Which of the hogs will yield the most meat?" Childress asked. "I say, the one in the center, eh? He'll look good, hanging from a meat hook." He translated his witticism into Spanish for the entertainment of the soldiers. They laughed, but looked uneasy.

"We're going to pay a little visit to Governor Armijo," Childress said, cheerfully. To the Mexicans he said, "Santa Fe, el gobernador."

They nodded.

"You should fetch a fine price at the butcher, my good man," he said. "Good flesh, but caved in a little."

Skye felt black rage permeate him, and gathered his strength. Any more of that and he would rise, tear apart those stakes, and land on Childress before anyone could stop him. But he knew better.

Tears had gathered in Victoria's eyes, which she artfully

brushed away under the deep shade of her hat.

"Tallyho, old boy," Childress said, and smacked the lines over the croups of his trotters. The black horses lurched forward, and the carriage swiftly passed the groaning carreta.

The old peon cursed softly. He didn't like rich foreigners, Skye gathered.

Santa Fe. Visiting Governor Armijo. What did that mean? He wrestled with it until he was dizzy. He wrestled with the whole idea that Childress was trying to help him, believing and disbelieving, unable to put it all together. But in the end, he thought that Childress probably was doing just that. Somehow, he had found the women and sprung them from Padre Martinez's grip, and that in itself was a feat. Where had they been hidden and how did Childress find them?

Skye lay back in the straw, his mind awhirl, barely noticing the foulness of the urine-soaked bedding. What did it all mean? He had no answers. Who was Childress? He had called himself most everything, and none of it was true. The man was an enigma; his purposes a mystery.

The swaying cart, pounding on its rough wheels, slowly lulled him into a nap, and so the day passed. By dusk, he was thirsty and still sick, but he had hope, and he knew that something was afoot.

thirty-six

The man called Childress was not a bit impressed. Santa Fe looked to be nothing but a gaggle of one-story adobe buildings that would wash away in the first deluge. If this was a capital of a province, what did the rest of Mexico look like? He saw no brick in the streets, or good carpentry, or any sign that these people had mastered the civilized arts and crafts.

The city was perched on an arid slope and watered by a poor excuse for a creek that was largely unbridged, sawing the town in two. At least the view east and north, into the pine-covered reaches of the Sangre de Cristo Mountains, was grand.

There was scarcely a pane of glass in the city, and people employed rudely fashioned wooden shutters to keep out the cold or let in some light. The clay streets were scarcely wide enough to allow the passage of a vehicle, and his progress through the northern reaches of the little town scattered old women in black, barefoot *trabajadores,* children, and women carrying impossible loads of food or merchandise on their slim backs. Such animals of conveyance as he could see were largely burros, plus a few mules, but horses were scarce.

On the tawdry plaza, ankle-deep in dung, some Yank ox-teams stood restlessly in their yokes while the scruffy frontiersmen gawked at pretty Mexican girls and guarded their trail-worn wagons. The girls tossed them bright smiles and swaying hips and shy glances. Some of the Mexicans wore capacious straw hats against the bright glare of the day, and most wore simple sandals of leather, and not a few carried a folded *serape* over their shoulders, and so were equipped for an instant siesta, Childress supposed.

For the life of him, he could find no public building, nothing that rose above the clutter of little adobe merchant establishments. Metal was obviously scarce: the buildings had none except for the hinges on their doors, and not even all of those were iron. Where was the capitol building or palacio?

He drove his carriage round and about, exciting glances among the warm-fleshed and cheerful crowds, who studied these foreigners closely, their gazes falling upon him in his black suit and top hat, and his two dusky passengers, who managed to absorb these wonders of Mexican civilization without so much as a gesture or exclamation. They played their part well, and the effect of their haughty silence was to make them look blasé and a little bored, which was perfect.

He finally returned to the plaza, having gotten himself lost in the warren of little callejas north and east of the public square, and here he stopped next to a scraggle-toothed Yank teamster who sported a beard that reached his waist.

"Childress here, my good man. Tell me, where is the governor's residence and seat of government?"

The teamster looked amused. He jerked a dirty thumb in the direction of a low building that embraced one entire side of the plaza, a building with a shaded gallery in front of it, and loafers parked in the shade. It looked no more like a seat of government than a country church looked like St. Paul's Cathedral.

"That's the palace."

"That? That warehouse? Thank you, Sah," he said, and wheeled his calash around the plaza once again to maneuver it into a suitable place to park. There seemed to be no order at all; one put his rig wherever one could, and if that bottled traffic, so much worse for the victims.

"All right, ladies," he said, having commandeered a spot. "Step lively. Now remember, let me talk; you look royal."

"Crap," said Victoria.

He handed them down to the grimy gumbo of the plaza, and they hunted for a door to this horizontal mud palacio, and since there were several it would be a matter of luck.

They entered, found themselves within a barracks room, withdrew, and headed to the next orifice, which admitted them to an antechamber of some sort, as plain as everything else in this disturbing city. But at least an orange and green flag of the Republic of Mexico stood at an inner door, and Childress supposed that might herald something.

He tried the door, found it open, and entered upon a shadowed office, lit only by a narrow window in the thick adobe wall. He thought it might belong to a clerk, but the portly man standing within was no clerk. This one stood over six feet, had a long acquiline nose, large features, dark flesh, and straight jet hair combed back. But what astonished Childress was the man's uniform, which was sky blue with white lapels, a crimson sash, polished black boots, a sword in a gaudy scabbard, and acres of gold braid at the shoulders and sleeves of his tunic.

Childress was quite taken with him.

"Señor?" the man asked, politely.

"I am looking for el gobernador," Childress replied.

"Armijo here, come in, and how may I be of service?"

"Governor! I didn't mean to intrude."

"Think nothing of it. *Nada*. That is the way of the Republic of Mexico, which rests upon the will of the people."

Childress listened to the rhetoric, assessing this amazing apparition, and then shepherded his women in.

"Your excellency, I am Sir Arthur Childress, Her Majesty's viceroy for Madagascar and Ceylon, here on a little journey on my own account, and not the queen's."

"Ah! The English! A great nation! And what brings you to our province of Mexico?"

"Ah, Governor, first let me introduce these lovely ladies, their royal highnesses the queens of Zanzibar and Sheba, who have traveled far with me as we search for suitable investments for their endowments."

The governor bowed. The ladies nodded.

"They speak not a word of Spanish, nor do they grasp any European tongue save for a few words of English, so their purpose here is to decorate our little meeting with their dusky beauty."

"Ah!" Armijo gallantly rounded his desk, and clasped the hand of each woman, bowing gallantly to them.

"Sonofabitch," murmured Victoria Skye, which Childress thought was appropriate.

"Now, your excellency, if you could spare us a few moments, I shall describe our business here, and perhaps you can advise me as to its prospects. As part of my task of governing the protectorates, it is my duty to seek financial opportunities for the royal households, and I am here because Mexico is ripe for development. In short, excellency, we are looking to purchase a large estate, one with cheap labor at hand, for it is with such labor that large bonanzas are made."

"Plantations? Don Arturo, this is an arid climate, and not suitable for plantations."

"Ah, yes, but there are gold and silver mines and great livestock holdings, and these are of some interest to me, on behalf of these great ladies, of course."

"Ah, si, it is so. The riches of Mexico are indescribable, and there is abundant labor, and more can be gotten. But tell me, have you spoken to others about all this?"

"Indeed, Governor, we have spread the word wherever we have been, starting in Taos, the ranchos there, and we will continue southward into Chihuahua, Sinaloa, and other provinces."

"And how, Don Arturo, did you come here?"

"By steamer to New Orleans, river packet to Independence, and out the commercial trail with a caravan, past fierce Comanches and wild tribes. But we were not troubled."

"Ah! You have seen the commerce."

"We think there is great profit in it. And I have good English capital to put into it."

Armijo flashed a great smile, baring even white teeth. "Then it is up to me to persuade you to invest in Nuevo Mexico, si?"

"Well, your excellency, you can start by describing the labor situation, for there is no profit to be gotten from an estate without plenty of cheap help."

Armijo shook his head. "Oh, some merchants here profit without very little help, señor, but yes, the great estancias, or haciendas, or mines, are built upon the backs of many hombres."

"What does it cost?"

Armijo shrugged. "What is the price of food and some rags?"

"How does it work?"

"The hacendado indentures his help, and pays them in food and clothing and shelter; it is very simple."

"And they work for that, excellency?"

Armijo shrugged. "Some don't."

"And what of them?"

The governor smiled. "Ah, this is the land of opportunity, my friend. Opportunity for you, and for me. I have many resources at hand, and can find just what you are looking for. Land, labor, mines, livestock, titles to property, influence. For a small consideration to the public purse, of course."

"Ah, Governor, how secure is it? I have heard that the wild men of Texas are even now marching. I must think of the safety of our investments!"

Armijo frowned. "Any invasion will be crushed swiftly. There will only be a crowd of vultures feeding on the gibbets."

"That is good news, your excellency. The Texans are a rabble, and have no regard for human life."

"They are braggarts, too, and cannot speak without exaggerating their powers and virtues. My English friend, consider me your reliable friend and the person in office who can steer you toward a successful venture."

"Well, your excellency, yes, there is something you can do."

Armijo's eyebrow arched upward.

"Labor is the secret! I should like a list of the hacendados and mining associations that employ much labor. And these I will visit and talk to at length."

"Consider it done. Come back before the sun sets, and I shall have a list for you. Are you sure there's no more?"

"Oh, your excellency, there is always more. What does one do for entertainment in this noble capital city?"

"How about an execution?" Armijo asked. "Only an hour ago, I received word by courier that a Texas spy will be here in the morning. We handle such things with dispatch, my English friend."

"Ah, yes, keep me informed. The queens are avid for executions," Childress said. "How will it be? By shot or noose or garrote or ax?"

"We practice marksmanship," Armijo replied.

Their business done, they were ushered out of the governor's chambers, and it was then, in that plain adobe antechamber, that Standing Alone shrieked and swooned, but Childress caught her just before she fell, even as a coppery serving girl gaped.

thirty-seven

Standing Alone collapsed into Childress's arms, a strange, guttural sobbing racking her. The thin serving girl stood, paralyzed, bewildered, and then began edging away.

Victoria cried out to her: "Wait!"

But the teenaged child, her gaze riveted to the woman in fancy clothes and a great hat, cried out, and then backed away.

"No!" cried Victoria.

But the girl vanished into the private rooms of the governor's palace.

Childress, seething with curiosity, helped the stricken woman to her feet, and signaled to Victoria, who began talking to the Cheyenne woman in the lingua franca they had worked out.

"Ask if that was her daughter!"

But Victoria had already done so. She nodded. "Yes, in all likelihood, but it happened so fast that she's not sure. The girl! Right age, right face. The strong cheekbones of her people. Little Moon is the name she was given."

"She must be sure. We need to see her. And then, if it's her daughter, we must plan. Fast!"

Standing Alone stood now, gulping air, staring at that

massive wooden door where the serving girl had disappeared. The gaunt girl was barefooted, wore only a simple shift of unbleached muslin, minimal clothing, the least possible cost for a slave.

"She must be sure. We must see that girl again. They must talk to each other! If this is her daughter, it's a stroke of luck! Maybe she knows where her brother is."

But Standing Alone was mute, staring at that forbidding wooden door with great iron straps holding it together, a door that must lead from this antechamber to the governor's private apartment in this long box of a building. He was tempted simply to barge in, take the women with him, and plead ignorance of local custom if they ran into trouble. Get a look at that girl one way or another. And if she was Standing Alone's daughter, begin to plan, plan, plan.

"Victoria, tell her we'll sit here in this waiting room. This is a room where people wait to see the governor. A reception room. See the benches. If this was her daughter, the girl might recover soon enough, and come peek, eh?"

Victoria nodded. She looked cross, as if Childress were intruding on some private matter, some women's prerogatives. But she led Standing Alone to the cottonwood bench, and there they sat. Childress didn't mind. His mind was teeming with ideas. He had Skye to worry about, and as yet he hadn't any notion of how he might free the man. Things were happening too fast. He had supposed he might have days, even weeks, to work out a scheme, a bribe, a trick, a political ploy, an escape. But this was Mexico, and trials and executions scarcely lasted fifteen minutes.

They sat in the anteroom, waiting. Occasionally Mexicans entered from the plaza, glanced at these exotic foreigners, vanished into one door or another. Others emerged from the governor's chambers, and left. The girl didn't return. Then, when the plaza door opened, Shine leaped in, and with a bound settled beside Childress, tugging his sleeve and reproaching him for ignoring his friend and ally. Childress rubbed the monkey's back, and the monkey chittered and delicately scratched his own belly.

The girl did not appear. Time was wasting! Childress's mind teemed with schemes, but nothing gelled. He strolled outside. His trotters were restless. They needed water and a rubdown and some good feed. But they would have to wait. He couldn't leave here. He surveyed the plaza quickly, noting its bustle, the babble of many voices from many lands, the street vendors, the carretas, burros, young women sashaying along, the dogs circling. When Skye arrived, these people would all amass right here, drawn by gossip and rumor and the thrill of death.

He returned and settled again on the bench in the anteroom. The women stared at that silent door, willing it to open, willing that child, not so much a child anymore, but a woman, to open it.

And she did, an eternity later. The door creaked. Deep in shadow stood that girl, peering at them, safe in there, ready to slam the heavy door shut in an instant.

Standing Alone had removed her hat, the broad brim of which had veiled her face during the first encounter. Now her sleek jet Cheyenne hair, parted in the center and drawn severely back, was not hidden.

They stared. Standing Alone groaned, and staggered to her feet. She said something in her own tongue, a name, Childress guessed. Little Moon. Little Moon! The girl cried out, looked about fearfully, and closed the door in the very face of her mother. But then she opened it a crack again, and Childress saw the mother reach out and touch her daughter, and her daughter touch her mother, and he heard the sound of soft keening in the gloom. Then someone came in the plaza door, and swiftly the inner one slid shut. But moments later it groaned open again, and there were furious whispers.

"Tell her we'll get Little Moon out," Childress said to Victoria, but Skye's wife glared at him, as if he were interfering with something sacred. Childress sighed impatiently.

Standing Alone was crying softly, and the girl, still deep in shadows and fearful to come out of the door, stood tautly, choking back her joy and terror.

He turned to the monkey. "Go," he said. The spider monkey sailed through the air, slipped into the darkened door, and tugged at that dim figure within, but the girl only squealed in alarm. There was a new volley of whispering between mother and daughter, and this time Standing Alone reached down to pat the monkey. So Little Moon was learning about the monkey, and that was the next step: *expect the monkey*.

It seemed a long visit, growing more dangerous by the second, but then the girl begged off. Standing Alone cried out, but the girl slipped that dark door shut. Only then did Victoria help her friend back to the bench, and the monkey joined them, clucking beside them.

Slowly Standing Alone translated, with fingers and words, everything that had transpired, until Victoria got it whole.

"It's her, Little Moon. She's not sick. She wants to go. She's damn afraid. She works for the governor, makes food, cleans up, and he's got big medicine that can track her down to the sunset or the sunrise and throw her into a hole. She's plenty sick with worry."

"How's Standing Alone?"

But he didn't need to ask. She sat there, rapt, her mind a thousand years away, something so sweet and beautiful on her features that Childress marveled. For all those years she had sat at Bent's Fort waiting for news, waiting for this very moment. And now it had happened. She had *seen her daughter*, whole and unharmed.

"Tell her that we'll think of something," he said gently.

Victoria nodded.

"Did they make plans to meet again?"

Victoria shook her head.

"We know where she is. We know how to reach her. Now

we've got to do some planning. Skye's coming soon. We have no time at all! I thought we'd have days to work this out."

Victoria stared at him so darkly, with so much pain in her eyes, that he was driven back by it.

"Come along outside now. It won't do to linger in here. I'm the royal viceroy. You're the queen of Zanzibar," he said.

She only stared at him. Right now she was no one but Victoria Skye and her friend was no one but Stands Alone of the Cheyenne people. Nonetheless, at his beckoning, they abandoned the Governor's Palace and stepped into the bustling plaza. No time, no time!

The horses were restless, but he chose instead to walk his women around the plaza. They needed to walk. It was as if walking was their salvation. He could not walk far, his enormous bulk paining him with every step, but this time he plunged forward, the women on each arm, Shine resting on his shoulder and drawing stares and laughter.

The plaza bustled with vendors selling dulces, tortillas filled with hot meat, and tamales, and he was reminded that he hadn't a cent. They hadn't eaten for some while. The horses needed feed and water. Yanks were haggling with Mexicans about the contents of those begrimed prairie schooners that had just come in from the States. Oxen drooped in their yokes. But no ideas came to him. Rarely had his good swift mind failed him so utterly.

The toured the plaza, and Childress settled the women in his carriage. He peered at their hungry, distraught faces, and then at Shine, who sat beside him, picking his nose.

He glanced about, fearful of discovery. "Fetch," he said to the little creature.

The monkey sprang gracefully to the clay, and then in bounds, clambered to the roofs, and dropped downward again, hidden from view. People squealed, jostled one another for a look at the little fellow, and he swung upward, the projecting vigas of the adobe buildings offering him his own walkway. Then he vanished. Childress waited patiently, trying to look as though he had no part of any of this. When the little fellow did appear, it was so suddenly that Childress startled in his seat. Shine simply bombed down from a rooftop into the carriage, one of his little hands clutching his loot, several steaming tamales wrapped in cornhusks, and carried in a sheet of coarse brown paper.

"Ah, the pirate has struck!" Childress said, his stomach growling with anticipation.

He doled out the meal, furtively watching the crowd, which had failed to notice Shine's arrival in the carriage. The monkey ate one of the tamales himself, licking his fingers and smacking his hairy lips.

And then, as swiftly, he was gone again, swinging casually along the roofs, unseen by anyone this time. Childress didn't like it. He wanted to get out of the plaza. The ebony calash and its handsomely dressed occupants were drawing too much attention in this rude frontier town. He waited itchily, irritably, and finally with anger, but the monkey did not reappear.

He turned. The women had finished eating, and were staring at him. The anguish in their faces touched him to his core.

Then Shine appeared, this time with more booty: a small burlap sack of white beans, rustled from some grocer. They would have to be cooked somewhere, but there was nourishment in them.

White beans. A plan bloomed in Childress, at last. He eyed the monkey, wondering whether there was time to train him.

thirty-eight

*M*aybe they were expecting him. As the carreta creaked into Santa Fe, silent crowds lined the narrow streets; almost as if they knew who he was accused of being, and what his fate would be. They craned their heads as the cart and the soldiers and the old peon walked by, but they weren't examining the soldiers or the hogs or the old man; they were studying Skye, the doomed.

It was hard to focus his mind. He had been four days in the cart along with two hogs, and most of it he had been fevered. But last night, at a village north of the town, he had felt a change within himself, and within the hour his flesh was cool. That crisis had passed; he now faced another, vastly darker and more menacing than anything he had ever experienced. All because he had been falsely accused by one who called himself a friend.

He had rocked along the stony trails hour after hour, the hollow plodding of the little burros carrying him closer to his doom with every passing minute. Santa Fe was oddly silent, as if all commerce had ceased; as if even the wind had turned timid. He heard only the heavy breath of the weary burros, and the ceaseless groan of cottonwood axle against hub, as the carreta grumbled toward the governor's palace where matters of life or death would unfold.

The crowds thickened as he approached the plaza. Most stared silently, but then a young man spat at him as the carreta passed. And often he heard that whispered anathema, "Tejas!"

These were mild people, neither fierce nor armed. They peered at him solemnly from faces used to sunny living. The bronzed laboring men, creased by sun and chapped by wind, watched impassively, but the dons, most of them tricked out in gaudy coats and white lace and fancy boots, nodded shrewdly and whispered to those beside them.

For all Skye knew, a Texan might be as exotic as a macaw or an orangutan or a rhino to them all. A shirtless little boy picked up some dried offal and flung it, but a woman's voice halted him in his tracks. These were civil people.

Skye cringed at their gaze. Ever since he had entered this nation, he had been paraded about, subjected to stares, made to endure the most humiliating of circumstances. Were not those gazes punishment enough for any man? But there was more to come, darker, crueller, the special fate of some in this nation that celebrated death, welcomed it with flowers, let itself be riveted by it, and looked for any excuse to experience it, playing it toward a climax of terror. A gentle people with a violent lust.

The old peon, whose name Skye had never discovered, began chattering with the corporal, and Skye understood at once: the man wanted his caretta and hogs back. The corporal nodded. The peasant would receive his property in moments, as soon as this enemy of the republic had been deposited at the palacio. The pigs stirred restlessly, knowing somehow that they were as doomed as the mortal between them. They squealed and grunted, and Skye thought they were even groaning. This was the end of the road for the three penned by walls of stakes rising from the cart bed.

Then, suddenly, the entourage burst into the plaza, and the corporal steered them straight to the low building commanding one whole side. Skye saw that ebony rig there, and knew Childress and the women were present, though he did not see them. He could not imagine what they could do: even if all three were armed to the teeth, they could do nothing. If Childress intended to get Skye out of the fix he had put Skye into, Skye had not an inkling of any way to do it.

The carreta creaked to a halt and the guards formed up at either side of the cart. The corporal lifted the rear stakes and beckoned Skye to crawl out. A silent gawking crowd pressed close now, eager to see the man who was now alive and soon would be nothing but a corpse.

They escorted him into a gloomy barracks, where a dozen soldiers had collected.

One spoke some English:

"There," he said, pointing at a pail. "Clean up. Then get into this." He gestured toward a bunk where some unbleached cotton clothing lay. "The gobernador, he hate smells. He got nose bigger than you, even."

"That would be a big nose," Skye said.

These men weren't abusive, neither did they push him around. They were gentle, at least for now.

He turned his back on them, pulled off his fouled shirt and pants, and washed. He doubted that he would get rid of the pig smell for the rest of his life . . . which might last one hour, maybe two.

He eyed the barracks furtively looking for miracles, loaded cannon, conspirators, rebels, hideyholes, anything. But there were no miracles in that whitewashed room. He tied the cord that held up his loose-fitting pantalones, and faced them. He felt himself tremble.

Then he waited. He sat, taut, waiting, waiting. He tried to pray, he tried to think of Victoria, of London, of blue skies. But he could think of nothing; there was only the endless waiting, and the desperate hope that he might be freed. What did they have against him?

He would make his plea, tell the exact truth, look for every chance, let nothing escape him. For he was not yet dead and as long as life pulsed in him, there was hope. But not much hope. He could scarcely fathom just how he had arrived at this place, to face this fate, when all he wanted was to free two children in bondage, and leave Mexico just as it was, a peaceful and friendly country for the most part.

The corporal nodded, and now the blue-clad soldiers formed lines to either side of him, and at a command they escorted him, boxed among them, through an interior door, into an antechamber, down a hall, and into a public room of some sort, high-ceilinged, with hand-hewn vigas supporting its roof. A crowd had collected there, and the air felt choking even though the shutters were all opened. Skye had the sense that not one more person could crowd into the chamber. They watched him silently, as the soldiers cleared a way to a dais.

On the dais there stood a tall man with hooded eyes and an air of expectancy, in a fancy blue uniform, the muted light glowing from the golden thread that decorated his epaulets and sleeves. The governor, no doubt. Armijo. The man who would turn thumbs-up . . . or thumbs-down.

The soldiers led him there, to a place before the governor, but lower, so that the governor looked downward, as if from some great height. The man smiled, nodded to a black-clad balding clerk, who rose.

The crowd hushed. At the rear stood Childress all got up in his new black suit, and Victoria, and Standing Alone. He stared at them, loathing Childress for all of this, loving his wife and their friend, seeing them for perhaps the last time, all the feeling within him caught in his throat. Victoria nodded, ever so slightly, but in the faint movement of her head lay a universe of yearning. For whatever reason, she could give him no more, and he did not question it.

The clerk addressed him: "The governor of the province of Nuevo Mexico has asked me to translate. I will truly tell you his every word, and tell him all that you say. He informs you that you are charged with spying for the army of the rebels of Texas, and that you may respond now."

Skye scarcely had time to think: all this was occurring with such breathtaking speed that he hadn't given much thought to anything.

He tried to speak, but his throat froze up; everything within him died in his mouth. He was not far from tears. Then from some far corner of his heart, he remembered a line from a psalm: "Yea though I walk through the valley of the shadow of death, I shall fear no evil; for Thou art with me . . ."

The terror lifted. He turned to the governor, who was watching him as a raptor watches a rabbit.

"I do not know why I am here," he said slowly, letting the clerk translate into sibilant Spanish. "I came here to your good nation peacefully. I am told I am a spy. I am not. I am not a Texan either. My purpose was to find two children of the Cheyenne tribe, and if possible, return them to their grieving mother. That is all . . ." He started to say he had come with his wife, but thought better of it; the statement might endanger her and Standing Alone. "I swear before God that I came here in peace; that I have no connection with the Texans, and have never been in contact with them."

He waited as the clerk droned on. The entire city, it seemed, was crammed into that tight space, and was listening closely.

"I ask you, what is your evidence? Where are your witnesses? Who accuses me? Do I have the right to confront my accuser?" He refrained from glancing at Childress with all that. "Where is a lawyer to defend me? What are the laws that I face? Can you show me any evidence? Any at all?"

He waited until that had been conveyed.

"I ask for a real trial; present your evidence; let me rebut it. Judge the case on its merit, and on its truths. I am innocent."

That was all he had to say.

They waited for more but he shook his head.

Armijo smiled and began speaking. "The gobernador, he says that the evidence is sealed and comes from a reliable informant in Taos, and without rebuttal, he finds you guilty as charged. But because there is some small chance that you are innocent, he will put the matter into the hands of God. He will count out nine black beans, and one white bean, and place them into this earthen pot. You will draw a bean. If it is white, you shall live."

That excited the crowd, which stood tautly. Skye knew how they were thinking. They were already seeing the execution, and feeling it in their bellies. They were hearing the snare drums, watching the condemned walk to the wall, listening to the padre recite a prayer, watching the jefe tie a blindfold over the eyes of the condemned, watching with morbid delight as the condemned was tied to a post before the wall, the man who was now alive, but in seconds would know nothing at all; knew the words that would come, once the soldiers lined up with their good clean rifles, and the command came . . . *fire!*

Yes, it was there in their faces, the swift intakes of air, the sweat, the eagerness, the fine, bright horror, the thrill that swirled through them all like a snake.

Slowly, the governor counted out the nine black beans and the white bean, showed them to all, and dropped them into the pot. Then he nodded.

But Skye stood still. "I will not participate in the travesty of justice. If I am to die, let the blood be on his hands, not on mine."

The clerk translated the response: "Draw a bean, or face the firing squad. If you are innocent, God will protect you."

Skye shook his head. So it had come down to that.

"If you will not, then I will," Armijo said.

Skye stared, refusing the participate in his own doom.

The crowd tensed. Armijo waited.

Then the governor reached into the pot.

thirty-nine

Skye stared at Armijo's nose as the man's hand lowered into the tawny earthen pot. He could not look at the man's hand.

"Don Manuel!"

The voice was familiar. The governor paused. Childress stepped forward, pushing his way to the front of the rapt crowd. A long dialogue ensued and Skye understood none of it. But strangely, Childress kept pointing at the monkey, and Armijo kept examining the monkey, as if Fate were somehow connected with the simian.

Skye felt his knees buckle. There was only so much a man could endure.

Then, finally, the governor nodded to the black-clad clerk who had translated for Skye. The clerk gestured toward Childress. "That hombre is a high official of the government of England; I don't quite know his title. That ape of his is a prodigy. What this Englishman said is this: Your Excellency, you must not take into your hands the will of God. Only a poor dumb creature like this monkey of mine should draw the bean. He does that all the time, reaches into things and pulls them out. Let him do it, and then the will of God will truly be known. And the governor, he says, well, he doesn't like that, but maybe it is best; the blood of a man will not be upon him but upon the monkey. And so it is to be."

Skye gripped himself. He was in the hands of that miserable little spider monkey. His *life* was in the monkey's hands. Well, no; his life was already over. Nine black beans, one white. The monkey would make no difference. This was nothing but another small entertainment for the Mexicans, and they would soon be calling Shine the Death Monkey.

Skye nodded. The mode by which he was to be condemned to death, by monkey paw or human, did not matter.

And with that, the clerk stepped back and Childress led the monkey by the hand. It jumped up to the table where the clay pot rested malignantly, its earthen belly filled with death and life.

Now the silence deepened into unbearable tautness.

"Fetch," said Childress.

The monkey peered in, rattled the beans, battered the sides of the pot until it rocked on the table, thumped and hammered, a living thing as the monkey's paw pillaged its interior. And then, slowly, the monkey lifted its paw and held it open for all to see.

A white bean.

Skye stared, mesmerized. The monkey held the bean high. White, *white*, no mistake.

Armijo stared at the monkey, stared hard at Childress, stared hard at Skye, stared bleakly at the women with Childress.

Skye felt wobbly, faint, and caught himself before he fell to the floor.

"Miragro," breathed the clerk. Miracle.

The monkey chittered and grinned and licked the bean.

Governor Armijo held out a hand, and the monkey dutifully deposited the bean into the governor's hand. He inspected it, peered into the pot, squinted darkly at Childress, and finally nodded.

"Ah, señor, he says, so be it. God above has spoken. You are free."

But Armijo was still muttering.

"He says, Señor Skye, that if you are guilty, you will be found out and executed without a trial, so that no monkey can conspire against the justice of the Republic of Mexico."

Skye nodded. "Tell him justice was done. That's all I have to say."

"Ah, señor, I will say so."

The crowd didn't drift apart; on the contrary, people gathered around Skye, touching him, this man saved from death. One woman kissed the sleeve of his rough shirt, and then made the sign of the cross.

But Armijo stared, first at Skye, then at Childress, and at the monkey.

Childress pushed forward, the women trailing.

"My dear sir, let me introduce myself: Sir Arthur Childress, first baronet of Wiltshire, and an emissary of the queen. Let me congratulate you on your good fortune, Sah."

Skye was speechless. The clerk hovered closely, registering every word. It would soon be filtered into Armijo's ear in another tongue.

"I wish to introduce you to two ladies traveling with me, their highnesses the queens of Zanzibar and Sheba. I am viceroy of Ceylon and Andaman Islands, looking for investment opportunities in this magnificent land."

"The monkey saved me."

"No, my good sir, it was the will of God."

Skye supposed he should be grateful, but the bitterness at having been betrayed did not leave him so swiftly.

"I will be on my way, sir."

"I hear some England in your voice, Sah."

"London."

"I thought so! A fellow subject!"

"I am no one's subject."

Childress looked astonished.

Skye moved away, not wanting any more to do with Childress.

"Wait, Sah, how about some tea, eh?"

"Some other time." Maybe Childress thought he was acting, for the benefit of the watchful governor, but Skye had no intention of rubbing shoulders with Childress again. There would be no more deadly accusations, or rescue by means of a clever monkey.

He pushed through the gawking people and out the door. No one stayed him. He sucked air into his lungs and surveyed the deserted plaza. His knees were close to buckling. People still swirled around him, pointing, whispering, the man who had escaped death, but he ignored them.

He found Victoria staring at him, and he nodded. There were tears in her eyes. Somehow, they would need to unite, but not now; not for this crowd to witness. He saw Standing Alone there too, and there were tears in her eyes. They simply stood in the warm sun, under the free blue heavens, and stared at him, and he stared back, shaken to the core.

Childress was smart enough to stay away. Skye was ready to punch him in his fat gut.

A Mexican approached him: "Come with me, sir," he said in flawless English.

Skye did.

The thin, handsome man, with a hawk's nose and a raptor's air about him, led him into a handsome mercantile on the south side of the plaza, built entirely of wood rather than adobe, and well stocked with manufactured goods that plainly came from afar.

"Manuel Alvarez, United States consul. I am a Spaniard, actually, not a Mexican."

Skye shook the man's hand. "Mister Skye, sir. Formerly a subject of Great Britain."

"And?"

"And now a man without a country."

"You must wonder why I've asked you to come here." He led Skye toward a large and cluttered desk in an elevated cubicle in the center of the store. "Here," he said, handing Skye a note.

It read:

> Steer clear. Shine will fetch you. We are
> working on plans. I have asked Alvarez to
> help you. He has seen this.

It was unsigned.

"I don't know what it means, Mister Skye, but I will assist if I can."

"Is there anyone who needs labor?"

He surveyed Skye, who remained clad in the soldiers' castoffs. "You have no means, eh?"

"None."

"What did you do before you came here?"

"I was employed at Bent's Fort."

"Bent! He is a great friend of mine." Alvarez paused. "You are on good terms?"

"Yes, sir."

The merchant seemed to be coming to some conclusion. "I suppose you could pick out your necessaries, and I could send the bill to William. Would he honor it, and would you repay him with labor or by whatever your means?"

Skye nodded, too exhausted to talk. He was so tired from his scrape with death that he couldn't speak.

"Help yourself, Mister Skye."

'Thank you." But Skye lacked even the strength to shop, and slumped into a chair.

Alvarez took one look at him and trotted off, leaving Skye to gather his strength. When the consul did return, it was with a steaming pot of tea and a cup.

"You English need your spot of tea," he said, pouring into the cup. The smoky pungence of Oolong filled the raised office that overlooked the whole floor.

Skye sipped, and nodded to Alvarez.

"Mister Skye, if you're not occupied, perhaps you will join my wife and me for supper. We follow the custom of our old country, and eat rather late by your standards. Around nine. When the bells of La Parroquia ring at sundown, that'll be vespers, and you just show up here after that. We're up-stairs."

"That's a great kindness."

"No, not really; I want to get your story. You interest me."

An hour later, wearing a blue ready-made shirt and gray twill woolen pants and some squeaking ready-made shoes that didn't fit well, Skye left the emporium.

He wandered aimlessly, still reeling, and found himself drifting along an alley.

There, before a butcher shop just off a corner of the plaza, hung the pink, fly-specked carcasses of two small hogs.

forty

ean Lafitte Childress took a swift inventory: he had nothing except time. Now that Skye was safe, matters weren't so urgent. He could go about his next steps without feeling the pressure that had harried him from Taos to Santa Fe in time to halt an execution.

The most urgent business was the trotters, which were drooping in their harness, played out by the hard trip and lack of feed. That posed a problem: that Taos seamstress and a few purchases en route to Santa Fe had cleaned him out; he didn't have a peso to pay for their care, and he knew there wouldn't be a blade of pasture grass within miles of this busy town.

He glanced at the women, who were settled back into their carriage seat awaiting his decisions. They would be all right, even though he could not put them into an inn or posada this evening. They were women of the tribes, used to hardships that would swamp white women.

"Horses next," he said to Victoria. She stared back at him so solemnly that he shrank from that gaze. Skye's ordeal had been her own, and it was not yet over for her; not until they were a thousand miles from this dangerous place.

He drove slowly through the plaza, stopping at last beside an ox-team and some Yank teamsters. The big, red-bearded oaf would do just fine, he thought.

"I say, Sah, is there a livery barn here?" he asked.

"Not as they call it," the Yank said. "But they got a yard. Just foller this creek that cuts the town, down a bit, and it's maybe a quarter mile below."

"They'll put up stock, hay, and feed?"

"They got plenty of hay, and mostly some grain too, but not oats. It's likely to be maize, or maybe barley, all depends. But it'll put some pull back into them trotters."

That was welcome news. "I, ah, haven't made my banking arrangements yet, just arrived, letter of credit to cash. Do they want something in advance?"

"Mostly, but you can allus dicker. I once traded a pound of nails for a night's feed for my whole ox-team, time I arrived late once. Nails is an item around heah, worth a plenty to people that don't have foundries."

"Just dicker, eh?"

"You got it, friend. Where you from?"

"Ah, Trinidad and the Azores."

"Reckon I don't know where that is, but I'd guess south."

"There, you know more than you think! Well, you've been a help."

The teamster waved. Childress set his weary trotters into a slow walk through town, struck the shade-dappled creek, and headed downstream until he found a large stockyard fenced with crooked cottonwood poles. A haystack rose nearby, and some rude adobe shacks lined the perimeter.

He approached the gate, and found a wiry Mexican hostler.

"You take care of these horses, hay and grain?"

The man nodded.

"How much?"

"Dos," he said. "Por dia."

"Pay you?"

"Si, Amando, that is me."

"All right, Amando, a generous feedbag for these nags, rub them down, water them, and put them on hay. There'll be a tip for you in it."

Childress helped the women down. Shine landed at his feet. The hostler drove the carriage through a chattering gate and closed it. It would be a long hike back to the plaza for a man of his girth, but he was determined to go. There was a girl to rescue, and a meal to be found, somehow. He eyed the monkey, his salvation in times when his belly rumbled and protested.

It struck him, as he stood looking at the adobes of Santa Fe just up the creek, that this was an uncommonly sweet place, nestled into the sheltering crook of the mountains. The pungent scent of piñon pine smoke filtered his way. Odd, how peaceful was this place, with its azure heavens, its pine-clad slopes, its earthen homes, its smiling warm-fleshed people. He had never been in love with any place, but suddenly this rural village smote him, and he could not say why. Only a few hours earlier he had seen this place as a miserable gaggle of mud huts.

He took in arm each of his woman friends, and strolled slowly back to the gentle village, admiring the great cottonwoods that lined the creek bank, the staircased tan adobe buildings, the velvety air, the riot of flowers here and there, where least expected, the strange light that sharply limned every building made the whole place seem almost holy, almost sacred. He wondered how such strange thoughts could stir him.

Santa Fe was an old city with old ways. They strolled up narrow streets, past languid people who were in no hurry, past a hostelry called the Exchange Hotel, and an adobe Yank store called Seligman and Clever, and when they finally reached the plaza, near dusk, they discovered that much of the town was strolling, apparently an evening diversion, many of them arm in arm, laughing, enjoying that heady cool air and the great hush of serenity that embraced Santa Fe.

The Governor's Palace loomed darkly, it massive doors closed, and no light rising from any of the narrow, grilled windows. But these public rooms were not the governor's private apartment. They strolled by, the women on his arm, Shine sometimes beside them, attracting much attention and whispers, and sometimes swinging along the roofs, from viga to viga, unseen by those below.

Somewhere, within that long low building, a Cheyenne girl toiled and pined for another life. He scarcely knew how to rescue her. He scarcely knew how to feed himself and these two women he was suddenly responsible for.

Off the plaza were gambling parlors and eateries, their windows bright with yellow lamplight. Shine didn't wait; at the next one, a place on San Francisco Street, he dodged in, startling people, chittering and nattering, catching bits of food tossed at him, popping the morsels into his mouth, licking his hairy lips, and finally absconding with some hot buns. These he deposited at the feet of Childress, outside, who plucked them up off the grimy clay, and handed one to each woman. It would be the start of a meal, Shine-style, one item at a time, rifled from a dozen sources. But they would be fed.

The plaza darkened as the twilight faded, but the paseo did not cease. People walked, gossiped, courted, flirted, and maybe did a little business as they strolled the streets at sundown.

When Childress and the women next passed the shadowed Governor's Palace, everything changed. Deep in the gloom behind a barred window, a girl cried out.

Standing Alone slipped close and whispered furiously, even as Childress stood casually by, hoping the strollers would not see anything amiss. They didn't. For a woman to be talking to someone within was as ordinary as a sunset.

"How do we get her out?" he asked.

Standing Alone's powers of speech obviously weren't adequate; Victoria strained to understand. But finally, it came clear: the great wooden doors were locked with an iron key for the night. The soldiers took care of that. But one way out remained, through the barracks and into the plaza, right past the soldiers.

Childress thought swiftly: "Tell Little Moon to try it; walk out past the soldiers. Smile and walk."

Another great whispering ensued, and finally Victoria told him that the girl could not do that: the soldiers would catch her and do bad things.

Shine jumped up to the window and sat there, nattering at them all.

"Try it, take him into the barracks, let him amuse the soldiers."

The girl absorbed all that, after Victoria had conveyed it to Standing Alone. The monkey squeezed past the iron grille and jumped into the darkness within, chittering softly.

"All right! We must be quick! The barracks door is right over there," he said, pointing at a narrow orifice cut through the thick walls.

He hurried the women to where the door stood, a silent barrier between an Indian girl and her mother, and a reunion long overdue. There was a lamp lit in the barracks; light filtered under that door.

For an endless time, nothing happened. Santa Feans drifted by, though their ranks were thinning now as night enveloped the city, and they repaired to their homes for their late suppers.

The stars were popping out. The vast black bulk of the Sangre de Cristos loomed in the east, dark and mysterious. A breeze brought upon it the scent of juniper, and cooking food, and maybe even the freshness of the peaks.

He heard muffled noise within, maybe laughter, male, amused.

He eyed the women. They had heard it too. He nodded: they would head straight across the plaza and vanish into a narrow dark alley. He didn't know what they would do if soldiers burst out, in pursuit of the little servant.

The door opened so suddenly that light seemed to explode from within. He heard laughter. Caught a glimpse of Shine, bounding out; then came the girl, stumbling, breathless, out into the dark plaza, ghostly in white. He closed the door swiftly, plunging them back into the sheltering dark.

"Ayah, ayah," cried Standing Alone, who was hugging this lost child of hers, this thin, haunted girl.

"Come," he whispered in a voice that brooked no dissent. How long would the soldiers take to decide something was amiss?

He hurried them into deepening dark. Light spilled from various windows in the plaza, but in its heart there was the sheltering gloom that fell over them now.

He heard the soft sounds of weeping, and then they were out of the plaza and into one of the little streets that would lead them downslope to the river. For the moment, they were safe.

But only for the moment.

forty-one

s weary as he was, Skye knew where he must go and what he must do after leaving Alvarez's store. He pushed one foot ahead of the other across the plaza, and then eastward on San Francisco Street toward the twin towers of La Parroquia. He clambered up steps; the church stood on a low elevation, and then he plunged into its darkness, which foreclosed a brilliant afternoon light.

He waited just within the nave for his eyes to measure the gloom, and then headed toward the gilded altar with its glowing reredos and golden tabernacle. He chose the foremost pew, for he wanted to be as close to the Mystery as he could be, and there he sank to his knees and buried his head in his hands, and thanked his God for deliverance.

"You have spared me the eternal night. You have brought me through the trial. By what means I don't know, but it doesn't matter. I know only that I live and You spared my life. That I breathe here before You, and that I am thankful for your mercy, and for the breath that ebbs in and out of me, and for the chance to be here," he said, aloud, his voice echoing.

He tarried there in the solemn darkness, cherishing the safe silence, barely aware of the comings and goings around him, for his soul was utterly devoted to this thanksgiving. He did not know why he lived; only that he did. He hadn't a cent, but at least he could give the thanks that rose upward through him.

He rested there in that safe pool of silence, drawing strength even as he gave thanks, and after some while he stood, bowed, and retreated through the nave, and out into the blinding sun of Santa Fe.

He was alone. His wife was somewhere nearby; the others were nearby too. But he could not contact them; they had to remain strangers. He ached to be with her, but she remained well hidden. Wherever Childress was, she would be. He could come to no conclusions about him: his rescuer, perhaps; his accuser for certain. But he was tied to him by Fate for the moment.

He trudged wearily toward the creek that bisected the town, the Rio Santa Fe, and settled himself against a cotton-wood tree, wanting only to watch the clear water from the mountains shimmer by. Children gawked at him, and he smiled at a girl who was frowning. She scampered off into the safe orbit of her mother's skirts. He had no children. Victoria had never conceived. Someday, God willing, he would have his sons and daughters.

And so he rested that sunny afternoon in the dappled shade of the riverbank, alone and penniless, yet rich, for anyone who lived was by that very fact incalculably wealthy. Nothing owned by Midas could equal the breath of air in his lungs.

Something about Santa Fe reached out to him; he could not fathom just what, especially since he had come so close to doom in this very place. And yet, here he was, filled with a strange, aching delight in these warm, unhurried people, and in this pueblo that seemed so close to the sky.

Time slipped by and he never noticed. Then the bells of La Parroquia lifted him out of his reverie, and he grew aware once again that he was deep in Mexico, that the sun had fallen below the western horizon, and that he was expected for dinner at the residence of the American consul.

He stood, summoning energy. He could not remember ever having enjoyed such a pleasant sensation before; the lavender twilight, forested green slopes, golden buildings, the windows spilling lamplight, the dry, piñon-scented air, the deep peace. He stretched, and walked back to the plaza and Alvarez's store, and ascended to the second floor.

The consul was expecting him, and led him into a generous room that overlooked the plaza and was furnished with mission-style pieces and fussy bric-a-brac. Handsome oil portraits of grandees hung on the walls.

"Mister Skye, make yourself at home. May I serve you some burgundy? My esposa will be here in a moment."

Skye declined. A glass would throw him into a stupor. He wondered if he could even stay awake through the forthcoming dinner. Alvarez poured himself a generous glass of ruby wine.

The thin, hawkish consul introduced Skye to his equally thin fluttery wife, who could speak no English but welcomed the visitor with a warm smile. These people were opening their home to him. The señora vanished into the kitchen regions.

"Here's to life," the consul said, lifting his glass.

Skye nodded.

Alvarez eyed him. "I confess to some intentions," he said. "I have heard something of your story, public gossip, but I should like to hear it from you if you wish to tell it. It behooves a consul to be watchful."

Skye wondered if watchfulness was all, but he didn't mind.

"It's no secret. If you wish to know, I will tell you."

He had always been frank about his purposes, but he wondered now whether to mention Childress, and decided that for the moment, he would be cautious about that.

"I came here to look for two Indian children who were

abducted from Bent's Fort four years ago by Utes, and who probably are in Mexico toiling as slaves, or indentured in some fashion. I have with me my wife, of the Crows far to the north, and the Cheyenne mother of these children, Standing Alone, who has kept a vigil all these years. At the moment, I don't know where they are. I had little enough to begin with, but we hoped we might purchase the liberty of these young people if we could find them . . . and if they live." He waited for some reaction from Alvarez, but received none. "But Jicarilla Apaches took all we possess, even our clothing. We arrived in Taos with nothing, and I soon was in trouble."

"A Texas spy, yes. They thought they had caught a dangerous man."

"I'm not a Texan. Not a Yank. There it is; there isn't much else to add."

"A strange story, a generous impulse, Señor Skye. There were more risks than you imagined."

"Still are," Skye said. He was fighting drowsiness and did not know whether he could stay awake through a meal. A brush with death had drained him.

Alvarez stared out the open windows, onto the darkened plaza. A breeze eddied piñon smoke into the room. "This nation of good people has certain arrangements that cannot stand much scrutiny, señor. The treatment of its Indians is one."

"Peonage?"

"Ah, that they defend gladly. The hacendados think it is a great kindness to the humble. The simple ones are guided; they toil, but then they are cared for until they die. But the Indians, señor, that can be another matter . . ."

"I guess every nation has its dark corners, Mr. Alvarez. Consider the Yanks and their slavery. The Texans are a slave republic."

"Mexico isn't, or so it says, but everyone knows better. And that is a warning for you. If you ask too many questions, nose about too much, you will discover enemies facing you, and they will be formidable, and if you do not flee them, you might find yourself in trouble just as grave as what you faced this day."

"Thank you for the warning."

"The Indians are used and thrown out, quite literally, in the mines. There are a few gold mines not far south of here, and there the Indians spend their lives climbing ladders made of notched logs, carrying heavy baskets of ore to bring to the arrastras, where stones grind the ore, and there the Indians waste and die for they are scarcely fed. In two, three, four years, they are gone, wolf-bait. That is the fate of so many. Terrible accidents, too. Nothing is done for their safety. The ladders fall or twist, spilling human life. A flood washes away the diggings. Dust and dirt ruins their lungs. Ah, it is a grim thing to see.

"It is worse even than the black slavery of the American South or Texas, where slaves are costly and most masters at least feed and clothe them, if only to protect their property. Señor Skye, there are many in those terrible pits who have no clothing at all, not even a cloth about their loins, and who must work in all kinds of weather, fierce heat, bitter cold, or they will not be given their gruel. There is no flesh on any of them, and within a year they are skeletal, and by the second year, they are weakened, starved, and sick, or dead."

Skye sighed. Standing Alone's boy, if that is where he ended up, would not be alive after four years.

"Ah, I have told you the worst! It is not always so bad. There is hope for you. A few captive boys are employed as herders on the great ranchos, and theirs is a better life. They eat; they are clothed and sheltered. But mostly the Indians go to the mines; the sons of peons are indentured as herders. The Indians don't seem to rebel; they work until they drop, and one hears nothing about uprisings."

Skye sighed, remembering his years of captivity, the pain,

the lashes, the toil inflicted on him when he fought his masters; the small rewards that came to him for causing no trouble: an extra morsel, an occasional light task.

"But let us talk of pleasanter things," Alvarez said. "You brought your wife?"

"We were separated. I am looking for her, and our Cheyenne friend."

"In Taos?"

"I was seized in Taos and brought here by soldiers."

"Ah, she could be far away."

Skye said nothing. He hated to mislead this hospitable man.

The hostess appeared, and with a nod invited them to her table, which was sparsely set. Bowls of leek soup steamed at three places.

"The señora invites us, Mister Skye."

Alvarez led his guest to the table, settled himself, paused to say a grace in Latin, and smiled at Skye.

"Start, señor, for much more comes soon, eh?"

Skye thought he would be starved, but found himself sipping slowly, all appetite gone, wanting only the solace of sleep. His kind host understood, ate quietly, and did not press conversation upon this man who had escaped death that very day.

Skye nibbled, struggled to stay awake, and stared out the dark windows, where the breezes of Santa Fe filtered in.

And there, sitting on the sill, was the monkey, peering directly at him, waiting for recognition. Skye startled, but the monkey was already gone, swinging easily into the night.

forty-two

here was no time for tears. Standing Alone threw a blanket around Little Moon, even as they hustled the girl away from the plaza, into the darkness of the street called San Francisco, and then the street called Galisteo, and then to the riverside street called Alameda.

There the night was so thick one could scarcely see. A little moon, only a silver sliver of itself, hung low, throwing no understanding on anything.

But at last they paused. The fat white man was puffing. Victoria of the Crows was beside them, guiding the girl. Standing Alone turned her child to her. She was a woman now, not a girl, thin, sad-eyed, but whole. The girl had scarcely spoken, but now she clutched her mother's arm.

"*Nah koa, nah koa!*" she cried. My mother, my mother.

So she remembered the tongue of the people. Standing Alone feared that she might have lost it after four winters of speaking the Spanish tongue.

"We have come," she said. "We will take you to the People. There will be great joy among us."

The girl, at last, trembled, and Standing Alone knew the tears would well up soon, but there was so much to learn.

"Are you sick, Little Moon?"

The girl sighed.

"Are you a maiden? Did you wear the rope?"

"They do not know the rope."

That was answer enough. "We will take you to the People, as one returned from the dead, and the corruption of the body will float away. The gourd singers will come and they will rattle away evil. We will purify you with sweet grass and juniper, and make the smoke flow over you, like the clean scents of the winds, and then all the People will rejoice, and bring you gifts, and we will be a stronger people because you have returned, Little Moon."

The girl's great courage seemed to leak away from her.

"Quickly, where is your brother?" Standing Alone dared not name his name for fear he did not live.

"*Nah nih,*" my brother. "I do not know. He was taken away by the men long ago."

"By the Utes?"

"No, the Utes brought us to the pueblo of the north called Taos, and then the Mexican men took us here."

"You know nothing?"

She hung her head, as if in shame for having no answer. "The last word the lost one who was my brother spoke, quickly, was that he would be taken to where the yellow metal is dug out of the breast of the world."

The mines. Victoria had told Standing Alone that the mines are bad, and now this bad news.

They hastened through the night, guided only by the burble of the Santa Fe River, the fat man leading the way, suddenly nimble on his feet. He had found a place for them to hide from the winds this night; inside the domed canvas roof of a big wagon that had rolled into town, now parked beside the yards for the horses and mules and oxen. This place he got for them by talking to one of the bearded white men who drove the oxen with whips. It would be a haven for this frightened girl, this girl of her womb, who had come back to her as from the other side, and now filled her with a joy that made her burst.

Victoria, who had excellent eyes for the darkness, led them to the place of the wagons, and soon they were sheltered within a big one. None of the bearded white men were around; they were in the earthen buildings of Santa Fe, drinking the whiskey there, and gambling away their money.

Little Moon shivered, and her fear permeated the inky place where they had found a haven. Standing Alone held the girl, her hands soothing and comforting, and felt the girl quiet in her embrace.

"Now tell me how it all happened, from the very beginning at the trading house of William Bent," Standing Alone said softly. "I will help our friends understand. We have words enough to talk a little."

"It was so long ago," Little Moon said. "These friendly old women of the Utes came to us, all smiles, and motioned to us to come with them. With signs they said they would give us gifts. Ah, gifts! We smiled back, and that was our mistake. My brother and I went to receive the gifts, walking across the grasses to the place where these Mountain People had made a camp, and as soon as we walked among their lodges, they threw blankets over us. I cried out, and so did the one who was my brother, but they wrapped us tight in blankets, and we heard the sounds of great effort: the Utes were leaving.

"And so we were taken away, the blankets over us, and I could hardly breathe, and no one cared about my tears. I was on a horse and someone was behind me. If I struggled, he beat me hard. It was a long time before I saw the sky again, and when they let us look around, I could not tell where we were, and the big fort was not in sight. And then I knew I would not see my people again, and I was a Cheyenne no more, and that I would face a new life, not a good life, very bad."

She fell silent, and Standing Alone did not urge her to talk. Little Moon was reliving so much in her mind that it was well to let her alone.

"We were watched," she said. "Always, someone was seeing to it that we could not run away. The one who was my brother tried to whisper to me, but they separated us so we could not make plans together. They gave us a little of their food, but we were not abused.

"Then, many days and nights from the white man's post, they began to slow down, and made camp, and hunted, and the band lived as if no one was pursuing them, but they were always careful. And then after maybe a moon, they started up again, and we were taken south to this land, through dry country where the water was poor, and this happened many days. I was not allowed to talk to the one who was my brother, but sometimes we waved; sometimes at night we whispered.

"We are going to the land of Mexico, he said one time. And that was so."

Standing Alone knew it had to be something like that. The Utes did that often. She listened as her daughter described the trip to Taos, the whispered bargaining with Mexicans in the night, and then the Mexicans gave the Utes four horses and blankets and axes and knives, and the powerful Ute warriors dragged the children into the light of a lamp, where they could be seen by the new owners, and then the Utes left.

"It was very dark that night; the one who was my brother was afraid of these new men who made us stand naked so they could see if we were whole. We whispered, but they told us to be quiet. Then they made him dress, and that was the last I saw of him. Just before they took him away, he said he was being taken to the place where the yellow metal is dug, and so I knew a little."

She wiped a tear from her eyes. "I have not seen my brother again."

Standing Alone translated for Victoria. The fat man, who spoke a little Cheyenne, listened intently in the dark, as the night breezes flapped the canvas of the wagon.

After Standing Alone had finished, Little Moon continued.

"I was brought here to this place, and there was much talk, and I was given to this chief of these people. He is very important, this Armijo, and he needed much help from women to keep his big house clean and his clothes washed and much food for many guests, and that is what I have done for four winters."

Her voice broke.

"What I do, it is never enough."

"Did you try to return to the People?"

"I thought much about it. But this Armijo, he has a man and woman who tell us what to do, and warn us that we will die if we do anything bad, like go away. We must be like this until we grow old, that is our fate."

"Until now."

The girl sobbed now, while Standing Alone conveyed the story to Victoria.

"We are going to find the one who was your brother, if he lives," Standing Alone said.

"You do not know . . ."

"We know it will be hard. But we have friends here, strong and wise to the ways of this country."

Little by little, Victoria conveyed the rest of the story to Childress, who sat silently in the dark. Then they talked in English, the tongue Standing Alone did not know well, and she wondered what they were saying. It was so hard, this traveling with people who did not speak the same language, and now they were in another country with still another tongue. The People possessed one tongue among so many, and that is why they were banded together, but knew so little of others.

Finally Victoria turned to her, and in their patois, she got the idea across. Childress, the fat man, was moved and grateful, and vowing to search to the ends of the earth for the missing boy. He was pleased that Little Moon was in good health, and soon would be in good spirits if that medicine was strong.

But now they needed to get her man, Skye; Childress knew how to do that. Skye would be with a merchant on the plaza if he had not found someplace else to sleep. It was time to go get him, while the darkness cloaked their movements.

And here Victoria's voice quivered, for she had not been with her man since the drawing of the beans from the jug, and there was such pain in her voice that Standing Alone grew aware that Skye had come to the edge of death, and all for her, because he and Victoria would not even be in this place if they had not agreed to help her find her children.

"Yes, go," Standing Alone said. "Bring him here, so that I can thank him and we can be together."

"I will go back to the plaza with the fat one," Victoria said. "And the Little Person, who will find my man for me."

"Ah, the Little Person! He is a great warrior."

Victoria snarled something. She never did trust that creature. "Maybe we will leave tonight. I don't know. But now I go back to the plaza," she said.

Standing Alone watched the others clamber out of the wagon and into the starlit night, and moments later their ghostly forms were gone.

She pulled Little Moon to her bosom, and held her daughter in the great sweet silence, and rejoiced.

forty-three

The American consul Alvarez lit the way down the long stairs with a candle lantern, and bid Skye good night.

"Señor, you have no place to go," he said, questioning.

"I have never had a place to go since I was a boy," Skye replied.

Skye stepped into the dark plaza, smelled the freshets eddying down from the Sangre de Cristos, noted the deep starlit heavens, the black rooflines of buildings around the square, and waited. The little monkey had summoned him; the monkey would find him. Victoria hated that monkey, and Skye could never understand it. The monkey had constantly aided them all.

Now he heard a soft chittering. He walked blindly into the plaza, following the sound, and suddenly found the others looming out of the depths of darkness.

"Skye, dammit," Victoria cried, and she wrapped her arms about him, hugging him fiercely, and he felt her thin, bony body pressed tight against him, and her hands possessing him. He hugged her joyously, this woman who had been his friend, lover, mate all these years.

"Victoria!" he whispered.

"I think maybe I never see you again."

"I'm here."

Victoria's hands found his face, the stubble of his beard, his neck. He scraped a rough hand down her back, the embracing filling and blessing him.

"Ah, Skye," said Childress. "Come."

Skye paused, his anger welling up in him, but he contained it. The man had gotten him into mortal trouble—and then had gotten him out of it.

They led him out of the plaza. He trusted Victoria's eyes because he could see so little at night and the sliver of moon didn't help any. Santa Fe this night was as dark as anyplace he had ever been.

He felt Childress's heavy footsteps beside him.

"I will explain it all," Childress whispered. "Rejoice! We have good news."

Skye thought the man would have a lot of explaining to do to make it right.

He was being led gently downslope and south and west; that was as much as he could fathom. But eventually they struck the Rio Santa Fe, and he was oriented.

"We have recovered Standing Alone's daughter," Childress said, after they had reached the river.

Skye stopped dead. "You *what*?"

"Little Moon had been employed in the very Governor's Palace where you spent a fateful hour, working for Governor Armijo. We ran into her utterly by accident. Standing Alone started to swoon; the girl fled. But we succeeded. We have her!"

"You have her now?" It was all too much for Skye.

"We do; we executed a little maneuver this evening."

"Is she well?"

"Ah, Skye, Sah, what is slavery but the destruction of dreams and hope, eh? She was a prisoner, what they call *criados sin sueldo,* servants without hire. A convenient set of muscles to be used at labor, a mortal without the hope of a life."

Skye marveled that this self-proclaimed privateer and pirate could speak so eloquently of slavery in its various forms and subtleties. But Childress was an enigma, and there was no point in wondering about him. Nothing on earth could explain the man.

They proceeded downriver to a place where livestock were penned, and numerous wagons lurked in the slight light of a sliver of moon.

"Here, Sah, is where we are domiciled," Childress said, steering toward one big Conestoga that he somehow singled out of the gloom.

He stood outside the mammoth conveyance. "Standing Alone, we are here," he said.

The monkey bounded inside and Skye heard a rustling and voices. Victoria clambered in, and soon stepped through the puckered canvas, followed by two women.

"Hey, this here is Little Moon," Victoria said, her voice crackling.

Skye found a gaunt Cheyenne girl, fear visible in her face even in that sparse light. But her mother was talking swiftly, and soon the girl's fears subsided, and she even smiled at Skye.

He held out his hands and the girl took both of them shyly. Standing Alone clasped her hands over the girl's, capturing Skye's hands in their embrace. They were thanking him with tears and clasps and sighs.

This was a strange, sweet moment. For just this had Skye thrown aside everything else and come here. Before him was one of the missing children, a young woman now, safe and free—at least if they could smuggle her out of Mexico.

He knew that Armijo would probably put things together: Childress, pretending to be a British diplomat; a girl vanishing from his staff; and Skye, released from death by Childress's monkey. Give those odd facts to a man as alert and suspicious as Armijo, and there would soon be a platoon of soldiers tracking them all.

He held these hands a long moment, for he shared their joy, and wanted them to know it.

They repaired to the dark confines of the wagon where they would be safe from wandering gazes, and there Skye learned their story: Childress's amazing acquisition of the carriage in Taos, obtaining the dresses for the women, a suit of clothes for himself, spare goods, a little food, a few knives, even a rifle, all by mortgaging his stock of goods up on the Arkansas River. All of it the work of a self-proclaimed pirate.

Skye sighed, unbelieving. What was Childress? Trader? Texas Colonel? Filibuster? Pirate? Rescuer of Indian children, a man absorbed with slavery and justice? What sort of alchemist was he, transmuting the base metals of his character into gold?

"I accused you, Mister Skye, Sah, because one of us had to escape and deploy. It worked, eh?"

Skye felt his rage boil up, but there was little to say. The man who had put him in such jeopardy got him out, somehow. Or the damned monkey did.

"Shine palmed a white bean?" Skye asked.

"Ah, Skye, I trained him to leave the black beans alone."

"It's *Mister* Skye," he snarled. "Mister Skye and don't call me anything else."

That ended it. Skye felt his rage and terror leak away, like blood from a cut wrist.

There was too much to absorb. Skye sat quietly, leaving his fate to the rest. His weariness was telling on him again. Victoria's hands found him in the dark, each caress loving him, each touch of a finger reaching beyond his flesh and into his soul.

Finally Childress broke the quiet. "We have a good idea where the boy, Grasshopper, is, if he's alive," he said. "The last thing he said to Little Moon was that he would be taken to where gold is scratched out of the earth."

Skye sighed. Chances were, the boy would be dead, then.

But at least they had fulfilled half of their goal; they had rescued a sweet Cheyenne woman.

"I made inquiry, Skye. As a Briton looking for a good investment, I had a perfect cover. I'm now a baronet, Sir Arthur Childress. Where would a man invest in gold mining? I asked. They said no foreigner could work the gold deposits. But that didn't deter me. I said I might make a considerable payment to the governor for some land in the goldfields. Well, Mister Skye, Sah, I got the whole history."

Skye nodded. Now Childress was calling himself a baronet.

"Back twelve or fifteen years ago, Sah, a herder stumbled on some placer gold, loose gold flakes trapped in gravel, you know, not far south of here on the east slope of the Ortiz Mountains. There's plenty of it there, and it's very pure, assays at .918 pure, almost as good as it gets in nature. But there's not much water there for washing it, so mining has been slow and most of the washing's done in winter, when snow can be melted. They have chopped deep into the gravel there, and employ slaves to do it, all Indians. Much of the ore is trapped in a conglomerate that needs to be broken up.

"There were some later discoveries of vein gold farther south, but most of the work is taking place scarcely thirty miles from here. They use the most primitive methods, Sah. Wooden vessels called bateas to wash the gold. Arrastras, rude stone grinding devices powered by bullock. Slave labor hauling the sands upward in baskets, climbing ladders fifteen or eighteen feet high, nothing but notches in a log. There's a bit of a town there called Dolores, and that's where we will go."

"All right."

"But there is risk, Sah. A few years ago an American named Daley headed that way, wanting to buy in, and he was murdered. The murderers never were brought to justice and Armijo did nothing, even under the most intense pressure from the Americans in the area, including the Bents. But what was a mere murder of a heretic Yank? So nothing happened. So the lesson was learned at the mines: outsiders are fair game. We'll need a plan, Sah. Arms, defenses, everything."

"You know how to get there?"

"Certainly. A British diplomat can find out anything."

"We go in that rig? Your black carriage?"

"It will convey us all. You shall drive; I and the three women will occupy the facing seats, and oh, what a fine sight we'll be, eh?"

"That's what worries me."

"Never fear, Skye. This little simian accomplishes wonders."

"It's *Mister*. . . ."

"Touchy, aren't you. Well, first we have a little problem to work out. I'm in hock. Have to pay the hostler here for graining and haying the nags. Haven't a cent of cash, you know. Pirates make a poor living, Skye, I assure you. It's feast or famine, but mostly famine. We're going to have to pay, or the hombre will set off alarms and we'll have a squad of dragoons riding us down."

"Daylight is our enemy, Childress."

"Can't be helped. But never underestimate my monkey."

forty-four

hildress padded through the murk of predawn
amid a hush that was not even broken by the
morning song of a bird. He had Shine bounding
along beside him in great frolics, plotting perfidy, and he had
Skye with him as well.

"All right," Childress said. "You get out on the plaza, stay
in shadow if there is any. Watch the barracks door. If any
trouble starts, just drift back here and let me know, and I'll
whistle Shine away from his nefarious duties."

"I don't like this," Skye said.

"Mister Skye, old friend, it's justice. We'll simply extract
from the governor a small repayment for the four years of
free labor he got out of that poor girl."

Skye stared. Childress knew what he was thinking.

"Sah, I know you don't approve. But we are engaged in
an act of liberation, not theft. Call it restitution. He paid her
nothing; now we shall extract a small price, and without his
consent. Nowhere near the value of her labor, Sah, but a small
recompense even so. By my reckoning we ought to extract a
hundred pounds from the devil to balance things up."

Skye nodded, and reluctantly headed for the silent plaza,
while Childress and his cheerful primate, who was growing
agitated, circled around to the rear of the palace where there

were barred windows, their shutters opened to the night breeze. The bars might foil a human but not the skinny monkey.

No one stood about. The predawn murk remained so thick on this southwest side of the mountains that Childress was all but invisible.

"Go," he said, and the monkey bounded up to the window in tumultuous leaps, peered about, and vanished within.

Childress waited nervously. Nothing stirred in the alley, but he heard the distant groan of a carreta. Some peasant on some early mission was passing by somewhere near.

Nothing changed. Childress paced. Then the monkey appeared on the sill, clutching something shiny. It leaped downward and handed Childress a silver candlestick holder.

"No, no, this will never do, you idiot. The hostler won't accept it and he'd report us. Take it back, you little bugger."

The monkey chittered and clacked his teeth. He could bite hard, and those clacking teeth were a warning that he was not to be trifled with.

"Shine, my apologies. Just try again. Something less, ah, incriminating."

The monkey bounded gracefully upward to the sill, bearing his candlestick holder, and vanished into the silent interior.

Childress thought he heard voices within, but strain as he might to hear, he couldn't be sure. He wondered how Skye was faring out on the plaza.

Then Shine materialized on the sill, clutching something dark, and jumped down to the clay. This object was mysterious, and Childress couldn't fathom what it was until the monkey handed it over. It proved to be a handsome humidor of enameled sheet metal with an elaborate design on it. Childress pulled the tight-fitting top, and discovered twenty or thirty fine cigars within, their pungence nectar to his nostrils.

"Ah! You little beggar, you've done it! Bravo, you little pirate."

The monkey bared its teeth and then sucked its thumb.

Childress hastened down the alley, rounded the corner, waved at Skye, and then proceeded away from the plaza. Skye caught up with him.

"A humidor full of fine cigars," Childress said. "Now, weigh this in your scales: any Mexican male, upon given a fat black cigar, will stuff his mouth with it, light up, strut and swagger, and make a great noise so that all the world can witness his machismo. I imagine it'll pay our feed bill, and the hostler won't suppose anything's amiss, either."

"You know Mexicans better than I do," Skye said, doubt in his voice.

They were soon out of Santa Fe and back in the livestock yards, still before sunrise. They returned to the big wagon and settled in without waking anyone except Victoria, though the Conestoga creaked.

Not until the wagon yard was stirring did Childress judge the time to be ripe for the exit. He lumbered over to the ancient hostler, who was shoveling hay with a big wood-pronged fork.

"Ah, señor, I have yet to manage a financial transaction so far from England. I have pounds but I am temporarily without pesos. However, I do have means," he said in Spanish to the wary and wizened man. "Look, señor, at these fine Havanas, eh?"

Childress stuffed one into the man's rough hands. "It's yours, all yours, *un cigarro*. Sniff it, taste it, roll it under your nostrils, covet it, you lucky hombre."

"Ah! Bueno!"

"I'll give you four, cuatro, more of these fat wonders for haying and graining my trotters, eh?"

The hostler was not about to surrender. He held up ten fingers.

"*Diez!* But these are worth two pesos each!"

The man wagged ten fingers.

"Ah, very well, ten it is," Childress said.

Ten fat cigars, payment in full, and now they could leave. He doled out his pungent payment, the hostler nodded, and pointed at the harness. Childress set to work.

A while later they were all seated in the ebony calash, and Skye was driving down an obscure dirt road that would take them to the Ortiz Mountains, which formed a purple sunlit mass on the horizon. The trotters were making music with their hooves.

Childress sat facing the women, enjoying the sweet chill air of early morning and the tawny and purple vistas of this arid land. They were off on the last lap, the final mission, and with luck, they would succeed. He opened the humidor and pulled out a cigar, debated whether to offer one to Skye, decided not to, and chewed on it unlit. When they came to a place where he could employ flint and steel, he would try to fire it up. Meanwhile he waggled it with baronial vigor.

Childress was in a very fine mood.

"Give me one of those," Victoria said.

"You? But madam . . ."

She glared. He surrendered a cigar and she stuffed it into her small mouth. The sight was disconcerting, but he began to enjoy it. What better than a fat cigar for the queen of Zanzibar?

The day passed gently; the carriage making good time over a bare excuse for a road. Perhaps by mid- or late afternoon they would raise Dolores, the hamlet where they intended to sojourn. They pierced deep into arid blue mountains, passing arroyos that carried no water.

"We should make plans, I suppose," Childress said, turning to Skye.

"It's your show," Skye said.

Childress watched him, concerned. Ever since Skye's narrow escape from the firing squad, he had not seemed to be himself.

"Well, we have to find out about the mining. How the Indians are kept in line; how they're punished or enslaved.

Their quarters, if they have any. Clothing. Have we spare duds? The boy will be naked or nearly so. We can't hustle him out of there naked."

"Will he know his mother?" Skye asked.

Victoria, who was listening, translated for Standing Alone.

"She says he probably would, but not in this stuff she's wearing."

"I don't want her to change, not just yet. I don't want anyone who might seem Indian looking around at Indian slaves," Childress said.

"I think we'd better wait and see," Skye said. "This is a gold mine. There probably will be guards. We don't even know whether we can buy the boy; simply pay for him and walk away without trouble. What's the price, and how do we pay?"

Skye's caution annoyed Childress. "Pah! We'll find him, just as we found Little Moon, and slide him out."

Skye said nothing and Childress took it for disapproval. Well, what did it matter?

They encountered more and more traffic, mostly people afoot, walking who knows where? But they also met with carretas, some carrying hay, others squash or produce, heading toward the mines. It would take a deal of food to keep hundreds of miners alive. Childress noted the garden patches, the adobe jacals, the herds of sheep, ribby cattle, and goats, often attended by a herding boy. But mostly this was a harsh land of barren rock, scanty grass, cactus, juniper thickets, and forbidding blue canyons that seemed to keep secrets.

The herders and peons gawked at them as they trotted by; no doubt they had never seen a rig so handsome, or men and women so fashionably dressed. The ladies looked elegant; Childress was the soul of gentility. A few of the Mexicans spotted Shine, perched beside Childress. They obviously had never seen a monkey. Shine licked his hairy lips and picked his nose, and sometimes bounced up and down on the quilted seat. That was good. Childress intended to make an impression, especially of wealth. Little could they guess, these humble, weathered, sun-stained people, that they had more wealth than everyone in that calash put together.

"Skye, we need a plan," he reiterated, annoyed at Skye's passivity.

"All I need to know is who you are and what we're doing here."

"I'm the viceroy of Borneo and Tahiti, that's who I am," Childress snapped. "And I'm here to look at obscene investments, and these are royal ladies of Timbuktu and you're my hired man." He laughed.

Skye stared at him.

They rolled into an adobe hamlet called Dolores, a scrabble of little square earthen buildings and a cantina in a gulch hugging a yellow slope. As humble as it was, it served the mines. They were in the Ortiz Mountains, and the last chapter would soon begin.

forty-five

Skye was discovering a new way to be a prisoner. He was helpless to resist Childress's follies simply because Childress could speak fluent Spanish while Skye could barely speak a dozen words. Wherever they went Skye was utterly dependent on Childress to deal with the Mexicans. He didn't even know what Childress was saying to them.

So Skye sat in the front seat of the calash, minding the horses, wondering what Childress would say to the people there in Dolores or to the mine owners, and it was not hard to imagine a dozen ways of getting into trouble.

One American had already been murdered here for poking around too much. Gold did that. Gold aroused passions and turned men into animals. And here was Childress, fluent in their tongue, floating one preposterous story after another, poking around wealth that Mexico guarded zealously. And there was Skye and the women, inevitable victims of any blunders Childress might make.

Skye halted the coach at the mercado, which seemed to be the only store in this rude settlement.

"I'll inquire," Childress said, lowering his bulky body to earth.

"I'll go with you," Skye said sourly. Maybe someone

spoke English, and if so, he wanted to know it.

"Yes, see what's in the place whilst I jabber with these people," Childress said, flapping toward the store like a penguin.

Shine landed beside his master and swiftly aroused the interest of half a dozen barefoot men, who eyed the monkey with amazement.

"Don't let that monkey steal one damned thing," Skye snapped.

"Tut, tut, Skye. You owe him your life and your liberty."

Childress plunged through a doorless doorway along with the little primate, and Skye followed. The dark interior revealed the simplest sort of store, with rough burlap sacks of beans and rice and sugar on the earthen floor, some crockery and tinware, sewing items, and little else. All lit by a late-afternoon sun.

Childress scarcely looked at the foodstuffs. He pulled one of his fat black Havanas from his breast pocket, lit it with a brand plucked from the beehive fireplace within, sucked and exhaled until the tip of the cigar glowed bright orange, and then approached a stocky woman with vast bosoms who seemed to be overseeing this rural emporium. Childress was soon talking and gesticulating and patting the stolid woman on the shoulder, while Shine cased the joint, looking for plunder.

Skye couldn't grasp a word of it. For all he knew, the Texas pirate was describing them all as buccaneers, bandits, crooks, abusers of women, escaped prisoners, heretics, murderers, and desperados. From time to time the woman glanced at Skye and at the monkey, and sometimes out the door toward the fancy carriage where the women sat expectantly.

But the Mexican woman didn't seem to grow excited. Plainly, she was giving Childress directions, pointing southward, lifting her thick arms up and down as she talked.

Childress nodded, patted her, and at the last, gave her a

fat cigar. She sniffed it, smiled, bit off the end, and stuffed it between her stained teeth.

Skye studied her and the other Mexicans lounging about. Plainly they were rural laborers, mestizos mostly. Nothing about them suggesting mining, and he doubted that any were miners. These were the weathered ones who hoed and scraped those fields they had passed, the ones who fed the miners if the rains came.

Childress bowed, lifted his silk top hat to the woman, settled it again on his sweaty brow, and retreated into slanting sunlight, beckoning Skye. The monkey followed, barehanded.

"There now, I've got what we need. There were seven holdings originally; now it's two after some consolidating. They employ Indian labor exclusively. She says the Indians make good workers and don't need the whip. All we have to do is keep on going. The first, the Blessed Saint Ignatius of Loyola Mine, is up ahead, and employs maybe a hundred, she thought, but counting that high taxes her mind. The other is smaller, Santa Rosita, and she couldn't say for sure what it employs. Ah, we'll find the bugger yet, eh?"

"Maybe. What did you tell her about us?"

"Is something wrong with you?"

"What did you tell her?"

"What does it matter? We're Finland royalty. I eat caviar. We have the queens of Van Dieman's Land and Iceland to amuse us, and are looking for gaudy investments."

"That's trouble."

"Ah, pah! Mister Skye, you're a worrywart. Leave it to Childress. Leave it to Shine, the phenomenal burglar."

Childress clambered into the calash, rocking it under his vast bulk. Skye settled himself wearily in the van, and urged the trotters forward. A thick coating of dust covered their sleek black hair.

The canyon widened abruptly ahead, forming a plain compassed by slopes. A dry riverbed ran beside the rutted road, and even though the summer had not progressed far, a great aridity marked the land.

A gash disturbed the rolling land just ahead, and as Skye drew close he beheld a giant pit swarming with human bodies. A single adobe shack stood on the brow of a hill. Off to one side stood some rude rectangular adobe buildings, probably quarters for the miners. A gulch had been dammed to provide some water.

But it was the pit that riveted Skye as he drove the trotters alongside the gaping hole in the earth. The solidified gravel rose in benches, which supported rude ladders of sorts, each hacked out of a single log. These were notched for the feet of those using them, but they lacked a handrail or any other means by which a person could steady himself. Yet the workers were climbing and descending these rickety devices while carrying huge baskets of ore.

"Look at those poor devils, Mister Skye," Childress said. "Swarms of them, like ants."

Skye slowed the horses. The sight horrified him. Those thin workers were bent double, no matter whether their baskets were loaded or empty. Years of brute labor and the weight of tons of ore had bowed their legs and twisted their spines, until not a one of them could stand upright.

Most were naked. A few wore loincloths of some sort. None had shoes or sandals. Nothing protected them from the harsh summer sun. They toiled ceaselessly, some at the bottom level hacking open the gravel, others loading baskets with crude wooden shovels, others parading up one ladder and another, delicately balancing the burdens while inching upward, one notch at a time until they reached the next narrow bench, and the foot of the next rickety log ladder. One misstep meant death. And there would be no pensioning of cripples. Above, somewhere out of sight, the ore was being heaped into a pile that jutted into the brassy blue sky. Skye wondered what sort of labor proceeded up there, and how the gold was extracted from this crumbling gravelly matrix.

He reined the horses to a halt, transfixed at the human anthill before him, where men threw long shadows in the low sun. These workers were small, wiry, bent, and bore terrible wounds across backs and calves and thighs. One labored with a stump of one arm. A few had tied a rag around their forehead to hold their jet hair back from their faces, but that was all the cloth Skye saw on most. He saw very little gray hair; these bent-over mortal males were young. Or were they all male? He studied them closely, his eyes uncertain. Maybe some were girls, but they all were so thin that none had breasts.

They did not notice the black carriage above, or at least pretended not to. Skye wondered where the overseers were, the ones who forced labor from this pitiful gaggle of captive mortals. He had been right; none of these had been at the mercado, and not one ever would enter those cool confines.

"The *gambucinos,*" Childress said.

"Slaves."

"Theoretically not slaves. No such thing in Mexico, they insist. Indentured workers on the books."

"Can they walk away?"

Childress laughed.

Below, a thin bent man stumbled on the second notch of a tall ladder and fell back, spilling his ore. Instantly, a crowd filled the basket again. The bent man shouldered it slowly, and stepped upward on trembling legs, one notch at a time. Skye thought that man was on his last legs, and wouldn't last another week.

"Skye, get on with it. The manager's up ahead, there."

But Skye was in no hurry. He waited to see if the trembling slave would make it. He looked for water barrels to satiate the terrible thirst of these miserable slaves, and found none. He saw none of them resting or recouping. There was only the sight of shining, bent backs of coppery little men, yellow dust caking their bodies, and the big gray baskets made of reed or something similar, all of it lit by a low sun.

"Skye, blast it."

"I am looking at hell. Nothing in the Royal Navy comes close, and believe me, I'm an expert on that."

"Well, that's not important. Are we going to rescue the wretch or not?"

Skye turned to see Standing Alone, who stared unblinking at the sight below her, the lines of her face taut. Victoria was holding her arm, cursing softly. All this was obviously beyond her most terrible imaginings. Skye could scarcely turn his gaze elsewhere, knowing that this awful pit probably claimed two or three lives each day, and what lay before him was an engine of death and pain.

At last he reined the horses the last two hundred yards to the squat, sullen adobe building ahead, where a thin, hawk-faced man in a white suit awaited them, backed by two burly segundos.

forty-six

The man in the spotless white suit a size too large surveyed the occupants in the carriage as Skye halted the sweated trotters. He did not approach the carriage, but waited, leaning into a gold-knobbed malacca.

"Ah, mi caballero," rumbled Childress, grandly, flourishing his top hat.

"Ah, the Right Honorable Lord Viceroy Sir Arthur Childress," the mine operator replied in sandpapery English. "Welcome to the mine."

"Ah, a Mexican who speaks my tongue! You have found me out with a glance. Permit me to introduce their royal highnesses the queens of Madagascar and Tierra del Fuego."

"Yes, very colorful, an entertaining idea, heathen queens skittering around rural Mexico to titillate us. I am Hector Ramon Pedro Marcus O'Grady at your service. And these gentlemen are assistant superintendents of the mine, Jesus and Pedro."

Skye thought that the assistant superintendents looked more like jailers. English! The operator spoke English and had an Irish surname. Skye supposed he ought to be glad, but already Childress was in deep trouble, and this was turning sour right from the start.

The mining man turned to him. "And you are a certain

Mister Skye, the one who escaped execution by the wiles of that monkey. I was there, you know. Yes, the governor was curious whether you would all link up. It seems you have. Just what business you're about eludes us, unless it's the business of a Texas invasion after all. But I am not being hospitable. Do step down and have some tea. I saw you coming and have some Oolong steeping."

Skye's stomach churned. Had they ridden straight into a trap?

"Charmed, I'm sure, Sah," said Childress. "Ladies?" he said, holding out a hand.

"Sonofabitch," Victoria muttered, stepping down. Standing Alone followed, nervous and uncertain. Little Moon sat, frightened.

"You sit right there, young lady," Childress said. He turned to O'Grady. "We have a servant girl, Sah."

"Yes, so it seems. The governor thought she might be found with you."

Skye sighed. So even that was no secret to this well-informed man. This was more than trouble; it was menace. He set the carriage weight on the ground, hooked the lines to it, and followed the rest into the rude adobe building. It was less rude within, and divided into several small warrens. But O'Grady led them into an office that resembled a parlor, and seated them upon stuffed chairs.

He spoke swiftly to a woman servant, and smiled.

"Ah, my Yankee friends, we shall have our tea in short order."

More trouble, Skye thought.

"Sah, not one of us is a citizen of the United States. I am a peer of England."

"Galveston Bay, I hear, is only a mile from London. Did you not engage in privateering on the Thames?"

Skye squirmed. All of Childress's wild stories were coming home to roost.

"And what are you viceroy of? Zanzibar? Van Dieman's

Land, Bermuda, Ceylon? Yes, and these charmers are, ah, queens of, ah . . ."

Childress laughed expansively. "You've found me out, Sah!"

Skye itched. He studied the thugs hovering about behind O'Grady, and thought he could take one, maybe both. He'd learned a few tricks in the mountains. Maybe he and the women could run for it . . . for a while. But not for long. This was looking more and more like a one-way trip in irons to the City of Mexico.

The superintendent's bright blue eyes locked upon Skye. "And you, Mister Skye, what brings the legend of the fur trade to Mexico, might I ask? You, at least, are an Englishman by birth. Have you been bought by Texas? Should you have been shot after all?"

Skye saw the question as his opportunity. "I am here on a peaceful mission, Mr. O'Grady."

"And what might that be?"

"We are looking for Cheyenne children who were abducted by Utes years ago and sold into slavery here."

"There is no slavery in Mexico, Mister Skye."

Skye didn't want to argue. Let them call it whatever they wanted, indenture, peonage. "We have reason to believe a Cheyenne boy works here. This is his mother, Standing Alone, of the Cheyenne people."

"Ah, yes, this woman is a legend. I know of her. The traders who pass Bent's Fort told us of her and her heartrending vigil. They speak of her with utmost respect."

"As long as you seem to know my purpose, and her purpose, then perhaps you'll help us."

O'Grady stared at Skye from rheumy eyes that revealed only clockwork.

Childress intervened. Ah! Señor O'Grady, my friend Skye here is straying far from our actual purposes," Childress said. "I'm looking for mining properties, something that will make me lasciviously rich, eh? I am the fiduciary guardian of the estates of these noble ladies, eh? Gold comes to mind: lustrous, soft, pure, delicious, glittering, heavy gold, to burthen the pocket, stuff the purse, suckle the loosest dreams . . . Señor O'Grady, Sah, you might join us in a great pecuniary adventure."

"The monkey is shaking its head and tugging at the leg of your trousers."

"Ah, wretched little ape. Simian Judas, scavenger, mountebank, obscene little animal! Never trust a monkey, Sah."

Skye had enough. If they were to leave this place alive and with Little Moon and his women, there would have to be absolute truth.

"Mr. O'Grady," he snapped in a way that subdued Childress. "Have you any Cheyenne working here?"

"Cheyenne? Mister Skye, what is your interest again?"

"Charity, sir."

"Charity, is it?"

Skye was boiling. "Is that something you don't grasp?"

"You puzzle me. But no, no Cheyenne. We employ Mexican nationals. We are forbidden to employ others."

Skye stared at the man, who smiled, nodded toward the steaming teapot.

"Tarahumaras, Jicarillas, Jumanos, Suma . . ." He shrugged. "They work well and hard for a while and then grow lazy, like so many of their coppery brethren."

"Does the other mine here employ Cheyenne?"

"Ah! You are behind the time. It is closed. It exhausted itself, and this mine alone survives."

"You speak English."

"My father, sir, was from Killarney. My mother is the Dona Olivera, of Chihuahua."

"My fine friend, do you want to dicker?" Childress asked, rubbing pudgy fingers together. "What's it worth, eh? I just might plunge."

"To a foreigner, nothing. It is forbidden."

"Well, there are always ways around that. Here, have a cigar."

"Yes, I believe I shall. It's just the sort enjoyed by the governor."

O'Grady plucked the cigar out of Childress's hand, but did not light it. The cigar vanished into a drawer.

"Well, delighted we have the same tastes!" Childress boomed.

The jails of Mexico City yawned wide, always assuming they made it that far before succumbing to whatever cruelties the federal troops might dream up along the way.

O'Grady stood suddenly, his gaunt frame scarcely filling his white suit, which flowed over and around his body as he moved. "This mine barely earns a profit. By the time I acquire, feed, house, and clothe my *gambucinos*, the cost of extracting the dust from this gravel nearly equals the value of the gold. You see how it is."

"No. How is it?" Skye asked.

"Come look. But sip your tea first, and rest. You've had a long ride."

Victoria listened silently, grasping most of it. Standing Alone sat mutely.

"Tell the Cheyenne woman her son died two years ago," O'Grady said.

"What?" The bluntness startled Skye.

"He is dead. Most die soon. I have never understood it. Sickness. A weakness in savages. The will of God." O'Grady shrugged.

Skye stood abruptly. "Dead? How do you know it was her son?"

"Four years past he was brought to me by the traders of Taos. About ten years old, big enough. Armijo took the girl, the one out there. I bought the boy. He didn't last. Pity, isn't it?"

Skye nodded to Victoria, who began translating into the

argot she shared with Standing Alone. The Cheyenne woman trembled once, but she said nothing.

"Come," said O'Grady. They followed mutely out the door and down a path to a lip of a hill overlooking the mine, and just a few yards from the series of precarious ladders leading to the stockpiled ore.

"Let the Cheyenne woman see for herself who walks up those ladders," O'Grady said. "All do. They take turns, every last one."

"Why are you bothering?" Skye asked.

"So that you will see I tell you the truth. You and I talk truly, even if this Right Honorable Viceroy Sir Arthur Childress fails the test. In Mexico, honor counts. It is the honorable life and honorable death we seek."

"And what else?"

O'Grady smiled. "Eldorado."

And so they stood at the pit, lit now by a low sun, watching each bent-over, twisted Indian struggle up the ladders with his basket of gold-bearing gravel. Standing Alone stood closest, her back arched, her body pressed against a rail, her black hair fluttering in the hot breezes. As each one approached, she cried out a word. Skye didn't know the word, but surely it was Cheyenne, and surely not the dead boy's name. But none of these twisted, ruined, ribby, gaunt slaves so much as glanced her way.

Her voice shrilled into the wind like the cry of a raven, harsh, painful, sibilant, tender, and the wind only blew the word back upon her. And yet she persisted, watching wretch after wretch wrestle his basket to the pile of ore.

"Come," said O'Grady, and he led them to a different area, where squatting naked Indians, older and more adept, swirled the gravel around inside of crude wooden bowls, using tiny infusions of water to spin the gravel away from the heavier metal. A dozen of these worked ceaselessly; all were gaunt. Standing Alone held her hat to her head, and said nothing.

"Come," said O'Grady, and he escorted them, past a compound where miners lived, to a dirt-strewn field lumped with unmarked graves. One open one yawned, and as they approached a pestilence of crawling and flying things and a foul stench shot toward them, nauseating Skye. Redheaded black vultures flapped upward.

"They do not last long," O'Grady said. "A weakness of those people."

forty-seven

Somewhere in this foul field lay the bones of her son. Standing Alone was careful not to say his name, or even think it, lest she disturb his spirit. The one who was once her son had not lasted long here, in this place of pestilence and starvation. They had worked him, starved him, beat him, and he had died.

Now she knew. But somehow she had known long ago, for the medicine seers of her people had seen this in the sweetgrass smoke and had told her. But she had kept her vigil at Bent's Fort anyway, for the daughter lived and might return.

The sun's light slanted across this place, but she saw the darkness of this land, as if no sun shone here. This boneyard held the remains of many of the Peoples, the ones who roamed this country before the white men came. She was familiar with torture, with slavery, with captivity, for her people had engaged in all of these things against enemies. But the slaves of her people, women and children taken in war, were usually treated well, soon intermarried, and became part of the band. Sometimes her people tortured enemies too. But this was different. This was endless women's work, this grubbing the soil and washing the metal from it. But she saw no women doing it; only men, who should be hunting or warring or protecting their People instead of this shameful labor.

And this toil was destroying them, just as it had destroyed the beloved one whose name must never again pass her lips. She stared bleakly at this witch-man in white, the mine chieftain who did not know *Heammawihio*, the Wise One Above. She saw a horseman patrolling the perimeter of this place, and knew why none of these *gambucinos* ran away. She stared, and wondered if she and Skye and Victoria and the fat one called Childress and her daughter would all be put to work here too, and soon die.

Aiee, this was something to think about.

She meandered past this place of bones, toward some open-sided buildings with thatched roofs, and here she discovered a kitchen of sorts and pots of thin soup hanging on tripods over fires. Was that all those people would eat, this watery soup steaming in iron kettles? Some stocky bronzed women of the Peoples were cutting thick roots and throwing them into the pots. Where was meat, which made men strong? This was not enough in such a meal to feed an infant.

She watched, learning much of this place. She could not grasp the tongue, except a few words. She did not know any of the tongues of the coppery slaves who starved and toiled here until they died, so she could speak to no one. She wanted to ask questions.

At this kitchen place sat two boys, huddled on the earth, neither of them at manhood yet. Maybe ten or eleven winters. Newcomers. Not yet worn down. Not yet twisted. Aiee! She knew their moccasins. Yellow dyed, like most Arapaho leather. Arapaho boys. Her people knew the Arapaho well, sometimes to fight beside them against the Comanches and Kiowas. Arapahos were friends, and spoke a tongue the Cheyennes could easily learn. These boys were newcomers, brought to this place this very day by slave traders, and soon to die like the one whose name could not be uttered, who had issued from her womb.

Yellow moccasins. Arapaho boys! Sturdy, not yet ruined.

Even as she studied them, an idea formed. She would snatch them from here, take them to her people and make them Cheyenne boys. The death of her son would be made right: the People would have two new boys for the one lost. Aiee! But how? She could not ask the fat one, or Mister Skye, for the want of their words. But she could talk to the Crow woman with signs and words they knew. Ah, she would do that, swiftly, for those boys might soon vanish into the pit and be lost to her forever.

They stared at her, not knowing whether she was a friend.

A fierce intention spread through her. She did not know what medicine might help her or what the augurs were. She eyed the boys again. They sat quietly, awaiting their fate, suspicious of her because she wore the clothing of white people.

But they might know the finger signs, or even some of her words. She drifted toward them, and now they studied her. They were stocky boys, still in flesh, their gazes wary. Had they been stolen by the Utes? Sold here? She made the sign for her people, the Cheyenne, and they stared at her, surprised. She saw light bloom in their eyes. She made other signs: Wait! Be ready. Friend. Run.

They stared, perturbed and silent. They were brave boys, scornful of their fate, but they had yet to lift a basket of rock, or stagger up one of those log ladders or feel the whip. How swiftly they would change under the lash of the man in white.

She did not waste more time on them. They had been informed.

The man in white was amiably escorting Skye, Victoria, and the fat one through the works, past the older ones swirling the rock in bowls, past the places were people slept. He looked like a hawk with a rabbit in its talons, enjoying the moment before he snapped his curved beak over the neck of the rabbit. Yes, that one, O'Grady, was a hunter.

What sort of man was he, who put so many men to this task? Did he care about any of them or only for the yellow metal? Did he free any? Was the only escape from this place the foul pit where sharp-toothed creatures ripped away flesh from bone? Did he have a wife and children who lived handsomely because of these men staggering up the ladders? Aiee, what a one was that man in the white suit, exuding darkness just the way this earth, here, radiated darkness and pain, so much so that it made her body ache and her own bones hurt.

She caught up with them, and motioned to Victoria, her fingers flying:

"Two Arapaho boys, friends my people. Just brought here," she said, making words the Crow woman would grasp.

Victoria glanced sharply at the boys huddled in the shade of the open-sided building.

"We must take them away," Standing Alone said.

Victoria stared at her and at the boys, understanding the urgency in Standing Alone's plans. The Crow woman would not have to be told that these would be a gift to the Cheyenne People, two boys to breed into fine warriors.

"How do that?" Victoria signaled.

In truth, Standing Alone had no idea. "Talk your man," she signaled. "He know. Don't tell fat man."

Victoria nodded and caught up with the others. The man in the white suit was pointing into the yellow pit at the swarm of men loading gravel into baskets, staggering up wobbling ladders, and pausing to catch their breath at the top.

Grief bloomed in her. Was that how her son had spent his last breaths, staggering under weight that bent him double? Was he alone, with no one to share his ordeal? Did he yearn for his people, and the tallgrass prairies, and the summer winds? Did he see the boneyards, and know he would soon be scattered across them, bits and pieces of himself whitening in the cruel sun?

Did he feel his medicine had been taken away? That he would bring no honor to the People? That he would win no girl of the People, no war honors, no admiration of the People? That he would have no reputation as a warrior? Aiee, his life was like midnight.

There was a tautness in the air. Something was going to happen and she didn't know what.

She saw Victoria whispering to Skye, and saw him listen intently. He looked strange in his humble clothes. Victoria left Skye and fell back to where Standing Alone walked.

"He says big trouble."

"I want those Arapaho boys."

"Skye says, maybe there is a way. But he don't know it. It would take money."

"I will give them to my people!"

Victoria shook her head. "Skye got taken away long ago and never saw his people again. He's not gonna help you give Arapaho boys to the Cheyenne. If he helps you, they will go home to the Arapaho."

A great rage built in her. She glared sullenly at Skye's woman, who was nothing but an Absaroka.

The wheeling vultures flapped into the field of bones again, and she knew they were feasting on the dead. She wanted to get out; if she could not take those two boys with her, then she was through with this place, and through with Mexico. Her work was done. She had her daughter.

They were gathering now around the black carriage. The man in the white suit was smiling but his eyes were cold. They were talking, but she didn't grasp any of it.

"What are they saying?" she asked Victoria by sign.

"The man Hector Ramon O'Grady is saying that it takes much labor to make gold, and he has many mouths to feed, and Indians are poor workers, and he does not get rich."

"Are we going now?"

"Soon. They are saying adios."

Standing Alone watched the hawkish man, and suddenly she knew what she must do. She raced up to him, and the words flooded out in her native tongue, Cheyenne, and she could not think of anything else.

"Take me and let those Arapaho boys go. I am strong. I am twice as strong as those boys. Take me so the boys can live. You bought them but I will do more work for you. I will carry more stone up the ladders. Take me! I am a Cheyenne and strong and I will make gold for you!"

The Mexican man O'Grady stared, and finally turned to Skye.

"You have any idea what the woman wants?"

Skye shook his head.

O'Grady turned to Victoria. "You understand her?"

"A little."

Standing Alone tried again, slow, her voice piercing, her fingers making words. "You take me. I work hard. I am better than two little boys! You trade me for them. Boys go with the carriage! I give myself to you. I do twice as much as they do!"

She stared at their faces, seeing the blankness in them. The curse of language was walling her off.

"I think she wants to trade herself for them boys you got over there," Victoria said.

The man in white studied Standing Alone. "She wants to trade herself? She's not worth two strong boys."

Standing Alone somehow understood, her small grasp of this English tongue giving her understanding.

She knelt before this man in white and clutched his leg, and wept, the hot tears rising from her eyes and flooding her face with her sorrow.

He kicked and tugged, and finally booted her free.

"Out!" he said. "Get the squaw out."

forty-eight

Skye helped the trembling Cheyenne woman into the calash, filled with pity and horror. Hector Ramon O'Grady was a swine.

"Wait," said the *mayordomo*. He stared at her, assessing her body as if she were a draft horse. "Some savage women are strong. Tell her to get out and stand."

"Leave her alone," Skye said.

But the mine superintendent held out his claw to her, and she took it and stepped down to the sun-baked clay. He walked around her, assessing, boldly examining her arms, her shoulders, her wiry legs. She stared defiantly, her gaze never leaving him.

"I'll trade her for one boy," he said. He turned to Victoria. "Tell her."

Victoria simply lifted one finger.

Standing Alone understood, straightened herself, and held up two fingers.

O'Grady thrust up one finger. "Tell her she can choose."

He turned to one of his muscular *capataces*, addressing him in Spanish. The man trotted toward the kitchen area, where the Arapaho boys waited.

"Señores, boys that young are almost worthless to me. I offered very little. They achieve little. They won't ever work off their indenture." He shrugged sadly. "No one else wanted them. I pitied them."

"Indenture," Skye said, knowing there was such loathing in his voice that O'Grady wouldn't miss his contempt.

"Would you care to work for me, Mister Skye? Actually, I pay well for brute labor, more than it's worth to feed and house these animals. You would be useful here."

It was a smoothly phrased threat, but Skye ignored it. "I saw black slaves in Missouri, and they were decently fed and clothed," Skye said. "I'll say that much for the Americans."

"We don't have slaves here."

O'Grady's *capataz* prodded the two Arapaho boys forward. Skye was shocked. One seemed barely nine or ten; the other a little older. They still wore the yellow-dyed loincloths and moccasins of their people, but that would last only days in rough rock.

Standing Alone studied the children; they watched her solemnly, their black eyes alive with fear. She pointed at the smaller one, the moonfaced boy who was half grown and far from possessing the bone and muscle of a man.

She spoke to Victoria in that patois of theirs.

Victoria translated: "Let this one go; give the other one an easy task, and I will trade myself."

Skye hated this trafficking in human flesh. He could scarcely bear to witness this brave woman's sacrifice.

Hector O'Grady nodded. So it was done.

Standing Alone spoke volubly to the boys, wanting desperately to say something to both of them even if her tongue was not theirs; and then to Victoria.

Victoria said, "She's saying that she wants the Arapaho boy to be given to her people, learn Cheyenne ways, but if the boy don't want to stay, he gets to go back to his people."

Standing Alone nodded.

So it had come to that. Skye thought back to the time at Bent's Fort when this woman had sought his help to find and free a Cheyenne boy and a girl. Now she would take the place of one, and her life would be short and hard.

"Grandmother," said Skye, "you won't understand my English words, but let the respect in my voice touch you. You are giving your life away, not for your son but for someone very much like him, that this boy might grow strong and come into his glory. I have never known a more beautiful and sad sacrifice. May you live forever in the memory of your people, and all people. I will carry your image inside of me."

O'Grady gestured. The *capataz* started to hustle the luckless older boy away. Skye watched the boy sag and stare at the yellow clay.

Standing Alone slowly approached the calash, where Little Moon sat rigid in her seat. She reached out to her daughter, smiled, touched her child's face, wiped her jet hair away from her eyes, and whispered things not meant for other ears. Tears slid down Little Moon's amber cheeks. Standing Alone whispered furiously, conveying instructions, requests, a hundred things, no doubt including a farewell to her husband, all of which rested now in the heart of the daughter she had found and rescued.

Standing Alone looked utterly beautiful.

"Damn it all," said Victoria. "Dammit, dammit, dammit."

Standing Alone helped the Arapaho boy slide into the calash and settle beside Little Moon. Childress for once looked overwrought.

Hector Ramon O'Grady took Standing Alone by the arm.

"A pleasure to show you our operation," he said to Skye. "And a word of advice, señor. Drive straight through Santa Fe. If the governor gets wind of you, he might reclaim his property."

"His property," muttered Skye.

O'Grady smiled. "Señor, you will thank me for the advice."

Skye watched the burly *capataz* herd Standing Alone away, until they disappeared in a distant adobe shack. The world somehow seemed smaller and harsher without her in it. Standing Alone had been like a pillar reaching the heavens.

"Ah, Skye, Sah, we'd better be off," Childress said nervously.

Skye slowly lifted the carriage weight and clambered to his seat in the creaking rig. He collected the lines in his rough hands and slapped them over the croups of the trotters, and slowly the calash circled away and a few minutes later a bluff hid the mine from sight.

Even Childress looked unusually somber. A great quietness fell upon them all, as visions of Standing Alone, courageous warrior woman of her people, filtered through their minds.

They had almost reached Dolores when Childress suddenly cried out. "I say, where is Shine?"

The monkey was not with them.

"Turn around, turn around," he bawled.

Skye found a flat where he could wheel the carriage around and collect Childress's rascally simian, and they slowly wended their way back to the mine as the sun was sinking.

A few minutes later they rode once again into the mining compound, and Skye headed up the slope to the building that housed the administration.

O'Grady emerged at once and stood waiting, while his segundos filtered out.

"We're missing the monkey," Skye said.

"Yes, he's here," O'Grady said. "There's his head."

There was Shine's little head swaying on a stake off to the side, its eyes lifeless, its lips opened forever.

"We do that to all thieves," O'Grady said. "It sets an example. Every once in a while a worker takes a notion to steal some gold. This is our response."

Childress groaned. The grinning head swayed on its crimsoned gibbet.

"Feisty little fellow. Hard to catch, but we caught him red-handed. Gold ingot in his little hairy hand. Pity, Skye. Too bad it wasn't a cigar."

Skye landed on the ground.

The mayordomo stepped back. "Touch me, you'll die," he said.

"All right, I will die."

He bounded into O'Grady and slammed him hard, knocking him down. Skye hammered the mayordomo, feeling his fists mash into the man's thin frame, feeling the air whoof from the man's lungs, feeling the man's teeth loosen in his jaw, feeling the bright light of justice in every blow.

But then the *capataces* landed on him, two, three, five, snaring his thrashing arms, yanking him off the *jefe*, kicking, jabbing, gouging. They pinioned his arms and returned his punches, booted him in the privates, doubled him over until he lay on the clay, puking, coughing, and even then they kicked him hard, tormenting his ribs.

O'Grady picked himself up, breathing hard. "Mean fists, Skye. I should make you one of my *jefes*." The man wiped blood from his nostrils. He turned and spat.

Then he snapped something in Spanish, and the burly foremen threw Skye onto the calash and slapped the horses. The carriage lurched. Skye wiped blood from his lips, seized the lines, and slowed the careening calash.

Childress sat moaning, his tear-streaked face buried in his hands.

They rode down the canyon and no one followed.

He felt Victoria's gentle hands dabbing at his face from behind, cleansing him, strengthening him.

He kept the trotters to a walk, not wanting to wear them out. He needed the cloak of darkness in Santa Fe, and that meant staying on the move if the horses could endure.

They passed through Dolores again, and no one stopped them. Below, he rested the trotters and let them graze on a patch of grass as twilight deepened.

Not a word was spoken all that while.

He studied the two Indians, the girl silent and somber and tear-streaked, the boy wide-eyed and wary. Victoria had clothed them in her love, and now they nestled into her, on either side. As always, the barriers of tongue prevented talking.

"Shine deserves the Order of the Garter," Childress said.

"I thought you were a Galveston Bay privateer."

"That, too," said Childress.

forty-nine

S kye kept the trotters to a quiet walk, conserving their strength. Childress slumped numbly, watching the hills unfold as the calash rocked northward over a rutted road. Victoria sat across from him, the young Indians on either side, each nestled into her for comfort. She was a reassuring presence to them, the one native person they had with them.

The trader quietly studied the young people. The girl, Little Moon, was composed, though he supposed her thoughts were back there at the mine with the mother she had seen for only a few hours; the blessed mother who had, after four years, come for her, found her, set her free. The most beautiful of all mothers. Little Moon now had her life before her, and would rejoin her people, marry, raise proud Cheyenne, and might well prepare all her people for the new world that was encroaching on traditional Cheyenne life.

The boy was more of an enigma. He had spoken his name this afternoon and pointed to himself, but no one could translate it. *Ouo*, he had said of himself. The meaning would have to wait. Skye would find out the name at Bent's Fort, where many knew the tongue, including Kit Carson, whose wife was Arapaho. *Ouo* was trying hard to be manly, to be a warrior, to be an Arapaho, and often he looked sternly about. He would become all of these now; at the mine he would have become only weary muscle and empty dreams and faded hopes. But sometimes *Ouo* looked ready to bury himself in Victoria's arms. Childress wondered whether it was all too late. The Arapaho might not yet know it, but their life would change as settlement progressed, and maybe they would die off, diseased and devastated.

Was it worth it? Yes, Childress thought. It had all been worth it. Little Moon was free. *Ouo* was free. Each could live the lives they might choose to live. And Childress had found out what he wanted to know.

But there was one who was no longer free, and Childress thought of her now. No doubt they had put her right to work, and even now, in the last light, she would be carrying terrible burdens trip after trip. From this day forward, her life would no longer be her own. And yet she had chosen it so that the boy nodding beside Victoria in this black coach might receive a life.

Childress studied the slumped back of Mister Skye, knowing the man hurt from his beating at the hands of the mine's ruffians, knowing also that without Skye's indomitable courage and strength, this strange rescue would not have happened. It might yet be thwarted if the governor had troops out looking for them.

Skye had begun this venture not for money, but to help a suffering woman, and her suffering children. That alone set him apart from the run of men. Childress loved the man for his courage and his honor and his artless integrity, and loved his wife, too, the perfect mate for a man of the mountains who scorned the wiles of civilization.

No one had spoken a word. No one wanted to. Childress knew that everything had changed, somehow. His work here was over, and he must wind this business up and make his report. His name was not really Childress; neither was it Jean

Lafitte or Sir Arthur. Neither was he an agent of the Republic of Texas, though his crew of traders at his post on the Arkansas River believed he was.

All those things had been camouflage, just as his gaudy cart, bizarre conduct, and startling dress had been camouflage, enabling him to probe where he wanted to probe, see what he wanted to see.

The monkey had been camouflage too, and now the monkey was dead, and everything had changed. He had loved that spider monkey, and grieved its sudden cruel death as if he had lost a son or a brother. That monkey had accompanied him for years, achieving what he could not achieve, sustaining him in bad moments, as if the monkey had a human intelligence, knew what needed to be done, and achieved it without even being asked.

Ah, Shine! Childress pushed that final image out of his mind and tried to focus on the graceful juniper-blanketed slopes around him, but there was only emptiness now. None of them, not Skye, not Victoria, not the Indian youngsters, would ever know what that little rascal had meant to him.

A chapter had ended. There were things to do now, in this darker, meaner world.

Skye rested and grazed the horses at a much-used spring as the slip of moon rose, bathing this land with a ghostly glow, almost phosphorescent. The scent of piñon pine sweetened the air. Victoria let the youngsters stretch their legs. Childress lumbered to the hard earth.

"Say, Mister Skye, we should talk a little."

Skye nodded.

"What time will we make Santa Fe?" Childress asked.

"Two, three hours. It'll still be dark."

"I'll be saying good-bye to you there."

"I thought you might."

"We've done what we could. You'll be heading out the Santa Fe Trail, back to Bent's Fort. I'll be going north to my post on the Arkansas. But we've some business to transact. I'll outfit you."

"Outfit us? With what?"

"This rig. It's worth plenty. We'll go see the American consul, Alvarez, most pleasant chap."

"I already owe him."

"Trust me. There's enough in this rig to put the four of you on horses and outfit you, too."

"What about you, Mister Childress?"

"I'll go back to privateering."

Skye laughed quietly. "Whatever you are, and I haven't the faintest idea, you were never a privateer."

"Then think of me as you will."

"Who are you, then?"

"No one you've heard of."

"We're talking in circles. What are you doing here? Are you an agent provocateur of the Republic of Texas?"

"For a while. It was a useful thing to be."

Skye shook his head. "I suppose you'll tell me if you want me to know."

"I'll say only this: our meeting was most fortunate for me, and by teaming up with you, I accomplished what I set out to do."

"You mean picking up the girl and the boy?"

"That, and letting me see how it all works."

Skye waited for more, but nothing more was forthcoming, so he smiled. "I don't suppose I'll ever know, then, mate."

"You're right about me, you know. I am a Londoner."

Skye nodded. He had plainly given up, and turned to stare at the darkened slopes. "I'm in your hands, mate. You're the only one among us speaks Spanish; you know what I don't, and you're not saying who you are. Keep us safe, put us on horse, give us a weapon or two and some food, a blanket apiece, and we'll make it."

"Consider it done, Mister Skye."

The man who called himself Childress wished he could reveal more, but confidentiality was important, and he couldn't break the seal.

As the night-chill deepened, Skye rounded up Victoria and the two Indians. "Two or three hours to Santa Fe," he said.

They rode through a soft summer's night without incident, and at midnight Skye steered the black calash through the narrow streets of the capital city until they were again at the plaza. He halted before Alvarez's mercantile.

"Wait here," Childress said, and mounted the long stairway, one step at a time, until he reached the vestibule and knocked. It took a long while before a yawning Alvarez opened.

"Childress? At this hour? Is there something wrong?"

"A moment, Señor Alvarez. Can you spare it?"

Alvarez studied Childress sharply, and waved him in.

It took some negotiating. Alvarez agreed to supply horses, saddle, tack, blankets, food, clothing, and a rifle and powder and ball to Skye's party. He would receive two matched trotters and a calash for it, and the only calash in New Mexico.

"And what of you, Mister Childress?"

"I have business here, some things to write and then I'll see."

"Business?"

The consul was fishing. Maybe, after Skye's party got away, the man who called himself Childress would explain. But not now. There were things to do under the cloak of darkness, and Alvarez swiftly dressed, lit a lantern, headed downstairs to his shadowed store, and set to work.

He opened the front door of his store, summoned Skye, and together they hauled the outfit to the calash.

"There is a livery barn out Palace Street. I will come with you," he said to Skye.

The calash creaked through empty dark streets.

The Mexican hostler sprang to life as soon as Alvarez

awakened him, and by the wavering light of an oil lamp, he caught horses and saddled them. In time all was readied for Skye and his party: the weary trotters rested in a pen, four horses stood ready, and a burro was loaded with a packsaddle and the new outfit.

"Well, Skye, this will see you through," Childress said.

"Some privateer you are, mate."

"I'm Her Majesty's viceroy for Borneo and Tanganyika, Skye."

Skye didn't laugh. "Whoever you are, sir, you're a nobleman and a prince."

"No, Skye, I am addressing the true nobleman, the natural lord of the wilds, generous and true and honorable. And his wife, who is all of those things, herself a duchess of this great realm."

Victoria looked ready to swear, but her gaze was filled with tenderness.

"Hurry, you'll need to be well clear of Santa Fe when dawn breaks."

"Dawn has already come for these young people, Mr. Childress."

"May it come for all enslaved people, Mister Skye. Be gone before daylight!" he cried.

Skye shook hands, and the mountaineer's grip was warm and firm, and he shook hands with the consul too, and then they mounted. Childress watched Skye, Victoria, and the savage boy and the girl ride softly into the soft night, and then they vanished from his sight, and he knew he would never see them again.

fifty

*I*n the Moon When the Cherries are Ripe, Skye found Black Dog's Cheyenne camped in a cottonwood bottom on Big Sandy Creek, enjoying the sweet harvest of late summer. He rode past buffalo hides staked to the earth to be fleshed, woven baskets burdened with hackberries, heaps of roots and wild onions, and racks where strips of buffalo were drying for future use as pemmican and jerky. The buffalo were thick, the berries ripe, and the People were happy.

When Skye and Victoria rode into the village along with Little Moon and Ouo, escorted by the ever-vigilant Dog Soldiers, women and children alike crowded about them, whispering furiously. Most of the men were off hunting. Little Moon cried out her greetings as she recognized childhood friends, kin, and Chief Black Dog himself, who stood waiting before his lodge as the visitors approached, lean, coppery, wearing only a plain loincloth.

Little Moon! This was news!

Even as these people welcomed the long-lost Little Moon with sharp cries, they studied the Arapaho boy, wondering about him. He came from an allied tribe, and their gazes were friendly. There were questions on their faces and Skye hoped to answer them all, despite the ever-present barriers of tongue.

These Cheyenne were friends of William Bent, and some would know a little English. But many more would understand Arapaho, and between them, Ouo and Little Moon could tell their stories. They dismounted from their weary horses under the watchful eyes of the Dog Soldiers, no friends of Skye or the Crow woman Victoria, but it didn't much matter.

Black Dog made them welcome, and heard their stories, one by one, while the Cheyennes crowded close.

Even as Little Moon was speaking, her father appeared, and there was a long, choked moment as they stared at each other, and his troubled gaze surveyed her strange cloth clothing and bare feet. The father, whose name Skye remembered as Cloud Watcher, was a graying warrior, flanked by younger wives, who eyed Skye and Victoria with frank dislike. He wore a necklace of human fingers and the ensign of the Dog Soldiers, a quilled dog rope looped over his shoulder, the warrior society eternally hostile to all who were not of the People.

But that changed, even as Little Moon poured forth the story of her capture by the hated Utes, life in Santa Fe as a drudge for the chief of chiefs, release from captivity by Standing Alone and Skye and Victoria and a certain fat man. She spoke of all that happened afterward, including the trip to the mountain place were yellow metal was clawed from the earth, and the amazing, beautiful sacrifice of Standing Alone for the liberty and life of this Arapaho boy, Ouo, whose name Skye learned was Raven.

The villagers listened in hushed silence, and when they learned of Standing Alone's self-chosen fate, they cried out in anguish. For now this little bronzed boy, standing uneasily before them, was vested with great medicine and sacredness by a woman of the People who had surrendered her freedom, indeed her life, for him.

Skye wished he could understand the tongue of these people, because some of what was unfolding eluded him. But more and more, the chief, Black Dog, eyed him and Victoria, and when at last the stories were told and retold, he motioned them to be seated in a circle, and an honored boy presented the chief with a sacred pipe of this band. Black Dog ritually pointed the pipe stem to the sky, the earth, and the four winds: "Spirit above, smoke. Earth, smoke. East, West, North, South, smoke." And they smoked quietly, each filling his lungs in turn. It was a peace offering and a bonding of them all.

Now a translator appeared, a youth who had tarried at Bent's Fort, and he explained, in halting English, that these people would rejoice for four days the return of their young woman.

"She make be purified," he said. "In a bower she be cleansed with smoke of sweetgrass, welcomed, and returned to lodge of her father. And much more happen, for the bravery and beauty of Standing Alone be honored. No greater woman ever live among our people."

"I agree, mate. She will always live on in my mind, and in Victoria's mind too."

"She make a damn good Absaroka," said Victoria, paying the ultimate homage.

"The Arapaho boy, he be gone into the lodge of his new father, Cloud-Watcher, and there he learn our ways. But in honor the wishes of Standing Alone, he be offered his liberty soon, few moons. But we hope he stay, and be a son, and replace the one who died."

Grasshopper, whose name would never again be spoken here, but who was missed and grieved by everyone in the band.

Skye dug under his buckskins and pulled out the sacred bundle that Standing Alone had given him. Slowly he lifted it over his head, and handed it to Black Dog.

He turned to the translator. "Tell the chief that I am returning the sacred bundle of his people. I have done what I was required to do."

Black Dog took it, nodded solemnly, and pressed a hand upon Skye's shoulder.

"You carried its power; you have honored it," the chief said.

The Cheyenne people stared at medicine bundle, which had inspired the man who wore it, and Skye sensed a gladness in them.

And so these people made Skye and Victoria welcome. They fattened Skye's rawboned horses, housed Skye and Victoria in a small medicine lodge heaped with velvet-soft robes, served them the most succulent ribs of the buffalo cow, while the Cheyenne women swiftly sewed a complete fringed and quilled doeskin dress for Victoria, and a suit of skins for Skye, dyed across the chest and back in strong red and black colors, and added exquisitely quilled moccasins for them both. Skye at once put away his cloth clothes and wore the new ones, tying back his long hair with a yellow ribbon.

On the eve of the second day, Cloud-Watcher invited Skye and Victoria to his lodge, and there at twilight, before the whole band, he adopted Skye as his son and Victoria as his daughter, clasping a hand to the shoulder of each, thus paying great honor to them both. And Little Moon proclaimed them her brother and sister. Even the shy Arapaho boy, Ouo, Raven, had a gift for them: a little medicine bundle he made for each, which he hung on a thong over Victoria's breast and the other over Skye's. The crowd admired that, and patted the boy happily.

Victoria had sighed as the boy honored her, and Skye knew how much she would have liked a son of her own, but her womb had always been empty. Now, at last, she had a son in this boy, and she smiled at him, and pressed his hands between hers, and found in him that which she had always yearned to have.

Skye noted that several of the young Cheyenne boys were paying court to Little Moon, though most stayed away. It was plain that most of the boys wanted nothing to do with her;

she had in their eyes been somehow demeaned by her servitude among the Mexicans. But one youth in particular, who had a mind of his own and whose war honors included an eagle feather, was playing the flute outside her lodge, and Skye sensed that soon Cloud-Watcher would acquire a son-in-law, and Little Moon, a sweet sixteen, would begin her new life in joy, living freely within the traditions of her people.

On the fourth day Black Dog himself held a ceremonial feast, at which he made Skye and Victoria members of the tribe and of his people, with much oratory, strokes of vermilion on the cheek, and fragrant smoke of tobacco mixed with red willow bark. Victoria, of the Crows, endured this with dignity, setting aside her own passions to permit this great honor.

"Almost like Absaroka!" she exclaimed.

"For you both have brought one of ours to us, and you both helped our beloved Standing Alone to fulfil her life," intoned the youthful translator. "And so you shall always be honored among us, and wherever the People gather, your names will be spoken of with respect."

Skye thanked them simply. He was glad.

The next morning he and Victoria loaded up their burro with its pack, saddled their horses, and headed away, escorted for half a day by an honor guard of the Dog Soldiers.

But at last they rode alone, ever north, through the tall tan grasses bobbing in the breeze, toward the land of her people, the Crow.

fifty-one

Santa Fe
Province of New Mexico
Mexico

17 August 1841

Thomas Fowell Buxton, Bart.
Castle Hedingham
Essex, England

Sir Thomas:

I am pleased to report that I have concluded operations in the Republic of Texas, United States Indian Territory, and the northernmost province of Mexico, on behalf of the British and Foreign Anti-slavery Society. A detailed report will follow in a fortnight but I will write briefly at once and entrust this to merchants en route to St. Louis over the Santa Fe Trail.

Slavery in the Republic of Texas is a variant of the sort in the United States South. The black is not a citizen of the republic, has virtually no rights, and serves entirely at the whim of the master, without hope of liberty. We should call

attention to this in parliament; United States ab-
olitionists can do little about it, operating from a
foreign nation, as it were.

In the unsettled portions of United States territory, the Ute Indians, in particular, abduct children and sell them in Mexico, where there are
traffickers of human flesh peddling wares to
ranchers and mine owners. In this they are very
like black African slavers. But the other tribes are
not free from the taint of slavery, though it is
milder, built around war captives, and usually
results in adoption into the tribe.

A much more subtle variety of bondage finds
form in Mexico, where slavery is theoretically
forbidden by state and church. There are several
types, ranging from the cruel and murderous
servitude imposed on captive native peoples, often in the mines, to more benign versions of slavery, such as the peon system which binds the
peon to his master through perpetual debt. Other
forms of indenture operate in Mexico as well.

I will recount my adventures when I return
to London. Suffice it to say that I employed my
usual stratagems, being highly visible, even
gaudy, to conceal my true purposes. I had the
good fortune to obtain a commission from Texas
President Lamar, which enabled me to study the
new republic without hindrance, and even better
fortune later on, when I encountered a famed
border man looking for enslaved Indian children
in Mexico. Both situations enabled me to discover everything the anti-slavery society wishes
to know, while my true purposes remained un-
detected.

I shall drop the nom de guerre Childress,
which is now worthless, and will let you know

317

by coded letter what new one I shall next adapt to my purposes. I leave shortly for the Mexican province of California, to examine, as you wish, servitude of the local Indians at missions and ranchos, with a special emphasis on their diminishing numbers, and after that I will take ship to Australia to see about forced labor in the penal colonies, especially as it involves spouses of convicts, freed women and children, and ticket-of-leave men unable to return to England.

A full report follows. I trust the work of the society proceeds well. Garrison and others in the States are furiously arousing sentiment against the southern system, which debases masters as much as slaves, but can do nothing about Texas or Mexico. We can do much.

I will sign myself simply,
W

Author's Note

This novel, like others in the series, is pure fiction, but is grounded in historical reality. The Ute Indians did abduct the children of neighboring tribes and sell them in Mexico, where the captives usually lived a short, brutal life. It is recorded that Kit Carson once took pity on a Paiute boy held captive by the Utes, and purchased his freedom for forty dollars, a large sum in those days.

William Wilberforce and others in Parliament worked diligently through the early part of the nineteenth century to eradicate slavery throughout the British Empire, as well as worldwide. His successor, Thomas Fowell Buxton, who was made a baronet in 1840, worked tirelessly to abolish slavery, and while some of his efforts came a-cropper, he exerted incalculable moral force against the institution.

Some of the characters in the story are historical. These include William Bent, Alexander Barclay, Lucas Murray, Juan Andres Archuleta, Governor Manuel Armijo, and U.S. Consul Manuel Alvarez. All of them have been depicted fictionally.

I am grateful to that formidable historian and editor, Dale L. Walker, for supplying me with ideas and material and encouragement.

RICHARD S. WHEELER
NOVEMBER 2001